I0684482

*To Shannon, the one woman I've ever
known that was "worth a dime". :)*

© 2014, Michael R. Holt; The Pen Is Mightier Productions - No part of this literary work may be reproduced, stored in a retrieval system, or transmitted in any form or by any means without the prior written permission of the author.

COVER PHOTOSHOP WORK by Assum Mirza (www.facebook.com/assum.mirza), who may be contacted via email at: assum.mirza@outlook.com

Acknowledgements

First and foremost (no matter how trite this may sound), I want to thank my *Mom*, Yvonne. Her constant outward, spoken faith in me (even when she must have surely doubted on the *inside*) and generous, charitable support during my four-month stay with her (during only *two* of which was I finishing the last 63 chapters of this thing)... as well as numerous *other* bail-outs in my life... have been the support (and sometimes *reproof*) that I so genuinely needed. We don't always *agree* (e.g. - on the use of life-like cursing in the narrative) and I've often had to stop and explain a word or idea from the book to her, but she has been the one reliable set of ears - always ready to listen to my latest chapter - that I've had for this grand journey. My one hope was for this to be published while she and my Father were still alive to see it... and I am just *so* excited that it's happening.

I want to posthumously thank the one and only Shakespeare for exciting my interest in the English language (and Sir Kenneth Branagh, for bringing his works to vivid, wonderful life) and my senior English teacher - Ms. Lewis - for making the language (and its *glorious* vocabulary) accessible even to me at that young age.

I want to thank the people (other than my Mom, of course) who have contributed monetarily to the success of this work: Elisabeth Bellville, who donated - *sight unseen* - to its future release... Mr. and Mrs. Ray Sailsbury and family, who have shown great interest in and support for their nephew's/cousin's work... and Mr. and Mrs. Michael Beard, long-time friends of the family, who are (*to this day!*) as in love as Frank and Mimi.

I also want to thank my online writer friends who have been anxiously awaiting this release as much as I: Opinionated Man at *Harsh Reality* and Erudite Knight at *Erudite Knight*. Thanks for spreading the word, you guys! I hope to get many more eyes on this work.

I want to thank my talented photoshop guru Assum Mirza for the long hours he spent with me on the cover (*Ugh!*). I know I was exacting (especially about the placement/coloring of my original Title Text, Taijitic Seal, and Xeresgatian Flag), but we ended up with something we were *both* proud of, didn't we? Seriously, other writers: if you need a photoshop guy, Assum is your man!

Lastly, I want to thank my Father, Stephen, and my Dagorhir "Dad", Blackhawk... for teaching me both the severity and levity of being a good Father. I've learned a lifetime's worth of wisdom from you *both*, and I only hope to someday be able to pass that wonderful gift on to my own children.

And to **YOU** - *Thanks for reading!* This wouldn't be possible without you.

Xeresgate:
The Castle Within
(A Novel)

By: Michael R. Holt

*(Turn the page **only** if you're ready!)*

Hi. My name is Malachi. You may not know it yet, but by opening up this book, you have released a little magic into the world. If you're really lucky, that magic will stay with you for the rest of your life. How do I know? The exact same thing happened to me once.

But I'm getting ahead of myself. Allow me to start from what I now call the beginning.

Most people in the world today will tell you that there's no such thing as magic. I used to be one of those people. The fact of the matter is that most magic in the world *is* gone… forgotten for too long while people contented themselves with bigger TVs, smaller computers, and fancier jobs. The sad truth is that magic, like most things, requires work and patience to perform – and a lifetime to master. As people grew lazier and more content with wearing suits and going to clubs than practicing the Art, magic began to be ignored and left behind… just like the gods of old.

But again, I'm getting ahead of myself. Don't worry, though – we'll get there. This book has more than an average share of magic in it, and a lot will be revealed as you read. You just have to be patient, and allow the magic to naturally wash over you like a gentle wave splashing against the beach on a breezy summer day.

Whatever you allow yourself to believe, though – you must know this: magic *is not* dead. Honestly, it *cannot* die… it merely changes hands. Most times, it changes hands unknowingly, passed down from Father to son or Mother to daughter. A very few times, it is relinquished by the magic user before he dies – placed into the vessel of the gods: a great crystal. These great crystals very nearly resemble apples (if one is inclined to draw a fruit analogy), and the greatest ever recorded magic transfer was in the very first book of the ancient Jamesian text known widely as "The Bible". Of course, by the time the story was recorded, it had become an allegory, so the truth of the first crystalline "apple" was reduced to nothing more than a prehistoric snack.

Think about it, though… why *else* would Yahweh have gotten so angry at the power transfer that occurred that day? From what I've come to understand, Yahweh was intending to keep the crystal a secret – to be revealed when he had chosen a champion from the lineage of man. But, as most gardens are, the first Garden was rather boring and Adam and Lilith (not Eve – *another* Jamesian fallacy) went spelunking in the nearby cave where Yahweh had hidden the crystal. It was the first really shiny thing either had ever seen, so they both went for it at the same time and *BAM* – all that magical potential was instantly split between them. Yahweh kept what had happened a secret from the two, but still acted like he was mad that they'd strayed from the Garden and "touched his stuff".

Lilith, who was generally more rebellious than Adam anyway, decided to leave the Garden and explore Earth on her own terms, and Adam stayed behind. A little extra sleepy-time surgery later, Yahweh had made Eve for him. (Odd how the Bible never mentions that Adam's torso is lop-sided and yet in order for that to have *not* been the case, he would have had to have been missing *two* ribs – one from each side. Even by the Jamesian account, Eve was only made from one. Christian doctors *never* take issue with this? Food for thought.)

So Yahweh went with Adam back to the Garden and Lilith was pretty much left to her own devices. Since Yahweh focused on Adam and his progeny almost exclusively, it was easy to quell talk of what actually happened that day in the cave, and to keep Adam focused on providing for his family. Personally, I tend to believe it was just decades later (after age had faded Adam's memory) that Yahweh re-told him the story of that day, replacing Lilith (who'd long been forgotten) with Eve – and the crystal that *looked* like an apple with the actual fruit. The Jamesian record bears witness to the latter account in any case, so that's what most people tend to believe. I mean, who argues with their own holy book, right?

Lilith, though? Oh, *that* was a different story altogether. This was the time in man's history when gods freely roamed the Earth, bestowing supernatural powers on mankind whenever they felt like it.

Yahweh was never big on sharing his powers (after the whole cave incident), but other gods did it all the time.

See, when the God of the Universe made this universe and all the galaxies, Earths, gods, and what-not, He gave power to these gods based on the number of followers they had. The real God is actually just a big fan of entertainment – and the struggle for power among gods over humans was His first "favorite show" to watch. And you have to admit that the premise is *funny*, if nothing else. Imagine if someone gave you and only three of your friends an ant farm – and whoever got the most ants to come to his corner would be rewarded with the most money. That's pretty much how things happened with the God of the Universe – except you and your friends were all the gods He'd made, ants were humans on all the Earths, and the money was supernatural power and influence. The more you (as a god) were recognized, worshipped, talked with, prayed to, given sacrifices, etc., etc. – the more power you were given as a god.

Yahweh took that idea and ran with it straight away, latching onto the practice of raising a certain "people" through procreation and family unity. The remaining gods were some of the more lecherous gods that showed up later in South American tribes and in Greece and Rome. *Those* gods were just taken with how beautiful Lilith was, and generally gave her powers and favors in return for sex. Needless to say, Lilith had already started off with a pretty big potential for power from her half of the Yahweh crystal – so *had* she devoted her life solely to magic, she would have been a lesser god in her own right. Sadly, she did not. Lilith lived richly, luxuriously – with every whim satisfied by her host of attentive gods. She gave birth to many demi-gods, who each had about three times more natural magic talent than any human from Adam's lineage.

The most powerful of these – I would know, then forget, then discover again – was my Father.

I'd lived in New York City for the majority of my life. I moved here from a suburban neighborhood just outside of Baltimore. I still miss their crab pizzas. *Man*, those things were good!

I originally moved here to go to college for acting. Two years into a four-year degree, I realized that my love of pizza and sodas (and ice cream and chips and other such wonderful treats of life) was turning me into less of a leading man – and more of a huge wall in the background. It was about that time that the college loans I *could* afford started running out, and I was forced to start working in security to maintain the meager lifestyle I'd become accustomed to... in the best (and easily most expensive) city in the world.

I've dreamed of great things all my life, but it was becoming painfully clear that – shy of a billionaire taking me on as his late-life god-son – I would never achieve even a *fraction* of those idyllic goals. In my thirty years on this planet, I've been taken by nearly every get-rich-quick, "become financially independent"-type scheme that has likely existed. All of these were things I couldn't easily afford, but that's what the *truly evil* people of this Earth prey on... the hopes and dreams of the less fortunate. By the time I was 27, I had allowed myself one last hopeful, silly, pie-in-the-sky vice: a weekly lottery ticket.

I looked at it as my dollar-a-week dream. My best friend, Michael, just tended to call the lottery what it was: "retirement planning for dumb people". I can't help feeling like he ripped that quote off from somewhere, because it's a little cleverer than he generally is. Still, by my age, I was starting to agree with him.

I still remember the last time we went out drinking together on the town. It was always a production for us. Long time bro-fans of Barney Stinson, we were always sure to "suit up" before heading to some franchise-type NYC bar to see what vapid, drunk sorority girls would also be out for "their special night".

"Duuuuude... tonight's the night, my man," Michael encouraged me, already emboldened by his pre-bar ritual of a few vodka shots (so he would end up spending less to get appropriately buzzed).

"...As opposed to every *other* night?" Experience had made me a tad less hopeful – and infinitely more cynical. "You always think that just because you got lucky with the first girl you hit on *that one time* that you're going to be able to do the same thing again – at almost a *decade* older and with *easily* fifty more pounds on you."

"Hey, man – game is game. You either have it or you don't," he emphasized the statement with his patented, douche-y "point, wink, and make a clicking sound" gesture. "Besides, why are you trying to harsh my buzz so early on, tonight?"

"I don't know... I guess I'm just sick of spending money I don't *really* have to come out to these things and meet girls that I'd really *rather not* meet, truth be told." Suddenly, as if to drive the point home, a sickeningly popular club song came on to replace the last one. "*Ugh!* And if I have to hear that insipid song one more time, I'm just going to lose it. I hope that sloppy mess of a singer actually *does* 'die young'!"

Michael's eyes widened as if I'd just slapped his Mom, and I realized that I'd said that loudly enough for several bar tables to hear me, one of which had an attractive girl dressed in the singer's same disheveled fashion. I apologized to Michael with my eyes... just in case he'd had any plans to hit on her. He expertly guided me to the back of the club where no one had heard me, and then looked into my eyes with the most focused concern I've ever seen him attempt.

"Dude... seriously?" His question wasn't of an accusatory nature – more of getting to the root of what had turned his mild-mannered friend Malachi into a fierce misanthrope all of a sudden.

"Honestly, Michael – this all turned into just a weekly hangout with you a *long* time ago. You just seemed to enjoy the 'game' so much that I couldn't bear to tell you that I'd rather be home watching DVDs or something."

"Yeah, but I *know* you, man. Something's eatin' ya – what is it, really?" his gaze had not wavered. He sincerely wanted and cared about the truth.

His concern broke down my last remaining wall. "It was at work two nights ago…" He nodded and leaned back, crossing his arms and biting his lower lip like he always did when he was going to intently listen to something.

I'd gotten a pretty high-profile security job at an upscale strip club about a year ago. Back then, it was a treat just to see so many physically gorgeous women take their clothes off nightly. I had hardly worked there a month before I'd seen enough to clue me in to the fact that there was nothing *basically* different about these women... if you didn't count their cocaine habits (that *most* had) and the fact that they all viewed men as ATMs – as suckers waiting to be taken for every dollar they'd brought with them.

Still, it had been an awakening. In just a year, I'd seen over a dozen A-list celebrities breeze in and out of the VIP portion of the club (really, just a slightly raised section of the club floor with more comfortable seating – that would cost you $700 before you could even *sit down*), dropping hundreds of dollars as easily as regular patrons doled out ones. We always tried to look our most intimidating when the celebs where in the club, for as my mentor James told me: "You never know when some new rapper or freshly-popular actor is going to need to round out their bodyguard numbers."

That was the "big win" for us as security. If an upscale strip joint was the majors, then a celebrity signing you to his multi-million-dollar crew was a grand slam. You could kiss all the thankless long nights for pitiful pay (nearly 30% of which you'd *never see* – thanks to the upscale places paying *above* the table, asinine taxes and all) goodbye, and build a life around a man who not only *recognized* your value as a guard, but was ready to hook you into any entertainment field you desired to pursue as a bonus! As a never-quite-made-it actor, the last bit appealed to me the most tantalizingly. After all, I'm pretty sure that's how Michael Clarke Duncan (May the gods rest him.) got his start.

Granted, I wasn't one of the bulging-out-everywhere-with-muscles types like Duncan, but then again, I couldn't afford a decent diet *and* a decent apartment on the pittance we made for nightly destroying our bodies. That, and have you ***seen*** that man smile?? It was like a sunrise over some majestic mountains that had yet to even exist!

The point being, we were always on the lookout for a grand slam. In fact, on the night I was busy telling Michael about, *I* was the security assigned to the VIP section when in walked the most talked-about celebrity of the past week: *Viktor Bender*.

...And he had *zero* bodyguards.

"*Jackpot!*" I exclaimed in my head. "I've even already seen his new movie that's got everyone talking about him!" I steeled my resolve – I would be *out of here* tonight. "That's it, Malachi," I told myself. "Just play it cool. You'll have plenty to talk about when he asks, and you can just casually mention his glaring lack of security... you'll be in like Flynn."

Right on cue, he proudly made his way over to the VIP section, and I made sure to seat him *directly* next to where I stood guard. If there was a snowball's chance in *hell* of my getting employed by this newly-popular millionaire actor, I would take it or die trying. He settled in quickly, and asked me for a bottle of our most expensive vodka. I deftly called a waitress over and relayed the order.

She gushed in Viktor's direction before she left: "Right *away*, Mr. Bender!"

While he waited, he was practically mobbed by every gold-digging whore of a dancer in the place, each cozying up to him, making their standard small talk before asking if he wanted lap dances. I had to hand it to him – fame had given him a very cool head, and he declined them all expertly. After a few didn't take the hint that he was just there to relax in the presence of some "nice scenery", he gave me the slightest of glances to rid him of them. I jumped on it like a soldier protecting his foxhole comrades from a grenade.

"All right, ladies... let's allow Mr. Bender to get comfortable for a while before we throng him, okay?" My patronizing tone was *not* reflected in my eyes, which stared daggers at them. They obeyed, leaving with all the indignation that strippers can muster without being coincidentally amusing.

"You seem to know your way around people, um… what did you say your name was, again?"

"Malachi, Mr. Bender," I almost boasted the name.

"Right. Malachi. So, have you ever done any bodyguard-type work, Malachi?" He'd asked the golden question. I was a shoo-in. The grand slam would be *mine*!

Just then, as luck would have it, a fight broke out on the other side of the club. Fights generally call for every available member of security – just to make sure that they are speedily quelled. I courteously excused myself and rushed into the fray. What, on any other night, would have been my impressive display of martial arts "excellence", was preempted when a brawler outside of my line of sight cracked me over the head with a bar stool.

The other security guys ended up stopping the fight, and by the time I came to, I could see (through a bloodied brow) that James himself was smiling and shaking hands with Viktor Bender. My chance… was gone.

Michael listened, his mouth agape, with his eyes as wide as saucers. "So you not only *met* Viktor Bender, but you could've been his personal ***bodyguard***?"

I slowly nodded. "…Emphasis on the *could've been.*"

"Damn, bro… looks like your mentor really screwed you, there." Michael had an uncanny knack for stating the painfully obvious.

"Yeah – by the time I'd cleaned myself up and staggered back to my post, Viktor was telling me how he wanted me to meet his new head of security. I later even *asked* James if he could get me in on the deal, but he said that 'Mr. Bender' was only looking for one guy for now," I involuntarily clenched my teeth. "…That smug, condescending thief!"

A far-too-chipper waitress appeared out of nowhere. "So, how are you guys doing? May I get you anything?" Michael reacted like a man on a mission. "Yes! Bring me two Hurricanes. This man here…" he pointed at me. "…needs to get *drunk*, but it needs to be *sweet*. You feel me?" The narrative was lost on the waitress, who was obliviously jotting down the order on a pad. "Okay, guys! I'll be right back with that!"

I shot Michael a mocking glance. "*Hurricanes?*"

"What? I saw it on *Archer*. I want to try 'em." This man truly had no shame.

"Anyway, that's why we couldn't catch 'Ladies' Night' yesterday – I had to go to the hospital to get checked out. You have to do that if you ever lose consciousness, so they can check for any neural damage," I was talking out of my ass, but I was *probably* right.

"Ah, don't worry about it, big guy. The same girls show up to those things every time. Now that we're coming a night later, we'll be able to catch the one-timers and the pub crawlers," his wink indicated that I should've instinctively known what his pick-up jargon meant, so I didn't bother asking. "Hold on a second, dude. I see a solo pair at eleven o'clock… be right back." Just like that, he was off to another corner of the bar. I watched, and he'd said maybe two sentences before he was bringing both women back over to where I was. I had to hand it to him: when he was good, he was *really* good.

"Hey, Malachi – I just saw a booth open up. Let's snag it," he said in passing. I couldn't help but roll my eyes, but I followed them all the same. Michael made a point of ushering the woman he'd chosen into the booth first – something I'd come to call his "cornering" technique. I entered the booth from the other side first, as I disliked having to constantly move for women getting up to go to the bathroom and what-not. In retrospect, it might have helped my case to do a little "cornering" of my own, but that just wasn't who I was.

Michael got in next to the one of them that I can only refer to as having "far too large of breasts for them to have been real" (He always *did* like big breasts.), and motioned for the other woman to take a seat next to me. "Kai, this is Tisha," he motioned toward his ample catch. "And that's her friend Katie there next to you." I could spy the waitress coming toward us, as she'd intuitively found where we'd moved to. Michael continued, "Today is Tisha's birthday, and…"

"*WOOOO!!!*" Tisha yelled, throwing her arms in the air. The waitress flinched at the outburst, but to her credit, she managed not to spill the Hurricanes. Yep – Michael *sure* knew how to pick 'em.

The waitress classily maintained her composure as she set the drinks down. "Would you like to open a tab, sir?" she asked Michael. "Absolutely, good lady! And two more Hurricanes for the birthday girls!" he took great pride in slapping down his gold card on the table, as if it were still 1980. The waitress retrieved his card and smiled, "I'll be right back with those for you, sir."

What followed was a blur of drinking and general game from Michael, who impressed the girls enough for the *both* of us. Tisha was a typical "bimbo" type, and Katie wasn't much better – even though you could tell that she *thought* she was. I always hated that: people that were too stupid to *know* they were stupid. As the night wore on, it became overwhelmingly obvious that Michael had tossed the contemptuously "intellectual" Katie-grenade at me, and I was expected to take one for the team. I was in no mood to be compliant, but the drinks were allowing me to stifle my disgust for every annoying thing that came out of her mouth...

"I got *my* degree online – only morons waste money on *physical* colleges anymore."

"Yoga is *so* the perfect way to keep your mind harmonized with your body."

"I *only* shop organic... I mean, we all have to do our part to save the Earth, right?"

"You know, I read online that they've found evolutionary proof that black people evolved from monkeys with less cranial capacity."

That was it. I was drunk, but I had *had it*. Ignorance, I can tolerate to a point; but bigotry and cultural elitism really ignites my wrath. "*FUCK you*, you arrogant, racist harpy!! Get out! Get the fuck out of this booth!" I shoved into her chubby side until she relented and let me get by her. "Michael, I'm sorry, but I can only take so much. Have fun with Tisha, but Katie here is *insufferable*." I left the bar in a rage, and somehow managed to make it back to my apartment safely, though ridiculously inebriated.

The next thing I remembered, I was waking up in my bed. My suit coat and tie were on the floor, but I'd apparently slept in everything else. The worst part was the gradual realization – through a hangover fog – that I was scheduled to work later that day. I thought about calling in sick, but my looming rent payment prevented me from seriously entertaining that thought for very long.

I picked up my suit coat off the floor and reached inside it for my wallet. If I'd unwittingly started a tab the night before whilst drunk, I hoped I would have at least had sense enough to get a receipt for it. To a mixture of relief and foreboding, I found the spot where I usually kept such things was empty. I was relieved that there was nothing there, but at the same time, trusted in my own history of addle-pated neglect to have left such a thing behind.

Leaving a tab behind you at a bar is bad for two reasons: 1) the bartender will naturally assume you were too drunk to remember what you ordered (and he would've been correct on *that* account) and add additional things to your tab to make the bar (or more likely, *himself*) more money, and 2) it leaves the "Tip" field blank. Anyone that frequents bars, dining establishments, or even has pizza delivered knows what I've known my whole life – not only is it *gracious* in modern society to leave an adequate tip (I generally would strive for 20%.), but servers and delivery people alike *remember* good tippers (as well as *cheap-asses* that stiff them entirely)… and treat you accordingly on your next visit. Suffice it to say: I was sincerely hoping I'd not left an open tab.

To my surprise, I found that I had managed to purchase a lottery ticket that night – just prior to the 11PM drawing. I could tell that I was drunk when I did, because I hadn't played my usual numbers… I'd just taken the random set that the machine chooses for you.

"Great," I thought. "Well, there goes *that* chance. Those stupid things **never** pick the winning numbers!" I trudged over to my recliner and slumped down into it, allowing the ticket to fall onto the "crate covered with a bedsheet" that was acting as my end table. I picked up my laptop from the floor, near the outlet where I'd carelessly plugged in its charger a *year* ago – and never moved it.

My first casual stop was the same as always… scrolling through pictures of the great castles of England and France and Scotland, imagining them in their primes. I wished every day – on everything I held holy and dear – that I could one day build a magnificent *American* castle… a monument to lasting greatness, a legacy whereby my name and the names of my progeny from here to eternity would be remembered. I'd even chosen a nice spot of mountainous land in the middle of a western state known to have the lowest property taxes in the country – and ready access to craftsmen that had been building castles (of a sort) since the 90s. It was a plot of *thousands* of acres, just *waiting* for some millionaire to erect a kingdom. "If only…" I heaved my usual sigh of quiet despair, and set about handling the remainder of my morning affairs as usual.

I figured I could check my email and still have time to browse some porn before work. (After all, like Sean Rouse said years ago: "You gotta get the poison out.") As always, small news blurbs would pop up on the email server's front page, so my eyes would naturally fall upon the most interesting.

It just so happened that there was a non-descript headline about the NY Lottery – apparently, someone had won the Mega-Millions jackpot. "Awesome," I mused, with ironic cheer. "Let's see who *else* gets to live their dreams instead of me." (Yeah, I'm a bummer when I first wake up, but who *isn't*?) I clicked on the article only to find that they only knew that that someone – one person, in fact – had won because they had been that one-in-a-*billion* lucky bastard that had won from choosing automated numbers.

Just… like… *I* had.

I allowed myself the spark of hope that I generally deny myself (but is *itself* the reason why people play the lottery in the *first* place) and turned quickly to retrieve the limp piece of paper that was my ticket from my makeshift end table. Activating a mental drum roll,

I scrolled the article downwards to the winning numbers, and checked them with the tenacity of a detective who's been given a hot clue.

What…

the…

HELL?!?

The numbers were a perfect match. I had just won *two hundred million dollars*! I checked again in frantic disbelief. I called up the official lottery website to confirm it. It was all there… in tiny little destiny-fulfilling pixels.

"*YES!!!*" I exclaimed, jumping up from my recliner with a roar that surely shook the pillars of the Earth. "Fucking *YES!!!*" My celebration was violent, profane, and utterly satisfying. Yesterday, I was Joe Schmoe Schlub – just some jerk on the street. Today, I was Mr. Fucking Moneybags, and my first instinct was to rub it in the faces of every enemy I'd ever had, every family member that thought I'd never amount to anything.

Fortunately, a cooler head prevailed. "No," I thought. "For once in my paradise-free life, I'd better plan my next moves carefully." And so I did.

Now, I'm not normally a spiteful person, but there has been one particular dancer at my work that – if she wasn't (for *whatever* crazy reason) the club owner's favorite – then I would have **long** ago told her exactly where she could stick it... whilst shoving her out of a window. You've got to understand, though: Vanessa was the kind of bitch that only other *bitches* flocked to. She was constantly talking about people behind their backs – even the security guys (And what kind of idiot talks smack about the guys that are there *for their protection*?)! I remember one time, about a month into my job there, that she just happened to be next to the time clock when I came to punch in. She offered the smarmy, back-handed comment: "Well, you're on *time* today! *That's* good."

My first thought was, "This bitch is *far* too invested in my work schedule." But knowing her connection to the boss, all I replied with was, "I've only been late *twice* in a **month**. That's *hardly* the kind of record that merits such derision. I'm almost *never* late."

She scoffed, "You're *never* late? Now *that's* a lie!" As with most bitches, she had irritatingly selective hearing.

"That's not what I...!" I couldn't bring myself to finish the sentence. I just turned away with a growl. I had a ten-hour day of standing on my already swollen, aching feet ahead of me, and I didn't need to be reminded that some whore (that had basically just called me an unreliable liar) was among them.

As with most objects of anger, however, your mind can't help but to focus on them. It's like an awful song that you just can't get out of your head. I watched her lazily "work"... overheard her disparaging security with another dancer... even had her tell *me* at some point (as if we were bitch-buddies) that a faithful club patron was a "douchebag".

Honestly, I just didn't get the appeal. I couldn't, for the life of me, understand *why* the boss favored this little blonde jerk. She would always brag about how "great" her tits were, but she failed to take into account three things that any observer of womankind would know in a week: she was short (Short women more easily have "curves".), she was *chunky* (Fat women also tend to have more pronounced curves.), and what little she **did** have, she was always augmenting with padded push-up bras. Her "great tits" were all smoke and mirrors – she was merely an average chubby, short chick with access to upscale underwear.

Keep in mind, for all her abusiveness and misplaced vanity, I'd never said even a cross word to Vanessa. I was barely making the rent as it was, and with James having taken my last foreseeable windfall opportunity, I needed the boss to think well of me. I couldn't have some uppity 22-year-old with a chip on her shoulder-fat keep me from *eating* and having a *roof* over my head! Suffice it to say, it was one of those unenviable situations that the common man finds himself in *all too often* in today's workforce.

But **today** was different. I had a paycheck coming – which I, thankfully, no longer needed – so I had one last good reason to march in there and give this spiteful harridan *what-for*.

I stopped off first at the bank where I kept a safety deposit box (I told you – *dreamer*.) in which I'd previously only kept one first-strike gold coin that I'd bought online for $1200. It seemed like it would be a good investment, but I'd almost spent $300 so far just keeping the *box*. (These are the kinds of things rich people never bother to tell you.) At any rate, I was glad to have the box at this juncture, because I could chance neither carrying the winning ticket on me *to* the job (in case someone decided to get brave and try to rob me), nor leave it at home (as the boss had my home address on file, and could have easily had any of his not-so-above-board "friends" go and fetch it from there while I was either incapacitated or *dead*). Like I said: I now needed to plan my moves *carefully*.

Once that was taken care of, I made my way over to the strip club. I strutted in with the kind of confidence that only a man with a new lease on life (wearing street clothes and sneakers instead of a work uniform and steel-toed boots) could have. I had always changed at home, and I was *hours* early, so all my "boys" in security knew something was up. A couple even filled in behind me.

"Dude… you're *early*?" "Hey, what's up?" they queried.

I instinctively borrowed a line from a Kevin Hart bit that I knew we'd all seen: "It's about *to go down*." Excited gasps and squeals of glee (uncommon in behemoth-sized security men) erupted from them both, as they continued to follow me. This would, at the *very* least, be a story that they could tell later.

I knocked loudly on the boss' door in every door's noisy, weak spot (the top corner above the handle – a trick you learn working collections for a rental company). It was loud enough that it could've easily been the cops. But had it *been* the cops (The boss had a top quality surveillance system installed.), he'd have had his two biggest guards blocking the door before the cops could even *get* there. "Come in, already… and quit banging on my door like an asshole!" I heard him bellow from inside. I could tell that I was going to *enjoy* this.

I threw open the door, startling the boss and causing Vanessa to fall right off of his lap. "Listen here, jackass!" I yelled with the authority of Genghis Khan. "I just came by to tell you three things: I don't need this *shitty* job, I *know* you've been skimming 10% of our paychecks under the 'taxes' section this whole time…" (At this point, I paused to turn to my security brothers and said: "It's true – the section of your paycheck under taxes labeled STRIPNY is *bullshit*. You should *sue* this motherfucker.") "…and that mouthy bitch-whore of a slut that just fell off of your fat lap just *also* happens to be fucking James!" The last part wasn't true, but the boss would never believe it wasn't. I left them all astonished and walked out like a proud hero, allowing Fate to let those three decide their *own* punishments.

It occurred to me just how many great working men of our age must have been being held down by the constraints of necessities. Have the mighty warriors of today become naught but wage slaves, embroiled in the daily struggle for shelter and sustenance? Indubitably. How many more good men would instantly rise against the affront of common tyranny if their very livelihoods did not hang in the balance? The world might never again know.

Stepping out onto the street, I faced the July heat wave bravely, knowing that it would surely not be long before I'd be resting comfortably in some nicely-equipped penthouse that was perennially cooled to a nice, livable 67 degrees or so. Then it hit me… why settle for the nicest that NYC has to offer? Surely, with $200 million, someone would be able to build, say, a *castle* of worthy proportions that would dwarf the finest cramped *city* dwellings, right? (I would later find that I had a *lot* to learn about construction and the things associated therewith.)

Still… my dreams were large, and they spurred me onward. And a small fact began to gnaw at me: I had yet to *claim* the fortune I'd won. It was a situation fraught with nervous energy – do I go ahead and claim it openly, and risk harm on the way to/from the awarding… or do I wait until I'd secured an adequate personal guard and risk another drawing being held (with a new winner voiding my claim)?

I decided to go for a third option, and called my best friend Michael, who was nearly as large as I. "Most people wouldn't dream of risking bodily injury to attack *two* big guys… even if they had millions in a briefcase handcuffed to one of them!" I mused, foolishly underestimating the desperation of the times. Michael answered, and was quick to give me hell for the previous night.

"*Dude!* What the *hell* was up with you last night? Tisha was a *lock*, and then her shitty friend decided she wanted to go to a different bar, like, ten minutes after you blew up and left! She *totally* twat-blocked me!" I chuckled; his 'game' jargon was occasionally quite funny. "What have I told you about *grenades*, man? Sometimes, you just have to nut up and take one for the…"

"Yeah, yeah, yeah," I quickly interrupted – I had no time for sports metaphors from a man that admittedly played none. "Look, Michael – I'm sorry, okay? But I don't have time right now to go into all that… I *really* need your help."

"Oh, so **now** you need…" I could sense the change in his tone, as if he'd suddenly acquired an unassailable upper hand. I didn't have time for that, either.

"**Michael!!**" I interjected again. "Seriously, dude? Not right now. I need to *bypass* all the normal B-S, because I *genuinely need* your assistance. Now, can you help me or not?"

"All right, all right – keep your panties on! You need me to come over to your place or are you in my neighborhood?"

Finally – some progress. "Meet me at my place as soon as you can," I instructed him. He told me that he was finishing up a lunch date in Manhattan, so he could meet me at my place in Brooklyn before the end of the hour. Trust me… in NYC, that's relatively quick.

When he arrived, I tried being vague about exactly *why* I needed him to accompany me, but ended up caving in to his constant, energetic barrage of questions. (Apparently, his lunch date was in a *coffee* bistro.) After some initial incredulousness on his part, followed closely by jubilation at the thought that I might *share* my winnings (I seriously was *not* considering it… not for *much*, anyway.), I managed to calm him down enough to have him put on a "game face" apropos enough to accompany me from the bank to the downtown office of the NY lottery to turn in my winning ticket. I was highly skeptical of even the lottery workers, but they assured me that signing the back of the ticket (along with all the pictures and videos I'd taken of myself *with* the ticket before Michael originally *got* to my place) was sufficient to prove that it was mine. (After all the shitty things people had pulled on me in my lifetime, I wasn't **about** to let my dreams be snuffed out by an opportunistic lottery office worker.) They then handed me a file claim ticket and told me they'd contact me in two weeks to arrange the award ceremony. After I left the building, I felt like I should've had the workers sign a notarized statement that they had, in fact, *received* my ticket as well, but Michael assured me that I was being a pain in the ass.

The two weeks of waiting were ***torture***, but I managed to pass my newly-unemployed yet still-pretty-broke time fairly quickly by watching a lot of old episodes of *Merlin*, *Legend of the Seeker*, and even some *Kröd Mändoon*. I also built pretty much an entire *city* out of obsidian in Minecraft (on a PvP server, with *no available mods*). I made a few decent sketches of some castle amenities and architectural structures that I liked from some of my favorite castle photo books, which I thought I could integrate into my American castle's final designs. I even re-watched some old BBC videos of Fred Dibnah hosting *The Art of Castle Building*. Other than the intermittent calls from Michael to see if the lottery people had called me early, it was a fairly ***focused*** two weeks, all things considered.

Then it came… the call from the lottery people. It was to be a small ceremony in the morning (ostensibly so I'd have enough time to deposit my ginormous check before the banks closed that day) with a light brunch (the only meal I've ever thought catered *exclusively* to White people with too much time on their hands). It was a closed affair, so they assured me that only one news outlet would be allowed to cover it (and only as much as I wanted), and no outside guests or panhandling charities would be allowed inside. It sounded heartless on its face, but I had to agree that making my way to the bank would be exponentially more difficult with a desperate crowd of people in front of me. I had even chosen a bank that also had a nearby branch in the state in which I was looking to erect my castle. It all merely waited upon my lifeless alarm clock…

I awoke to my alarm the next day like a kid on Christmas morning. For the first time in almost two *decades*, there was something worth getting out of bed for that was truly magical and exciting… *my destiny*! As I stumbled over the mess I had accrued in almost a year in this cramped, rented Brooklyn room, I thought – with relish – how this could very possibly be the absolute *last* time that I would ever do so. My small, cynical troll of a subconscious tried to talk me out of this reality, as if it were all just an incredibly unbelievable dream that I was long overdue to wake from. I ignored him.

Michael was over my place in a span of time so short that it seemed like he was camping out on the sidewalk in front of my building. He wore his snappiest suit, and the look of disappointment on his face at seeing my attire of jeans and my favorite t-shirt ("All your base are belong to us.") was the icing on my pleasant cake.

"What the *hell* are you wearing? Didn't you rent a tux or something??"

"Hey, man – millionaires can dress however the hell they want!" I beamed with joy. I was clearly not all he expected a rich friend to be. Sensing that making me displeased might adversely affect whatever small fortune he expected I might share with him, he cleared his throat and thought the better about further admonishing me.

"Well, Everyman, we'd better hurry up and catch the subway if we're going to be there on time."

"Don't worry, Michael… I saved out *just* enough money for us to travel in *style*…" his eyes perked up as if I'd ordered a limousine. "The cab should be arriving any minute." He wrinkled up his nose at first, and then smiled at my simplicity.

"Oh, well… I guess it's better than waiting to change subway trains in that July *oven* of a station at Franklin Avenue!"

"*Now* you're thinking!" I praised him. "And besides, who wants to waste money *and* draw unnecessary attention to themselves by taking a limo?"

He grasped the end of his chin, thinking. "Hmmm... I guess you're right. Wow, you've really thought this *through*, huh?"

I clapped him on the shoulder and looked earnestly into his eyes. "You have *no idea*."

The ride to the Manhattan Hilton was pretty quiet, as I'd instructed Michael not to talk to the cabbie. He just spent his time giggling and making faces at me, like some kid trapped with his brother in the backseat of a long family-car road trip. I couldn't help but smile as well. After all, my life was about to change *drastically* for the better. The cabbie probably thought we were nuts.

We were warmly greeted in the lobby by a lottery staff worker who had been given my picture (I'm guessing from the surveillance footage at the lottery office). She ushered us quietly into a small conference room, the likes of which I'd seen many a time at various "get rich quick" seminars. "What a coincidence," I thought to myself.

So few people were there that it caused Michael to scoff: "So where's the marching band? The dancing girls? Did you just win $200 *million* or two *thousand*?" The lottery lady jumped on the question quickly. "Oh, everything is as Malachi here has requested." She turned to me, embarrassed. "*Oops!* Should I even *call* you Malachi, or should I call you Mr. ...?"

"Malachi is fine," I stopped her. She nodded politely and led me to the small dais.

"Picture for the paper, sir?" the one press photographer spoke up.

"No," I answered. "And I'd like you to keep my *name* out of the paper as well." He turned away, grumbling into his cell phone, "Well then what the hell am I even *here* for, Sheila?" He packed up his camera and I thought I heard a shutter snap – without a flash. I glared at him angrily.

"Oh! Sorry there, big guy… just a misfire." His grin was not comforting, but I chose to ignore it.

"We have all the paperwork right here for you to sign, Malachi," the lottery lady directed me toward a small, red felt-covered pedestal. "This is the amount you'll have deposited here…" she pointed to a number clearly less than $200 million.

"Whoa! Hold up!" I protested. "This only says $125,633,334! What did you crooks do with $75 *million* of my money?!?"

Calm as a cucumber, she pointed to another section of a previous form where I had agreed to a lump-sum payment. "The lump sum payment is *always* less than if you waited years to get your money. Plus, if you look at the final line, sir, you'll see that you only get 75% of that thanks to federal resident withholding." My jaw hit the floor, and almost to add insult to injury, she leaned in and whispered, "And I probably shouldn't be telling you this, but federal taxes will take about 39.6% of that immediately, as well as New York taking 12.7% since you won this as a New York resident."

"*Jesus fucking Christ!*" I exclaimed. Michael, a superstitious Catholic, gasped. "Sorry, man," I apologized. "Nah," he said. "I kinda get it. That's pretty fucked up right there." I took a deep breath and asked her to do a quick calculation. "So, what are my *actual* winnings today?"

"$94.225 Million…" she proclaimed stoically. "And you'll owe $49.75 million of that in federal income taxes and $15.96 million of that in state income taxes by the end of the year."

"**Shit**. The IRS are the *real* winners. *How do they pull a scam like that?*" I wondered.

With the realization that I only *really* had a claim to $28.515 million out of my ***$200 Million*** jackpot, I left the Hilton a little crestfallen. Sure… $28 million is still nothing to sneeze at, as it was *light-years* from where I'd been before, but it was still like the kid on Christmas morning being told he's getting a new Playstation, who runs downstairs expecting a PS4 and gets a PS2 "refurb" from a discount shop.

Michael shared my chagrin, though not entirely. "That sucks, dude," he offered, loosening his tie. "Still, though – we should *party*! We need to go out and do it up like millionaires do!" I had just been told that I actually had a little over 10% of the money I thought I'd actually won… I was in no mood to party.

"I'm sorry, Michael… I just want to stay in by myself at some hotel and order room service. I need to gather my thoughts, okay?" The sadness in my eyes coerced his compliance.

"All right, bro. You do what you need to do. But *call me* when you come out of your shell, okay? You know I always love hearing about your crazy ideas!" That was true. He always had.

I stopped by the bank to get the withdrawal card for my new account. They wanted me to stay and talk to one of their VIP account advisors, but I just wanted to crawl into a hole and be *sad* for a while. I stopped by my apartment to pick up my laptop, and checked into the nicest hotel (with Wi-Fi) that I could find. I slumped into the goose-down comforter on the king-sized bed and stared over at the 60" LCD HDTV in my suite.

I *should've* been as happy as a clam, but all I could think about was how much *less* of a kingdom that I could buy with the stymied purchasing power of only $28 million. I needed to get my head into a better place, so I decided to do the only thing I could think of… visit the hotel bar.

I hadn't even changed out of my silly t-shirt and jeans when I arrived to see that most everyone else in the fancy bar-space was appropriately "suited up". I didn't care. I flashed my room card at the host like an ID badge and asked if there was any room at the bar. He gave my attire the once-over before informing me, "Oh... geez... um, it's a jacket-only dress code tonight. I'm really sorry." His tone was one of regret, instead of the normal snooty, dismissive uptown attitude. For that reason, I reached into my pocket for the few thousand dollars I'd taken with me from the bank earlier (my "walking around" money) and slipped him a hundred.

"Will *that* take care of the dress code?" the money gave me an uncommon confidence.

He looked at the money in his hand in shock, as if I'd just handed him the last smoldering chunk of the family barn. "Oh, man... I'd love to, really, but the maitre d' is kind of a jerk." He was probably the only honest, sincere host I'd ever met in my life.

Then, a lightbulb lit up in his head. "I know!" He began removing his own suit jacket to give to me. "Here... take this. I'll just go get my spare that I keep in my car!" His small-town genuineness was actually touching. He signaled to a nearby waitress, "Hey, tell Claude I'm going on a quick break, okay?" and then he was off. I was almost stunned out of my funk... *almost*.

I crossed to the bar and took the only available stool. Apparently, rich hotel patrons have either a lot of sorrows to drown in alcohol or a lot to celebrate. Generally, the cynic in me would opine that the latter was the case, but the somber mood of the place denied the accusation outright. Even the jazz that softly played over the sound system was depressing. This wasn't a place to *escape* my gloom; it was a place to *nurture* it. I was past seeking freedom from my despondent bonds, and was to the point where we all get as humans – where we almost *enjoy* the depression.

The bartender was surprisingly prompt. "And for you, sir?"

"Just gimme something strong… and lots of it." Having been lower middle class for the majority of my life, I was a *pro* at being depressed. For whatever reason, my response had sparked the interest of the man on the barstool next to me.

"That's a pretty heavy order, friend. What's eatin' ya?" The voice was soothing and familiar, but I couldn't quite place it. I turned my head for a casual glance at the man, and quickly did a double-take. It was *Nathan fucking Fillion*!

My eyes no doubt became as wide as the bar napkins, while my chin could've told you what grain the hardwood floor in the place was. This was *Nathan Fillion*… Rick Castle… Cap'n Hammer… Captain Mal *Reynolds*, for fuck's sake! He was the singular reason I'd stopped correcting people when they shortened my name to "Mal" instead of "Kai", like I'd always preferred. I mean – yeah – his Mal stood for a different *name*, but it was close enough for me! I looked up into the irises that appeared to hold the power to stop time itself… and immediately realized that the puzzlement they expressed was in response to my having been frozen in awe-face for nearly half a minute.

I regained what little of my composure that I could, and cleared my throat. "Ahem! Oh, sorry… I was thinking of something… else." I winced at my "recovery", but smiled like the *non*-craziest person I could think of being at the moment. He chuckled, a little amused at my awkwardness, and extended his manly hand.

"Sorry for the intrusion. I'm Nathan Fillion. And you are…?"

I almost forgot. "I'm Malachi Hunter. Nice to meet you." Short of mild recognition, one has to feign ignorance of the personage of a celebrity lest they become quickly weary of an obvious fan's exuberance. Needless to say, my depression had evaporated.

If my luck included both winning the lottery *and* meeting Nathan, the odds were good that the Universe was now swinging the fortune pendulum *decidedly* in my favor. I must've subconsciously figured that one never knows when that great cosmic weight will start swinging in reverse, so it's best to just enjoy life's pleasures while they sit before you... quite literally, in Mr. Fillion's case. I was really just shocked that he was *alone*, but of course decided not to pry.

After my first horrifically strong drink was done, I began joining Nathan in his favored drink – rum and coke (with Dr. Pepper instead of actual Coca-Cola). It was an unassuming, yet adventurous drink. Or, as he put it: "Who wouldn't want to be a pirate, right?" It was too early in our acquaintance for me to know whether or not he was joking, considering he'd *already* been a superhero, millionaire playboy, and cowboy spaceship captain. Come to think of it, if he ever has kids, he's already starred in all of their possible bedtime stories.

After he put my wealth in perspective ("You're bummed about $28 million? That's easily four *times* my net worth, and I'm *famous*!"), and I told him about my plans for a castle and all ("Not a bad plan, if you can pull it off. If it ever becomes a medieval community, let me know; I'll stop by to say hello and feast."), I was feeling like I had won the lottery *twice*. The man was generous with his time and counsel, and worldly-wise without being world-weary.

We had a few laughs, and then called it a night. My head was spinning from both the company and the alcohol at that point, and I retired to my room for the evening. I wasn't sure how exactly I got undressed (or anything *else* I may have done), because I was still in that after-glow you have once you meet someone famous and they turn out to actually be *cool* in person. The liquor had merely prolonged the effect.

I awoke the next morning to the incessant buzzing of my cheap cell phone. I groggily answered, only to find that it was Michael on the other end. "*DUDE!*" even the first word out of his mouth was like a punch in the face. "You meet Nathan gorram *Fillion* last night, and all I get is a drunk-dial afterwards?? Why didn't you have him call me and leave a crazy message or something? Or even better... why didn't you *invite me the hell over* to wherever you were and let me **meet** him?? How could you..."

"*Whoa!*" the only word I could think to stop his reckless assault on Fort Hangover. "Take it easy, man... we were drinking... *a lot...*"

"Pffft... well, *that* much was obvious from your message," he'd mercifully applied the brakes to his ramming-speed charge. "So... why didn't you at least take a *picture* with him or something?"

"Well, he gave me his business card," I found, as I multi-tasked the conversation with my ritual post-drunk wallet search. "Besides, my phone doesn't *have* a camera. You know that!"

"*Seriously?* **Still?** Why do you keep that piece of crap phone anyway?"

"I keep it exactly *because* it's just a phone!" I retorted. "If you'll recall, it was a major selling point when I originally went to get it!"

"Yeah, that and you're cheap," he muttered.

"I'm not *cheap*, you ass! Phones were meant to be just that... *phones*! Not computers, not cameras, not super-mini movie theaters... just **phones**! Maybe the *rest* of you clods could get decent reception and not have calls dropping left and right if your phones didn't have all that unnecessary **crap** clogging up the space that *mine* uses for just a dialer and a digital antenna!" He'd brought this rant on himself, and the exasperated sigh on the other end of the line meant that he was resigned to take it. "And since when is *texting* supposed to be a step *forward* in progress? Oh, I forgot... it's for all these twenty-somethings and under that never knew how shitty it was to take *typewriter* classes! It just so happens we *already have* a magical device that sends your fucking *voice* through the air so that neither you nor the person on the other end has to bother with *word-processing*… it's called a ***PHONE!***"

"Are you done?" his sarcastic tone was palpable.

"Mostly," I paused for a decent breath or two. "But while I'm on the subject…" I could hear a drawn-out groan on the other end. "These young yuppie-spawn socialites with their camera-phones are *really* annoying. I could see this couple of idiot blondes not *three tables away* from where Nathan and I were, snapping pictures all damn night – of *themselves*, mind you – as if being out at a bar is now somehow a 'memorable' occasion. Yeah… the hotel and sports bars are now the new Pyramids and Great Wall. Fucking morons," I grumbled. "It's like – give any kid an iPhone and all of a sudden, they think they're Jimmy fucking Olsen or something."

"You realize how much of a crotchety grandpa you sound like right now, don't you?" he jeered.

"I don't care. It's bullshit," I was done. "Besides, you know how cranky I get after I drink."

"Yep," he said, brightly. "I definitely do. Now why don't you pop your patented painkiller cocktail and meet me for lunch, huh?" If anyone knew me, it was Michael… and I definitely needed an excuse to clean myself up and get out in the sunlight. That, and I had to return that nice host's suit coat, which I'd apparently worn out of the bar.

"All right, man. Just give me a few minutes to get straightened up, and I'll give you a call." I wanted to roll back over and go back to sleep, but I'd made plans, and adults *keep them*.

I met Michael at one of his franchise-type bar haunts on the Upper East Side that also happened to serve pretty decent food. The place was surprisingly tolerable in the middle of the day.

"So you're finally calmed down, grandpa?" he wryly asked, as we took a seat at one of the many open booths. I was willing to overlook the jab, as my synthetic opiates were starting to kick in. "Oh shut up, you doofus," I smiled.

A bored-looking waitress took our order and then promptly shuffled off without so much as a pleasantry to either of us. Had I not been chilling on my prescribed drugs (As a security guy, lower back pain from standing long hours is pretty standard.), I might have said something acerbically snarky, but I opted for enduring her "lack of social courtesy" slight... and for enjoying spit-free food.

"All I'm saying is that Nathan is like a giant..." Michael annoyingly continued, even though I thought we were done with the subject.

"He's only 6-foot-1. Hell, even *I'm* 6-foot-4!"

"That's not what I meant, and you know it. It's a metaphor... *duh*."

Had he not added the "duh" as if *I* were the simpleton, I might not have corrected him. "Actually, you said he was '*like* a giant'. That's a **simile**. A metaphor would have been if you'd said he actually *was* a giant," I paused for effect. "*DUH*."

He gesticulated his consternation: "Gaaah! *Whatever*. He's like some sort of mythical beast that – when you see it – you feel the overwhelming need to take a picture with it, or you will literally die."

"*Figuratively*," I was just being a jerk now, but it was fun.

"What??" he hadn't caught it quickly enough to know what I was talking about.

"No one literally dies from failing to take a photograph. You would *figuratively* die," I sipped slowly from the straw in my water to mock him. (And while I'm remembering that detail, who puts *straws* in their drinks anymore? Does the straw salesman have some sort of mafia-like deal with NYC restaurants, or do they just have *such little faith* in their dishwashers/dishwashing machines to do a thorough enough cleaning job? Sorry… it irritates me.)

He caught on. "Yeah? Well, you're a jackass when you're high," he slouched backwards and crossed his arms like a scolded eight-year-old. I sipped a bit more to drive the point home that I'd won, and sincerely hoped we'd not be talking any more about my night drinking with Nathan Fillion.

The waitress appeared again, nonchalantly dropped off our order at the table, and lazily asked, "Will there be anything else?" Michael – always quick to rebound – responded, "Sure… how about a smile?" I was actually a little relieved that he had noticed her surliness as well. She flashed us one of those "I'm not really trying."-grins before she listlessly made her way back to the waitress station.

"Is it just me, or is she just not *giving* a flying fuck today?" I asked Michael, who had already shrugged off the waitress' cold manners and was mid-way through a bite of his burger. He took the time to chew before swallowing and answered, "Yeah, bro. She's a bitch."

I looked at him knowingly. "Nine cents?"

He nodded his agreement to my proposal, "Nine cents." (See… I once dated this cute girl named Shannon that I recalled had dug through her purse to get the proper coinage for a nine cent tip, for a waitress that she had said – and I quote: "Wasn't *worth* a dime." Michael and I had thought it so clever that we made a habit of never going out to eat without nine pennies… should the occasion ever again present itself.)

We continued eating happily in the otherwise dismal bar, and discussed the plans I'd come up with for my American castle in the west. He proposed that I hire the castle-building team from the state I'd talked about, but that I should also think about hiring a qualified architect/engineer to oversee them. By this, he meant himself, even though he'd only taken *one year* of both subjects at a community college in the state where I'd met both him and Shannon. "It's okay," I figured to myself. "I should have him involved in *some* kind of way. I'll just tell the workers to let him *think* he's in charge, and then present any glaring faults with his propositions to him in a way that would make him think that *he* had thought of the perfect solution for them." And yes… my thoughts are often very long.

"Before I can really do *any* of this stuff, though… I should meet with the realtor handling that huge property and tell him of my interest in it."

"Yes… quite," Michael adopted his most "advisor-like" chin stroke. I got the express feeling that Michael was beginning to think he'd have an automatic position in my future "Royal" household. He probably would, but I hadn't even *begun* (at that point) to consider the laws and governance of what had the potential to become a full-blown modern day medieval society… and not just a grand castle.

We finished the lunch – some of the driest burgers we'd ever eaten – and ceremoniously slapped nine cents onto the table (on top of our credit card receipt, in which we'd written in the "Tip" line: *Grow a decent personality!*) before we left. I made a few last-minute arrangements and got us both first-class seats on the next plane to the land of my future castle.

I managed to get two seats right next to one another in first-class. It was the first time I'd ever *been* in first-class, but Michael had won a trip several years ago to some fancy-schmancy time share that flew him there first-class. When he tried to leave without buying into one, I think they tried to have some thugs beat him up (if I recall correctly). Still, it was a nice departure from our normal lower class, cramped lives – if only for seven hours (including our obscenely long layover in Salt Lake City).

I had chosen the window seat, so I wouldn't have to be getting up if Michael needed to use the bathroom during our flight, but also so I'd have the tiniest window (*heh*) of opportunity to scope out the mountains of this state during the hour-long second leg of our journey. Michael had consoled himself with the fact that he'd be able to at least hit on the stewardesses during the flight, but we were seated and served by two of the most horribly ugly geriatric female flight attendants that I'd ever seen, so for our first ten minutes in the air, all I did was glance over at him and snicker intermittently. He was not amused, and sat with his arms crossed like a spoiled little kid.

Once we landed in the capital city, a private plane (a single-engine Cessna) was scheduled to fly us further into the backwoods of the state – the truest mountain country, which appeared (at my last Google Maps perusal) to be surrounded on most every side with National parks and forestation. Carting our luggage and various bags over to the relatively tiny plane was a shocking wake-up call. We were going from reclining, first-class seating to pretty cramped quarters. And our deep-voiced, slumber-inducing, militarily-uniformed pilot was replaced with someone who reminded me of Jack Dalton from *MacGyver*... only he was older, had a bushier mustache, and his leather flight jacket looked like it had seen *far* better days. You know what? I take that back – he looked like what would've resulted if Jack Dalton and Sam Elliott were somehow able to have a son. Yeah... *that*.

As he unceremoniously crammed our luggage into the Cessna's rear storage, I let Michael into the plane first, as I was planning to take the seat next to the pilot. Michael took his rear seat, pouting: "I suppose I should just be thankful that I get a *window* this time, huh?"

"Oh, don't be childish. You didn't pay for *either* of your tickets, dude." He harrumphed. I hadn't meant to be so curtly matter-of-fact, but it *was*, after all, true. The pilot (whose name I never got, now that I recall – we'll just call him "Jack"), after he'd slammed the luggage compartment door closed, climbed up into his place behind the control yoke. He looked over at me quizzically, as I sat behind similar steering controls meant for a copilot.

"What do you think you're doing, sir?"

"Uh... what? What do you mean?" I hadn't caught on yet.

"This isn't an episode of *Wings*, sir. You are not allowed to sit up here unless you're an FAA-licensed pilot."

He *looked* serious, but as a knee-jerk reaction I asked, "*Seriously?*" Heck, for all I knew, he could've had a state-specific sense of humor that I just wasn't accustomed to. His expression remained grimly serious and he crossed his arms, waiting in silence.

"Geez, okay!" I relented and climbed in the back with Michael. He laughed, taunting me for having to share the same quality of view as his. I probably deserved it. Still, Jack was the *only* plane that flew from the capital city into the small mountain airport near the isolated hamlet to which we were headed. One doesn't argue with the owner of that kind of monopoly.

After he'd taxied to the lonely runway assigned to him – behind 747s that looked like absolute *behemoths* in comparison – he pushed the throttle in completely and the plane rattled to a much noisier degree than either of us were used to *or* comfortable with. "Hang on to your hats, gentlemen... here we *go!*" It was the first thing he'd said with any passion at all, so I figured it was the closest he'd get to actual humor.

It was almost ten whole minutes of Michael and I admiring the views out of each of our tiny windows before Jack's voice broke the silence that we'd been blissfully unaware was filling the cabin like a fog. "So what brings you gentlemen way up here?" Our city slicker auras were most likely *glaringly* apparent. I decided to be forthright with him, even though he really had no business knowing.

"I'm gonna be looking at some large-acre mountain plots, as I've just come into some decent money," I revealed.

"*Decent?!?* Hell, if *that* isn't the understatement of the y…!" I quickly shushed Michael physically with a finger over his lips. I didn't need every person in this Podunk town we were headed to knowing that I was a millionaire.

Jack acted as if Michael hadn't said a word. He probably knew full well that the larger acreage plots for sale were priced in the millions of dollars, anyway. "There's some really good land up there in the mountains… worth every penny." I couldn't help feeling like maybe he *knew* one of the men potentially selling some of that prime real estate, and meant to talk it up rightly. No sense in giving the city slickers a *local*-quality deal, after all.

When we landed (which was rough as well), Jack taxied into his own personal hanger, which was opened as we neared it by a stunning redheaded beauty… the finest young woman I've ever seen in jean *overalls*, I'll tell you *that* much! After we came to a stop, Jack climbed out and got our luggage for us. Pointing at the young woman, he said, "My assistant there will drive you gentlemen to our local hotel, if you like."

She gently placed her hand in mine. "I'm Vera. Nice to meet you."

As awkwardly silent as I had been upon meeting Vera, Michael had not wasted a single second. He swooped in like a fat woman onto a buffet after a week of Weight Watchers. Vera was, of course, both flattered and even a little intimidated by his big-city "game", so it was a little like watching Pepé Le Pew all over a red-headed Scarlett O'Hara. I honestly expected her to chime in at any moment with some sort of mountain folk version of "I do de-*clay*-yah!"

Having seen Michael work his magic before (and still feeling a twinge of culpability over *what's-her-name* from less than three weeks ago), I went ahead and let him scoot into the middle part of the "one long seat" of Vera's rusty 1970s Ford truck. Making a dude deliver his game *over* a middle person (*especially* if that person is *you*) is tantamount to cock-blocking, after all.

As it turned out, the drive from the one-plane airport to the nicer of the two hotels in town (*Both* were little more than glorified motels.) was not a very long drive. Michael was able to interject so few words between Vera's first "Oh, you *rascal*!" and her announcement of "Well, we're here!" that I considered it verifiable *magic* that he was able to talk her into showing us the local night life.

I went ahead and checked into the hotel while Michael was busy getting in some last-second flirting (I could tell by Vera's effusive giggling.). I booked us one of their best rooms (two *Queen*-sized beds as opposed to Twins!) for a week, so I'd have plenty of time to haggle with the realtor without having to worry if I'd be over-stepping some arbitrary check-out time in this ghost town.

The "Mama Fratelli"-looking front desk clerk had been giving me the stink-eye, as she saw that I was getting a room with another *man*, but after Vera's display of ardor for my companion, her eyes softened to what I can only describe as a sort of gentle acrimony. As Vera drove away, I was receiving the room key from – I looked down to her askew employee nametag – *Helen*. When Michael finally came in the front door and we began making our way down the inside hallway of the first floor, I could hear Helen bellow, "And *no shenanigans*, you two!" Had she been a younger, less-*troll*-like woman, I'd have had some manner of smart-ass query on deck as to what entailed said shenanigans, but I held my tongue.

"I guess some people are just naturally inclined to discourteousness," I thought. Michael just looked back at her oddly, then at me, and we both laughed.

About four hours later, I was in the tiny hotel room's bathroom, adding a splash of cologne to my "goin' out" ensemble. For the first time in as long as I could remember, I was about to go out on the town with Michael *without* wearing a suit. I had on a black Bon Jovi 2010 "Circle Tour" t-shirt and the darkest jeans I owned. Hell, I would've been King of the Bouncers if we were in *Jersey*. Still, I knew Michael would have something to say about my attire.

As I opened the door, I caught him in the middle of saying, "Thank *God*, Kai! If it wasn't for cable, this town wouldn't even have *three* chann…" and then he caught sight of my outfit. He was dressed as slick as a whistle – head to toe Armani – and the glimmer of his diamond cuff links shone brightly in the reflection of his perfectly polished dress shoes. Needless to say, one look at me, and he was gobsmacked.

"What the *fuck*, dude?!?" I smiled at his inevitable disapproval, which further annoyed him. "Seriously, bro – get back in there and *suit up!*" The astonishment hadn't even faded from his eyes before I calmly replied, "Look, Michael… for *years*, I've suited up to be your wingman, have I not?" He begrudgingly nodded. "Well *now* I'm just going to go out, get a feel for this town, and be ***comfortable*** while I'm doing it for once! Okeedokee?"

"Fine!" he groaned. "But you are the slacker-iest millionaire I've ever known!"

"Just how many millionaires *have* you known?" I teased.

"Oh, shut up."

Michael and I walked up the narrow hallway toward the front desk and the only hotel exit that wasn't an emergency one (so that Helen could keep an eye on arrivals and departures, I supposed). "Goin' out tonight, Mr. Hunter?" I heard from the room behind the desk, where Helen's scraggly face was bathed in her TV's light, giving it an eerie pallor. (Turns out my supposition was *correct*.) She leaned over a bit and quipped, "…and I see you've brought your mortician as well! At least you're ready for anything."

Michael's jaw dropped open, and for the first time that evening, he was speechless. I *had* to laugh. I told Helen we'd see her later if she was planning to be up late, and she waved off my courteous gesture with a shooing one of her own. I was sure that her low, incoherent grumbling meant that we were now on friendly terms.

Vera met us in front of the bar (which was *directly* across the street) a few minutes later. After she'd hopped out of the cab of her truck, she gasped at seeing Michael. "Dear Lord! Who died?" I stifled a chuckle as Michael rolled his eyes. "Oh *har* har, guys! Let's just go get *drunk*, huh?" He offered Vera his arm and she took it as if it were a privilege. We managed to get in with only a *little* further ribbing from the front door bouncer, and I was not surprised at all to find out that it was a Country bar (I mean, Vera *was* wearing red boots with her jeans!).

A few rounds later, I excused myself from the giggle-fest that was going on between Vera and Michael and made my way to the men's bathroom. I was actually relieved that all the urinals were taken, as peeing next to strangers was never my favorite thing to do. As I positioned myself in front of the one empty stall's toilet, I looked up to find that someone had written a poem on the wall above it. I read it, and was immediately taken aback at how similar life in this tiny town sounded to life in the urban sprawl of New York City.

> *"I stand in a puddle of sweat and beer,*
> *wond'ring what other men were here.*
> *This town, devoid of dreams and hope,*
> *(where drinking is the cheapest dope)*
> *pairs us with harpies, fat and plain*
> *(as if their pathos heals the pain).*
> *It steals our money, calls us "jerk",*
> *then sends us – drunk – back out to work."*

It was the finest poem I'd ever seen in a men's room stall. I even looked to see if anyone had signed it, as it was quite insightful. The closest name to it, however, was scrawled in a different hand and just read: *"BUBBA WUZ HERE!"* I smirked as I thought, "Heh – small town territory-marking at its best."

By the time I'd washed my hands and left the bathroom, Michael was already gratuitously making out with Vera. I took a page from the wingman's handbook and just diverted my course to an open seat at the bar. I was already buzzed enough to be amused by the crazy line-dancing antics of about half of the bar's patrons out on the dance floor (a *flagrant* misuse of prime real estate, by NYC standards), so I just ordered a Pepsi from the bartender.

"We only have Coke... will that be okay?" he asked placidly, as if it were the hundredth time he'd had to say that exact phrase.

"Um... *no*. That's disgusting," I sneered. Coke always seemed like the cheaper alternative of the Big Two, so it was *hardly* surprising that this backwater bar had devoted its soda gun's soft drink button to it. Of course, I felt like a big city *jerk* to have reacted so harshly to the poor fellow behind the bar. I tried to cover for my knee-jerk meanness.

"You know what? I'm sorry – it's not your fault. Just... gimme a big water with some lemons in it. I need to hydrate anyway." He rolled his eyes, and began making what my drunken brain realized (too late) was a *free* drink. Considering we'd all been sitting in a *booth* up to this point, it was entirely possible that this guy had no idea how well I'd been tipping our waitress this whole time. To make sure he knew what was up, when he brought my lemon water, I dropped a $20 on the bar for him. He silently gave me the man-nod, so I knew we were cool.

An obese man (who bore an odd resemblance to the "Rich Texan" on *The Simpsons*) – who, I'd guess, would look out-of-place anywhere *else* in a state this far north – spun on his bar stool toward me. "*Whoa* there, pardner! Ya don't want to go overwhelmin' yer girly stomach with a drink with *lemons* in it, now do ya?" A couple of nearby yokels (coincidentally, *also* wearing cowboy hats) started to laugh, and even the bartender chuckled a bit. We were no longer cool.

Drinking tends to make me lose my normal "social courtesy" inhibitions, so I was in no mood to either humor or ignore him. "You know what, fat old cowboy? I wouldn't mind taking my time to slowly *destroy* you tonight, but I can see that that particular gauntlet has already been taken up by *diabetes*!" The yokels now stood with their mouths open, shocked yet entertained. They looked expectantly back at their hometown fat-ass barfly for his retort.

"Yeah? Well you ain't that much skinnier than me *y'self*, ya dang city slicker!" he narrowed his eyes for war, but it was quite obvious that he was too drunk to do battle with someone that would've been his intellectual superior even if he were *sober*.

"*Heh* – nice comeback," I scoffed. "Did that come free with that shitty suit and bolo tie that you bought *in the eighties*?" He looked insulted – apparently, no one in this town had ever thought to say that to him. We were now beginning to draw a small crowd.

"You big city cow pie! I oughta…" he balled up his fists and rose up from his bar stool. Unflappable at this point, I calmly remained seated and interrupted, "…hop a time machine back to the 1850s, where you could still *impress* people?"

A few gasps escaped the crowd, punctuated by one ridiculously off-beat white girl yelling, "*Ooooooh, snap!*" I winced involuntarily. The obese old cowboy was visibly seething, but his age won out over his swagger.

"Ya know whut? You ain't worth it," he snarled through clenched teeth before he turned to make his way out of the bar. Driving the final nail in the coffin of his utter defeat, I called after him, mocking his southern drawl: "I'm-a just gonna finish ma big city waw-tur nah-yuh. How do ya like suckin' on *them* lemons??" Raucous laughter erupted from the crowd and even the bartender… the hometown giant had been toppled, and I was the bar hero of the night.

"Oh *man*, dude! That's the first time I've ever seen *anyone* put ol' Jim-Bob in his place!" one of the random cowboy yokels congratulated me. "How about a drink on the house?" offered the bartender. "Anything you like!" I ordered a Long Island Iced Tea, just to drive home the fearless outsider image. He smiled and cheerfully began making it.

"I'm Billy Watson," the yokel (who was *far* too old to still be going by the name Billy – you know, and not be a voice actor) introduced himself. "What're you in town for? Just seeing the mountain sights?"

"No, Billy… I'm here to buy some mountain property for myself," I revealed, reaching for the drink the bartender gave me. Billy's eyes widened. "Really? Oh, *man*… don't you know there's only one realtor in town?" I took a sip of the drink. "Yeah? Well, what's his name?" He pointed toward the still-swinging saloon doors of the bar. "Jim-Bob Abernathy."

I spit out what little drink I'd had and thought, "*Shit*."

I switched back to lemon waters for long enough to partially sober up… and see that Michael and Vera had no plans to do the same. As the night wore on, the Country music remained depressing and ridiculous, but the line dancers became worse and worse. (*Funny* how booze tends to affect people's coordination in that way.) We'd ended up staying until closing, and I managed to convince Vera that it would be safer to cross the road and sleep it off in our hotel room than risk driving her clunker Ford to God-only-knew where. (Like I think I've mentioned before: I am a ***helluva*** wingman.)

I left Michael and Vera to their own devices once we arrived at the room, announcing loudly and deliberately that I needed to go "take a long walk and look at the town". Michael gave me a wink that was about three seconds too long (because he was *plastered*), so I knew that he got what I was implying.

Even though I figured that they'd be done within the hour, I didn't want to potentially startle them by coming back at that time (That's just bad wingman territory right there.), so I resolved – half drunk – to take in what sights there were to be had in a secluded mountain town at 4:30 in the morning. The crisp, clean air (a stark change from NYC) was actually rather invigorating, so it was no surprise when I found that I had walked clear to the eastern edge of town (at least according to the East/West street name signs) before I had really given it much thought.

I'd never really stayed up late enough (or gotten up *early* enough) in my life, prior to that point, to have seen a sunrise; so the silvery-yellow lights I saw spilling upward over the eastern mountain ridge… well, I just assumed they were the first rays of a new dawn. Of course, who *knew* what was in those mountain drinks? I very well could've been *hallucinating*, even though it seemed unlikely at the time.

The house nearest the town's edge had an absolutely *Mayberry* look to it – white picket fence and everything. Fortunately, it also had some low-hanging apples off a tree or two in the front yard –

one of which I **barely** had to lean over the fence to pick. It was a succulent, juicy red apple (of the State Fair variety, I would later learn), that settled so well in my stomach that I went over and sat comfortably on an otherwise sturdy wooden bench across the street.

My eyes drifted lazily between the lights over the eastern horizon and the quaint yard from which I'd "borrowed" an apple. "There couldn't be any *busses* here," I thought. So, I began to imagine what the use of this wooden bench I was on might *be*. My imagination almost turned sepia as my mind conjured images of country boys in overalls and long-sleeved cotton shirts throwing acorns at each other and hurdling over the bench. I could see old men with Wilford Brimley moustaches slowly whittling away at chunks of wood, laughing with each other, and intermittently spitting globs of chewing tobacco on the ground. I imagined a *simpler* time.

I never got the chance to see the sun come up, but before I knew it, I was being poked by a man in a police officer's uniform. "Sir?" he jostled me with his nightstick. "You can't be sleeping out here off a public street." The sun had long since risen, and my back ached like it belonged to someone that had been sleeping on a hard wooden bench for hours. My morning yawn was ill-advised, as it ended with my unintentionally blowing a mouthful of old alcohol-breath into the cop's face.

"Oh! For crying out…" he began. "I guess you've been acquainted with our town's bar." I managed a weak smile. "But considering I know everyone in town – and I don't know *you* – I'd guess you're just paying us a *visit* here, am I right?" My head was aching, so I was in no condition to launch into my actual real-estate-purchasing reason for being in town. I slowly nodded assent instead, as I sat up straightly.

"Well, we'll just let this be your *warning* about public drunkenness, okay?" he smiled with his admonition, putting me slightly more at ease than waking up in Central Park. "Thank you, officer," I consciously turned my head away from him a bit to spare him my awful breath.

"Call me Deputy. I'm Deputy Meyer," he lowered his voice as he leaned down to my ear. "And considering the apple core at your feet, I'd be willing to bet the widow Athelas was the one who called in the complaint this morning." My embarrassment at being caught must've been apparent as he stood back up. "But she's a nice enough lady. Wouldn't want to go making a bad impression in town on your first visit, huh?"

Still partially fearing retribution, I quickly shook my head no. "Good, good," he widely grinned. "Then I won't ticket you for anything if you go on over there and apologize, okay?" I looked up at the man, who loomed over me like a poster advocating 50s virtues, and realized that he must be serious. "No time for that big city snarkiness *now*," I thought to myself.

I gathered myself up with a deep breath of determination, crossed the empty street, and slowly opened the widow Athelas' creaky white picket gate. I hadn't felt this much like a kid since the summer I hit that baseball through old man Rafe's kitchen window. Still, my Dad made me go and apologize for it, and even though I had to mow Mr. Rafe's lawn every weekend for the rest of the year to pay for it, it had taught me a lesson about personal responsibility that made this mountain pill a bit less difficult to swallow.

As I made my way up the widow's front walk, I caught a glimpse of the front curtains rustling closed (through which she'd *obviously* been watching the whole thing). I knocked softly on her door, fearing the worst. When a tiny old woman half my size opened the door, I did my best to apologize without chuckling at how small she was. She was gracious about the apple, forgiving me at once, and even invited me in for some morning tea, but I told her that I needed to check on my friend back at the hotel and couldn't stay. Deputy Meyer bid me a cordial farewell once the deed was done, and all I could think as I walked back was, "*Man*, Michael – you really *owe me* one."

16

I made my way back to the hotel, and managed to arrive around noon, judging from the sun… and the clock on my cell phone. When I arrived at our room, I found that Vera had long since left, and Michael was sprawled out across the more disheveled of the two beds. The remote control was nestled in the sheets just out of his reach, and the channel menu display on the TV betrayed Michael's late night interests… *Spanktravision*. I surmised that he'd not gotten as far as he intended with Vera after I left. For whatever reason, it was a little comforting that his night hadn't gone that much better than mine.

I decided to let him continue sleeping it off, as he'd done *quite* a bit more drinking than I had. I went ahead and took a quick shower, brushed my teeth, and changed into a different t-shirt and jeans. It was glaringly apparent that I was going to be one of those *comfortable* millionaires.

I made my way up to the front desk and could see that Helen was watching her soaps in the back room. Without even turning her head, she sensed my presence at the front desk and yelled, "Yeah? What can I do for ya?" I didn't mind. "Helen, I was wondering if you could tell me where the realty office of Mr. Jim-Bob Abernathy is." She spun her head around so quickly, I thought she'd snap her old neck. Her wide eyes softened into a teasing grin as she chuckled, "Yeah, I heard all *about* how you and Jim-Bob locked horns last night."

"Ruttin' small-town gossip!" I mused. Out loud, I only said: "Yep. And as you probably know, I'm in town to look at some real estate, so it wouldn't really do me any favors to have the man be all cranky with me." Helen had made her way over to the front desk counter, as my predicament was vastly more entertaining than her soap operas. "Honey, you sure enough said it. What do you reckon on doing to patch things up?"

"Well, that's just it!" I said. "I don't *know* the man! Hell, I wasn't even in *town* long enough to know he was the **only** guy you could buy real estate through around here!" I slumped onto the counter, defeated. Helen patted me warmly on the shoulder. "Aw, don't feel so bad, sweetheart. Remember - ol' Jim-Bob stands to make a *helluva* commission if you buy y'self one of those big mountain parcels, so he really oughta be apologizin' to *you*!" Her reasoning was sound, so I perked up a bit. "You really think so?"

"*Sure*, honey. It's just that what I think don't make much of a difference. Jim-Bob's always been kind of a highfalutin jackass, ever since he sold his first multi-million dollar parcel. Nowadays, he won't hardly even *talk* to somebody unless they're worth a good six figures. And in a town this size, sweetheart, everybody *knows* what you got." That was hardly reassuring, considering the low profile that I was attempting to keep. Things were looking bleakly.

"I know!" Helen snapped her fingers with a sudden burst of inspiration. "Go on across the street there to The Rusty Hoof..." I looked at her quizzically. "The bar where you all *were* last night, you dobro. Ask Hank the bartender to recommend the best brand of whatever Jim-Bob normally drinks, and then take him a bottle of it as a peace offering!" She smiled widely - almost eerily. I had to admit that it was a great idea, so I hugged her as thanks for it and quickly headed across the street to the bar we'd visited last night.

I made my way across the street, still a little surprised that there was no real traffic to dodge in the process. The bar had opened less than an hour ago, yet there were already three sad patrons seated on their lonely stools. Hank spotted me as soon as I walked in and nodded in my direction with a smile. He had dragged one of the barstools behind the bar and was leaning back against the far wall near the portion of the bar that swings up - passively reading some sports magazine. "Hey Hank," I said with a furrowed brow. "I'm hoping you can help me out, man." He let out the kind of yawn that one tends to when you've been tending bar all night only to wake up the next morning and start the following shift as well. Folding in the page of his sports mag to hold his place, he placed it on the bar beside him and in one clean motion, allowed his barstool to rock forward, hit the floor, and jettison him into a proper standing position. "I'll see what I can do... uh... Malachi, was it?"

"Yeah, that's it," I smiled - momentarily thankful that the same small town pipeline that had fed me *his* name had also fed him *mine*. "Look... I find myself in sort of an unwelcome situation with Mr. Abernathy..."

"Oh, yeah! You're in town to get some land; an' he's the only old fart you can go to to buy any, right?" You really have to give a small town's gossip mill credit for efficacy. "Well, yeah," I reluctantly admitted. "Here's the thing - I was wondering if you (being his regular bartender and all) were party to the type of drink he generally orders..." Hank raised a wry eyebrow. "...and I was hoping that I could maybe take him a bottle of it as a show of good faith - kind of reconcile things, if you know what I mean."

"Trust me, Mr. Hunter... I get it. But you've gotta understand that though ol' Jim-Bob throws back his fair share of Jack Daniels here, I doubt he's in short supply of it at his office."

"Crap!" I was defeated again.

"Although..." Hank's eyes rolled backward like he was searching his brain for the perfect answer. "Yes?" I expectantly prodded.

"Well, I've got this bottle of Jack Daniels Single Barrel - the most expensive whiskey I carry. I normally don't get much call for it unless someone's having a baby, or getting married, or coming home from war or something, and this particular bottle has yet to even be *opened*."

My wallet was already out. "How much, Hank?" He knew that he was my only shot at this purchase. "$150, Mr. Hunter... I'll give you a deal, since you're in a pinch." I knew he was ripping me off, but I took the bottle anyway, slapped down $200 on the bar, and left.

17

I strode quickly across the street to the hotel, hoping Helen might give me the directions to Jim-Bob's realty office... and maybe a bit of ribbon to tie around the bottle's neck (to give it more of a "gift" look). She did not disappoint, and produced both the directions (down the main street toward Athelas' place and off the first street on the right) and a nice, red velvety ribbon for the whiskey. I gave her a $20 as a tip for all her help, and she tried to refuse it, but I left it on the counter for her anyway. She giggled, "Oh, *you!*" as I hurried out the front entrance.

As I made my way to Jim-Bob's office, I ran through every horrible scenario in my head - every possible way in which the coming interaction could go wrongly - as it was generally my habit to prepare for the *worst*, and be pleasantly surprised if anything *better* were to happen. I imagined him pulling a six-shooter out of his desk and just blasting me through the chest, then later burying me in some obscure mountain cave, where he and Deputy Meyer would just clink their glasses of beer together, satisfied that they'd ridded the town of another "pesky city boy". I imagined him breaking some half-empty bottle of scotch over my head and then smothering me to death beneath his fat, old ass. Generally speaking, I am not the most optimistic of people.

When I arrived at his building (not surprisingly, garishly labeled "ABERNATHY MOUNTAIN REALTY"), I found it to be the most well-maintained one on its street... as well as the *only* brick building I'd seen in town. The large wooden sign over his front entryway gave the whole thing a decidedly "Wild West" look (which is probably what he was going for *anyway*). I couldn't help but get a "showdown at the O.K. Corral" vibe while plodding up the stairs to the wooden double doors.

The door creaked as I opened it, and the barely-lit front room had a lone desk in it - upon which sat an older model computer and an old, black rotary phone. I heard the muffled clacking of some high heels from a side room, and sure enough, a young woman appeared through the door nearest what was obviously her desk. She simultaneously wiped the smudged lipstick from the corners of her mouth while straightening her ruffled skirt before attempting to surreptitiously take her seat. Once seated, she looked up in my direction as if she'd been seated the whole time. "Hello, sir! Welcome to Abernathy Mountain Realty! How may I help you?"

I stifled a snicker and managed to ask, "Ah, yes - is Mr. Abernathy available?"

"Certainly, sir. May I have your name please?" she was relentlessly perky.

"Malachi Hunter," I replied, matter-of-factly. Her eyes widened as if she'd remembered seeing my name on a "To Kill" list. She reached for her phone without allowing her shocked gaze to leave my face. "I'll check if he can see you now." The phone had apparently been rigged to operate like an intercom system, though it hardly looked the part. She pressed a button I'd not previously noticed on the phone before speaking, "Mr. Jim-Bob? Mr. Hunter is here to see you... should I send him in?"

"Son of a *BITCH!*" I heard through the wall, almost clearer than through the woman's phone. I heard the kind of rumbling you hear when a large bull of a man is struggling to get out from behind a desk and is also busy knocking over boxes that (in an enraged state) he didn't quite realize were in his way. He flung open his door, enraged and exasperated, gasping for air and clearly trying to find the right words to terrify and berate me. I quickly decided that a preemptive strike was in order.

"*Whoa* now, Jim-Bob! I come in peace!" I blurted, extending the gift bottle in both hands.

"You dang city-slickin'..." he began, before setting eyes on the whiskey. His expression melted from rage into wide-eyed awe. "Is that Single Barrel Jack?"

"Yes, Mr. Abernathy. I wanted to show you that I truly meant to put last night's silly drunken encounter behind us. I hope that you'll take this as a token of my earnest desire for that resolution." I continued to present the bottle, as he practically salivated over the prospect of enjoying it. He shook his head quickly, as if to throw the cobwebs of anger from his skull. He uneasily laughed, "Well now, Mr. Hunter, I can't... uh... see how I could manage to *not* forgive you after such a fine gift!"

I swung for the fences. "Call me Malachi."

"Sure! And can call me Jim-Bob!" It worked. "What can I do for ya?"

"Well Jim-Bob, it just so happens that I'm in the market for a sizable plot of mountain real estate... and folks around here tell me you're the man to see about getting a quality parcel." I tried my colloquial best to sum up my intent.

"As a matter of fact, Mr. Hunter... uh, Malachi..." he corrected himself. "I have the best acres for sale in five whole counties, and let me tell you - counties in this state aren't exactly *small*." He guffawed. I joined in so as to set him at ease. "Come have a seat in my office and tell me what sort of plot you're in the market for!" He clapped his arm around my shoulder, lifted the bottle from my hands, and led me into his office like an old friend. "Jennifer darlin', hold all my calls."

He closed the door behind us and began humbly picking up the boxes he'd knocked over in his previous wrath. "Oh, don't worry about those, Jim-Bob," I reassured him. "Let's just talk turkey."

"Good man - right to business. I like that." His eyes twinkled. "Now what kind of acreage ya lookin' for? 20? 50? 100?"

I looked him straight in the eyes. "I was thinking *thousands*."

18

Jim-Bob wasted no time, opening up his biggest acreage maps and bragging about the best selling points of all the largest available plots. I looked on intently, studying the lay of the land, sizing up amounts of available wood and building-stone, following the courses of nearby rivers as they wound around (and sometimes through) the plots he showed me. It was a glorious hour of overhead maps and personally-taken photos - during which he opened and shared his new, delicious whiskey with me over freshly chipped chunks of "glacial" ice - before I decided on a particularly choice piece of land to ride out with him and view.

It was a plot of over four thousand acres that was selling for a relatively modest $3 million. It looked as if it had everything I could ever ask for: easy access to town and the airport, plenty of mountain land for quarrying castle stone, lush green forests of fir, spruce, yew, and pine for wood and hunting, and water coursing through it that flowed from a spring that originated *on the land*. As if that wasn't enough, the plot was surrounded on three sides by National Park lands, so I wouldn't have to worry about encroachment from over-zealous neighbors. Smelly, camping *hippies* maybe... but not neighbors.

Jim-Bob took pride in showing me every scenic view, pointing out every beautiful corner of the gorgeous land. "Yep, this particular parcel even comes with a herd of cattle - some Kobe/Angus mixed breeds from some Fukutsuru bull or somethin', if I recall correctly. The current owner just doesn't want to be as big a rancher anymore, and figures whoever buys the land wouldn't mind having a hundred head or so of quality cattle... with all the necessary shelters and fencin' for 'em, of course." I tried my best not to let on that I *really* wanted this place.

"Are wild animals much of a problem in this area?" I hoped to downplay the land's desirableness a bit. "Not really. I mean, you'll get your odd grizzly or wolves through here on occasion, but if you ever have any kind of actual problem with 'em, either the ranch hands you hire for your herds or even the local park rangers would probably be sufficient enough to handle 'em." Rather than dissuading me from my purchase, his story instead started me daydreaming about standing up to a giant grizzly bear, armed with nothing but a spear - like the world's bravest hunter. Heck, I could even see myself wearing a mantle made out of its pelt like those Saxons from that *King Arthur* movie.

"Is the price non-negotiable?" I asked, shaking my brain free from my wild imaginings. "Well, nothing's *entirely* non-negotiable," Abernathy answered. "But the owner *did* seem pretty firm on it. Still, if you're interested, I can let him know and maybe he'll entertain a lower offer. What would you ask him to consider?" Honestly, I would have been happy paying the full $3 million, but you can never tell a realtor that. After all, the more they convince you to pay, the higher their commission is, so they really don't have much of an incentive to find you the "best deal" - no matter *what* they say.

"Ask him if he'd be willing to accept 2.5," I offered, as if I'd made such offers before.

Jim-Bob scoffed, but knew that as the agent for both of us, he'd have to appear to be acting in *both* of our best interests. "I'll see what he says."

"Excellent; now let's drive back to town. All that talk of cattle makes me want a big, juicy steak!" I was being sincere. "Do you know of any good steak places in town?" His face twisted into a pained expression as I asked the question - the kind that either meant that this tiny mountain town I'd found myself in raised the tastiest beef known to man and then sold it *all* elsewhere... or else that he knew of *exactly* such a place and would be unable to come because of prior commitments. Thankfully for me, it was the latter. Exactly two doors down from The Rusty Hoof was the Meyer Steak House. I thanked Jim-Bob for the recommendation, and then had him drop me off back in town at the hotel.

As I closed the door to his truck cab behind me, I heard him put its window down electronically. "So I'll just go ahead and ask Mr. Mey... *ahem*... *my other client* if he'd be willing to accept your offer of $2.5 million and get back to you in the mornin'. Is that all right?" he yelled out the open window, a bit louder than I would've liked. I spun around and held my hands up the way you do when you're trying to get someone to quiet the hell *down* already and answered, "Shhh! Yes, yes... that's fine. Call me in the morning." Not one to take hints, Jim-Bob's didn't bother changing his volume. "All right, Mr. Hunter! See ya then!" He sped off down the near-vacant town street to God-knows-where.

I figured since the sun was already half set behind the mountains, that Michael had had plenty of time to recover and might feel like joining me on my quest for a delicious filet mignon. I gave Helen a thumbs-up as I passed by the front desk, so she'd know it went well and she flashed me a quick smile before turning back to the flickering of her old TV set.

I opened the door slowly and easily, knocking quietly - on the off chance that Michael had convinced Vera to come back over to engage in some further shenanigans. Michael practically bounded up out of the standard "one comfy seat" across from the room's television. "And just where the damn hell have *you* been all day? It's not exactly one thrill after another in this gawd-awful town, you know! And before you answer that, why wasn't I *with* you??" He stood, like a spurned wife, with his hands on his hips, tapping one of his feet, and with an exaggerated frown on his face. The overt dramatic posturing made me chuckle a bit.

"Nice to see you too, *dear*," I drew out the last bit for emphasis.

"I *mean* it, you assbag! First you drag me out here, Vera turns out to be some waiting-for-marriage *tease*, and then I have to sit here..."

"Shut up, you drama queen!" I interrupted him, amused at his belly-aching. "And hurry up and shower off - turns out there's a 'right dee-lish-uhss' steak house off the main drag and I'm buying." His mouth snapped shut long enough for him to pout silently for a few seconds. He crossed the room and tossed me the remote, "Fine... I'll be out in a minute."

19

When Michael emerged from the bathroom in his same suit from the night before, he was pleasantly surprised to find that I'd changed into a decent suit that I'd brought with me for just such an occasion. His face beamed with delight. "*Finally!* My bro suits up!"

"Yeah, sure - I figured *one* of us shouldn't be a whiny little bitch tonight," I winked.

"Ass!" he smiled. "But yeah, you're right. I should be thankful for the steak offer." He slapped me loudly on the back. "I am, and let's go!"

That was our general bro-reconciliation. Names would be called (in jest), laughs would be had, and troubles would be forgotten - no long, drawn-out, insincere apologies necessary. It always worked, and was always quick. I couldn't help musing that perhaps every single bitch I'd ever known could take a lesson from the way we did things... you know, if society hadn't pre-programmed them to think "humility" was a four-letter word.

We looked from across the street, and saw that "Meyer Steak House" was lit up in neon just two buildings to the right of The Rusty Hoof. "I can't believe we missed that before," Michael commented. "I think perhaps your attention was being monopolized by some rather ample redheaded boobies at the time, good sir," I reminded him. He smirked at me, "Yeah? Then what was *your* excuse?" "Touché, brother. Touché."

We laughed as we threw open the heavy, wooden double doors to the steak house, and were both surprised to find that it was not the rowdy saloon-like atmosphere that we'd imagined (given our previous night's experience). The doors slowly closed behind us as more than one family/date looked our way. Michael awkwardly cleared his throat.

"Sorry, folks - we're not the floor show tonight. You may return to your meals," I shooed their gazes with both hands, satisfied that my NYC wit was sharp enough to disengage their social disapprobation. A cute little wisp of a hostess hurried over to us, menus in hand. "Could I show you gentlemen to a table, or would you prefer a booth in the back?" It looked as if her eyes were desperately urging me to take the second option, so I played along. "Yes; the booth sounds fine. Right, Michael?" "Oh yeah!" he quickly replied. "Booth. You betcha." As the tiny brunette took a path around the main tables in the front area (with us in tow), I began to consider that getting the booth in the back would *also* mean that we'd be in the company of people that *hadn't* seen our raucous entrance, and reassured myself that it was the right decision.

The hostess led us under an archway with heavy velvet curtains that had been pulled back and tied with elegant, thick golden cords. We continued down a dimly-lit hallway that was just wide enough for two people to walk shoulder-to-shoulder. I was admiring the half-timber British-style interior design when it hit me what the place looked like... an old "Steak and Ale" restaurant. She stopped in front of the curtained archway nearest the back (and the bathrooms - still wasn't sure whether or not that would be a *plus*) and extended her arm inside of it. "Will this room do, gentlemen?"

I peered inside. The smallish room had two empty booths against the far wall, two empty booths on a wall that was also surely the flip side of at least *one* of the bathrooms, and two booths on the opposite side to those - one of which was occupied by a very obese, sad-looking man who was taking lonely bites of what was easily the largest steak I'd ever seen. Two tables had also been pushed together in the center of the room to make enough seating for a rather noisy family - made up of about six different *loud* kids (two of which were up and chasing easy other around the table), one obese woman who took turns either shoveling food into her mouth or yelling at the kids, and one skinny, beleaguered man staring blankly ahead of himself (no doubt wondering how he'd ended up the Father of such an awful family).

I looked back at the hostess with a look that read, "You've *got* to be kidding me!" so plainly that she chirped, "Oh, I think they're just about done."

"Fine. We'll take one of those booths in the back," I surrendered. She led us quickly to the back booth furthest from the epicenter of Hurricane "Brats" and sat a menu in front of each of us. "The salad bar comes with all our meals, and is right at the end of that hallway," she pointed back toward the archway. "So help yourselves. Also, may I tell your waitress what drinks to start you off with?"

"Jack and Coke," Michael had always had that drink with steak for as long as I'd known him. "And for you, sir?" Her cheeriness was starting to get on my nerves now.

"I'll have a Pepsi."

"Will Coke be all right?"

"Ugh - no. Dr. Pepper?"

"We have Mr. Pibb..." she offered hopefully.

I let out a groan of disgust. "Yeah. Yeah; just bring me one of those." She left, obviously thankful to be out of the worst room in the restaurant. Once she was out of sight, I looked across the table at Michael. "What the *fuck*, dude? Does Pepsi not have a delivery truck that comes through this asshole town, or *what?*" My outburst drew the attention of the fat wife, who chided, "Excuse me, sir, but this is a *family* restaurant. You should watch your mouth." I wasn't having it. "Oh yeah, Hogatha? Well when I want your fat-fuck opinion on anything from manner of speech aaaaalllllll the way up to how to raise a whole brood of out-of-control *jackass* kids, *I'll fucking ask for it!!*" Her mouth stopped flapping for the first time that night, and a spoon full of mashed potatoes fell impotently from her hand to the floor. As she hurried to gather up her kids and leave, I'm pretty sure I saw her husband silently mouth a prayer of thanks to the ceiling. Once they'd all left, the obese man turned around in his booth to tell me, "*Noice.*"

20

"Did you say this was the *only* steak place in town?" Michael anxiously asked me. The look in his eyes brought me back down from the celebratory mental plane of victory. "Oh shit," I thought. I did my best to encourage him, "Uh... yeah, the odds that that middle-aged battle-ax is getting the management right now are like..."

"One to one?" his eyes darted toward the curtained archway, where a rather familiar-looking man in a dark suit was already approaching our table.

"Um, good evening, gentlemen... is there a problem back here?" My recall caught up to my present state of mind and I recognized *him* before he remembered *me*. "Deputy *Meyer*?" I asked, incredulously. He sighed the labored sigh of a man that had been mistaken for someone else a hundred times before. "No, that's my *brother*. *I'm* the manager here."

I snapped my fingers. "*Now* I get it - *MEYER* Steak House!"

Michael was lost. "What the *hell* are you talking about?"

I ignored him for the moment. "Look, I'm sorry I snapped earlier, Mr. Meyer. There was a pretty rowdy family here... about a dozen kids... I promise it won't happen again. We're just here for what I've been told is the best steak in five counties." I looked up at him, confident that that last little lie would do the trick.

I was only half-right. "Well, we *do* serve that, but we're *also*..."

"Come on, Larry," the obese man piped up. "Don't give him that 'family restaurant' B-S. I mean, we're *already* back here in the fuck-off room, what more do you want? I'm **glad** that fat biddy and her little brats are gone! He oughta get a *medal*!"

"All right, Sam. But *still*..."

"Look, Larry, was it?" I interrupted. "My friend and I here are going to order *two* of the best, most succulent steaks you have - **each** - and in addition to paying and leaving a nice tip for *whatever* brave waitress you send back here, I'll also leave the generous tip that I'd practically guarantee that that loud family *didn't* leave on their way out. Okay? Would that square us, Larry?" I looked directly into his eyes, which were empty from trying to manage a steak house in the middle of nowhere.

Larry took a deep breath and let out a lengthy sigh. "Sure. That'll square us. Just please - no more swearing or outbursts, okay?" I did my best to throw up a scout sign, "I promise." Larry smiled and shuffled away. As he passed under the archway, Sam cheered after him: "Atta boy, Larry!" Michael smiled, shaking his head at my audacity. "Oh, come on, you doofus," I slapped the table in front of him, then got up to lead the way to the ample salad bar that awaited us.

I was so proud of my now *two* victories, that I went ahead and tried practically everything on the cornucopia-like salad bar spread before us. (The biggest surprises for decent salad ingredients? Dill pickle spears and baby corn. Honestly; I had no idea.) By the time we both made it back to our tables, our phantom waitress had our drinks waiting - in the appropriate places, no less! We hungrily devoured our salads while we waited for her return (Which, incidentally, is *not* my general order of doing things... I typically prefer to eat my salad *after* the meal like they do in France, because the roughage helps to push whatever artery-clogging crap you've just enjoyed out of your system like an over-zealous street sweeper.).

When she arrived (another wispy brunette, by the way), I remained true to my word, and Michael and I ordered two nine ounce filet mignon steaks apiece. They were indeed the Kobe/Angus mix of beef, and let me tell you... *they were **divine***. By the time we were done, we were both loosening the belts on our suit-pants and patting our bellies like fat husbands after a well-catered sports game in a sunken den.

"So... what do you think? Bar?" Michael asked hopefully.

"What... are you hoping Vera'll be there *again* tonight? After all the shenanigans you two were up to last night?"

"Maybe," he sheepishly admitted. "Well, that and it probably wouldn't *kill* me to learn a line dance or two."

This really was too much. "You... line dance. Need I remind you that you balked when a NYC stripper with *double Fs* asked you to join her at her dance class to learn the Electric Slide?"

"And need I remind you..." he looked quickly around for any eavesdropping Larry-types. "That there is *fuck-all else* to do in this less-than-one-horse burg?" He had a point. And considering my "vast" experience here had only encompassed a low-grade hotel, a one-plane airport, a nosy old lady's yard, a fat drunkard's realty office, and this particular steak house, I had no footing from which to argue. "Fine," I acquiesced. "But if we're going *again* tonight, you have to wear the same thing *I* do." He grumbled, "*Uuuuuuuugh!* All right, but I'm breaking out my Ed Hardy shirt that you said looks douchey!" I rolled my eyes; it was obvious that *neither* of us was going to fully enjoy tonight at the bar. "That's fine - but I'm telling you... wearing a pair of bedazzled angel wings on a tight-ass t-shirt doesn't make you look hardcore. It makes you look like you should be collecting Lisa Frank stickers on your *My Little Pony* Trapper Keeper!"

We got back to the hotel, changed as fast as two 30-year-old guys (who'd basically wolfed down three NYC-quantity entrees) could, and then made our way over to The Rusty Hoof for the second time in as many nights. Michael looked ridiculous, but managed to have some fun awkwardly learning some Cotton-Eyed Moe dance (or something - I forget) and did, in fact, end up making out with some random blonde at the end of the night. I kept an eye open for Vera (who never showed), and eventually just helped Michael back across the street and to bed.

21

I was awoken by a knock at our hotel room door. I stumbled lazily out of bed and managed to cast a glance backward at the clock out of hotel habit. "Ten o'clock AM," I read in my head. "Huh - most checkouts aren't until at *least* eleven." My mind goes to paranoid places when startled from sleep.

"Mr. Hunter? Sorry to disturb you. Could you come to the door, please?" It was Helen. Thinking quickly, I grabbed some sleep pants from my duffel and slid them on over my boxers. "Just a second, Helen!" I bought some time as I made myself decent. As luck would have it, I'd slept in my Bon Jovi t-shirt, so my "upstairs" was already presentable. I slowly cracked open the door and prepared to feign a yawn, just so it seemed like slightly more of an imposition than it actually was. (Hey, you have *your* defense mechanisms; I have *mine*. Don't judge me.)

The first thing I saw was Helen in her rollers, looking with a modicum of panic toward the front desk. "Now, hold on, Mr. Meyer! You said you would wai...!" Before she could even finish her sentence, a large man shoved her to the side, burst through the cracked door, and practically knocked me over to come into my room. The man wore black leather cowboy boots (complete with actual spurs!), dark, worn blue jeans, a black-and-red flannel long-sleeved shirt, a large black cowboy hat with a braided leather hatband at the base of its crown, and (considering the rest of his get-up) a rather modestly-sized silver belt buckle. He was the first man I'd seen in quite some time that was any taller than I was, and he was built like a brick shithouse. His rowdy entrance had startled Michael (drowsily) awake, but when he saw that monster of a man standing over him, he yelped and instantly gathered the covers around him like the man was his Dad walking in on him jerkin' the gherkin.

The man spun around, fixing his steely gray eyes on mine. His *tone* carried none of the apology that his *words* did as he said, "I'm sorry. If I'd a' known you weren't alone, I wouldn't a' burst in like that." His hand passed for a moment in front of his rigid Sam Elliott-like mustache as he reached for something in his front shirt pocket. He flipped out a business card (without ever breaking his stare) that seemed to snap in the musky hotel air like a whip. "Name's Meyer. Frank Meyer. I believe you've met both of my boys by now." I had no response to that. "Look - this obviously ain't the place to discuss this, but Jim-Bob told me about your 'offer' on the land I'm sellin' round here."

"That fat asshole! He's supposed to keep his buyers' identities a *secret*!" I thought, but then remembered how he'd almost let slip Mr. Meyer's name here the night before. Having now caught sight of the man, I dare say that his name would catch in *my* throat as well. "Now maybe you're too much of a big city-man to know how much that particular figure is *horse shit*, but I'm gonna give you the benefit of the doubt that you weren't tryin' to blow smoke up my ass and tell me it's summertime!" I think I heard myself noticeably gulp.

"If you've got the balls, son, you meet me at the address on that card. We need to have a talk - *man to man*." His eyes seemed like they would burn a hole through the back of my skull if his gaze wasn't averted in the very next second, but fortunately, it was. He stormed back through my open hotel door, tipped his hat toward Helen in the very mildest of gentlemanly deference (as Helen had been knocked over but had managed to get back to her feet in the interim), and was gone like a tornado... leaving nothing but confusion and disbelief in his wake.

"I'm so sorry, Mr. Hunter. Frank promised me that he'd wait back by the front desk while I got you for him..." Helen offered apologetically. "It's all right, Helen. He seems like the kind of man that would just as soon kick you as kiss you." She giggled at my impressive grasp of the local jargon. "Yep. He's not to be trifled with... probably the only man around here that can make even ol' *Jim-Bob* quake in his boots," she agreed.

I honestly had no idea what to make of the situation. "So what do you think, Helen? Does he want me up on the backside of some out-of-town mountain so he can *shoot* me for besmirching his honor or some shit?" She bit her thumbnail in anxiety (or *thought*... it was hard to tell at this point). "You know, I can't recall him ever killin' a man in anger - well, one that hadn't tried to kill him *first*, of course." The implication that the man was a seasoned killer did ***not*** set me more at ease. I think Helen could tell that my expression was one of trepidation, so she attempted to quiet my thoughts. "Really, though? I think you should see what he has to say. I don't know that anyone outside of a ranch hand or his own two *sons* has ever gotten an invitation to his mountain cabin, which..." she bent the card in my hand down so that she could see it. "...Yep! That's the place, all right."

"Mountain cabin" just conjured up more images of some remote, snowy location - the kind of place where you could easily cover up a gunshot, and then bury a body or two under some kinda crop that you would use to slowly eat and digest your enemies... all while your Deputy son covered up the official investigation. I shook my head of the thought - and reminded myself that Stephen King-esque things tended to happen quite *rarely* in real life.

"I know this much, Mr. Hunter... if you want to buy that land he's sellin' up in the mountains, he's likely to flat-out refuse the sale if you don't go up there and have that manly chat he's after."

My big-city umbrage was activated. "Isn't it *illegal* to refuse to sell something to someone just because you don't like 'em? Like, discrimination or something?"

She scoffed, "Shoot, Malachi - you's both White! And even if it *was* against the law, do you think anybody in ***this*** little mountain town would give a squat about it? Half the time, the city court is presided over by Deputy Meyer just so the regular judge can get in a nice afternoon of *fishin'*!" I hated to admit it, but Helen was right. Michael and I got showered and dressed like we were preparing for our own funerals, and then headed over to Abernathy's office, hoping to catch a ride up to Meyer's cabin.

22

Jim-Bob took a pretty decent amount of convincing to give us the ride in his fancy truck, but the winning argument ended up being my implication that Frank would somehow blame *Jim-Bob* if we weren't able to make it up to his cabin. I didn't feel any amount of remorse for deceiving him, considering it had been Jim-Bob's fault that Frank practically assaulted me in my underwear that same morning.

The ride out of town and up to Mr. Meyer's cabin was a short but treacherous one. Parts of the rocky mountain roads were so slender that Michael and I were both surprised that the hefty truck we were riding in didn't tip over altogether and tumble down the steep hillside. Jim-Bob seemed a bit more unnerved by the prospect of being seen by Mr. Meyer than by careening down a rocky mountainside... a fact which in and of itself made me all the more worried about what Frank's true intention might be for summoning me to this remote location.

As we rounded the final bend, all three of us set eyes - for the first time - on the unprecedented spectacle of Meyer's cabin. It looked more like a Northeastern ski resort than the tiny log cabin that we'd all been expecting. "Well, I'll be a monkey's uncle!" Abernathy exclaimed. The driveway led up to the double front doors in a posh, asphalt circle that boasted a marble fountain in the middle that seemed *really* out-of-place. Jim-Bob was too flabbergasted to drive the truck under the ample driveway overhang in front of the entrance, but merely sat like us - drinking in the wide front of the log "cabin" that seemed to be built from logs borrowed from California *redwoods*, they were so immense. "Holy... shit," was all Michael could say. "I concur," was all I could respond.

After what seemed like an eternity that we all sat transfixed by the palace (masquerading as a cabin) before us, I saw one of the two heavy wooden doors swing inward to what looked to be the gaping maw of Charybdis herself at that point. "Well, boys - I'm pretty sure that's y'all's cue," Jim-Bob urged. I was frozen. "So drive us *up* there, you jackass!" Michael replied, a bit too overly-familiar. "In a pig's eye!" he yelled. "If you wanna get within rock-salt firin' distance, you go right ahead. My truck stays *here*!" I didn't know what rock-salt was, but it didn't sound pleasant. All the same, I snapped out of it and opened the passenger door to get out. "Come on, you pussy - if he's mad at someone, it'll be *me*, not *you*," I figured a little mockery might get Michael on his feet. He reluctantly crawled out of the open door. "Thanks for the ride, Jethro!" he shot back at Mr. Abernathy.

When I shut the door, Jim-Bob began to back the truck up. I clutched onto the open passenger window, "Whoa, whoa! How're we gonna get back to town?" Once he'd backed up enough to turn around, he shifted the truck into drive and called out as he accelerated, "I'm sure Frank'll get you two back to town! *Bye!*" I was flung helplessly off of the truck as it sped away. Whatever our fate, we were stranded here now.

"Great," Michael ironically quipped. "I'm telling you, though - if I hear banjos, I'm *out*!"

We turned to look back at the front doors, and in the previous gap now stood a thin, older woman in jeans and an apron - with a tray of what looked like cookies. "Hello, you two! Come on in! Welcome!" she chirped. It's hard to describe the vibe this woman gave off, so I'd describe her thusly: imagine if Aunt Bea had the body of Christie Brinkley, with majestic gray hair down to the middle of her back. That was pretty much it. The tray did, in fact, have cookies on it... little gingerbread men shaped like cowboys. I can't recall the last time I'd seen baked goods (even in NYC) that had had so much apparent time and energy put into perfecting their every last detail. To top it all off, they were *delicious*.

We followed her inside, where there was a massive stone fireplace against the far wall of the great room. I'll put it this way - the room was so spacious that there were three full leather couches arranged in a semi-circle around the fireplace, and there was still *ample* room to walk around them. As if to solidify our impression of the Alpha that *obviously* lived there, each couch was covered by the largest whole-bear fur blankets I'd ever seen. The old lady motioned to Michael, "You go ahead and make yourself comfortable over there - I'll bring you out some nice drinks to go with the cookies." "Thanks!"

Michael shot back, obviously relieved that his hide *wasn't* to be added to the ones already so prominently displayed.

I began to follow after him, when the lady suddenly clutched my arm. "*Oh* no, not you," her smile was eerily hospitable. "Frank wants to see you out back. Follow me, dear." I sincerely hoped that someone who would call me "dear" in such a friendly voice wouldn't be leading me to my own execution. I followed her through a kitchen that looked like it belonged on the cover of a Better Homes and Gardens kitchen magazine... the kind of space that would probably make Martha Stewart herself have an involuntary orgasm. She led me out of the kitchen's back door, and right by the largest tree stump I'd ever seen. The double-headed ax firmly planted in its center sent an ominous chill up my spine.

We walked between two very well-tended garden plots, one which looked to be growing vegetables, and the other which seemed to be yielding herbs. "Wow," I marveled. "You must have quite the talented gardener on staff!" She looked over her shoulder with a smile, "Well *thanks*, sweetie! Actually, I tend these little plots myself to make sure I've got quality produce for the house. 'No sense in hiring somebody to do the work that family can do,' Frank always says." I was desperately hoping that his country sensibilities extended to *not* killing folks that had insulted him.

She led me past a barn that had pens for pretty much every farm animal one could imagine *being* on a farm, and I couldn't help wondering how all this livestock made its way up that dangerous mountain road in the *first* place. After what seemed like a silent eternity, we rounded the back corner of the barn and she motioned toward Frank, who I could see was leading two large stallions toward us on foot.

"Time to ride, kid," he bellowed.

23

Admittedly, I didn't know how to ride a horse, but it was one of those things that I'd always imagined I'd be able to easily learn. I mean, I was always good with everything from dogs to ferrets to Scarlet Macaws... surely that kind of animal kinship could carry over to large, snorting beasts of burden, right? As if Frank could read my mind, he jeered: "You've never mounted a horse in your life, have you?" I put my left foot in the nearest stirrup and grasped the pommel of the saddle like I'd seen a hundred cowboys do (in the movies) in my time and went to effortlessly swing my right leg over and onto this mammoth beast, intending to fire back something snarky like, "How hard could it be?" Unfortunately, I only *actually* made it about halfway up the side of the horse, having misjudged the amount of effort it would take for a paunchy city man (like myself) to fully mount an equine behemoth like this one.

When I landed impotently back on the ground, Frank, as if to mock my obvious inexperience, mounted his steed (which was at least a half a head taller than mine) with ease, sliding into his saddle like a graceful foot into a custom slipper. He trotted his horse around mine until he was on the same side of it that I was, bent down and grabbed the back of my jeans by the belt, and lifted me up like a feather until I landed in my saddle with a *plop*. "Don't worry, kid. Nobody gets it perfectly their very first time!" he said with the kind of reassurance you'd give a child who'd managed to topple a bike with training wheels on it. He continued on with a cursory lesson in horsemanship that was surprisingly easy to follow, and by the time he galloped off, beckoning me to follow him, I felt comfortable enough to do so without hesitation.

We rode through an apple orchard from which he picked an ideal apple without even slowing his horse's gallop, and then up the side of a mountain so green that I could swear we were riding through a *Highlander* movie location. By the time he slowed his horse, we'd reached a lush plateau of grassy mountain earth that appeared to overlook practically the whole world. We were so high that I could see clouds rolling through the valley beneath us, and above us was nothing but the clearest blue sky that a noonday sun had ever had the good sense to illuminate. He grabbed the reins of my horse as I got close enough - probably so I didn't end up doing something stupid like spurring us both off the side of the mountain.

"Look, Mr. Hunter," he said gravely (although I was relieved he wasn't calling me "kid"). "I know you didn't mean any harm by offering what you did for my land, but I've got to tell you: this place up here is God's country. I've never felt closer to any town or stretch of earth than I have *this* town... this county... this state. I raised my kids on my land just like my Father before me, and provided quite a few jobs to some real good ranch hands and farm workers. This kind of country isn't meant to be merely *owned*... it's got to be a **part** of you. The rivers that run through it are your blood, the mountains are your skin, and the wind is your breath. I always imagined my boys would find the same passion for the land that I have, but they haven't. So before I go sellin' you almost a third of the land I own - for *three* million dollars, and not a penny less - I need to know, Mr. Hunter... are you gonna be good to her?"

I was moved by his speech, and not just because in the short amount of time I'd been in these mountains that I *too* fell in love with their beauty... but because I felt for the first time that someone was truly speaking *my* language - the language of my heart - the language of a true *man*. This man had lived and experienced everything short of an actual castle (though his cabin seemed to be castle *enough* for him) that I'd ever wanted for *my* life, and I honestly envied him. I couldn't help but ask, "Forgive me for this, Mr. Meyer, as I'm not generally in the habit of shooting myself in the foot..." He raised a single eyebrow.

"But why exactly *are* you selling part of your land? If I were in *your* shoes... er, boots... I don't think I could *ever* trust another man to love my land the way I do." I felt like he could sense the sincerity in my tone. "Well, that's a real good point, young man," he ceded. "But the truth of the matter is that the long arm of the tax man has finally caught up to me... with a vengeance. I need every penny of the $3 million to pay back-taxes and fees!" I was shocked that anyone could even do enough business up here in *three* lifetimes to rack up that much federal debt. "Yep - even when you think they ain't keepin' tabs on ya, they sure as hell are. It's like they wait for the worst possible moment to..." he stirred from his own mental riot rally. "But shucks - those are just *my* worries. I wouldn't be so firm on the price if I didn't know the land was worth that much and more. And I'm sure you know that."

"It definitely seems that way, Mr. Meyer. This really is beautiful country up here - and though I was raised in the city, this is always what I imagined heaven to be like." As I finished saying it, he smiled so widely that it turned his stern moustache up at the corners. "I was hopin' you'd say somethin' like that."

It suddenly hit me that perhaps his cowboy sensibilities and my medieval sensibilities might be at aesthetic odds. "Oh! And I want to be as completely honest with you right now as you have been with me about your tax situation... which I completely understand, by the way." He nodded for me to continue. "Well, the fact is, ever since I've been a kid, I've always held a special place in my heart for the mountains - not just for their quiet tranquility, but for their unmistakable ties to the earth... to things that are grounded: truth and the old ways. That sort of thing." He looked as if I'd struck a chord with him. "Go on..."

"So, those old ways (to me) are best summed up in the romantic tales of the knights of old, of fair maidens, of justice, castles, and men working with their hands. None of these gadgets and gizmos that seem to permeate society today and put us all at arm's length, but the kind of community thinking that bonds people of all colors and cultures under a common bond... friendship, loyalty, respect, and working for goals that *matter*." It was at that moment that I saw his gruff exterior armor crack and fall from his metaphorical shoulders, as a single tear welled up in the corner of his eye. He brushed it away with his riding glove like he'd gotten a speck of dirt in there, but I knew what I'd said had spoken to *him* just as surely as his words had touched *me*. "Well sir, to be honest, I never expected to see a *castle* put up in these here mountains, but I don't rightly see how that would be a *bad* thing either, given the manly heart you just showed me."

24

Frank leaned over and clapped me on the back like the son he'd never had and then pulled me in for a manly hug. It was clear that I'd found a kindred spirit, and that he'd have no compunctions whatsoever about selling me his land. As we rode back toward his cabin, he told me how it was all probably for the best anyway - that his "little woman" had been after him to cut back on his work *anyway*, and that selling the land made him feel less responsible to always be riding across it, checking on it. It sounded to me like the land *really was* his baby in his mind, and that he was irresistibly compelled to constantly make sure she was in the best of condition and health.

He reminded me of Vinnie from back in Brooklyn when we were growing up: the guy who bought a nice Camaro early on in our high school years, and seemed to be working on it *every* weekend - fixing it, tweaking it, improving it, washing it, shining it. Only these mountains weren't mere "car love"... this was "love of the land" - the kind of passionate thought that encompasses the care of crops, livestock, buildings, and the people who tended them all. Land-love even extended to those things we hadn't even put there: the trees, the rivers, the mountains, and the wildlife. And I was *determined* to find a way for them all to coexist peacefully.

Once we got back to the cabin, his wife had already grilled up some delicious steaks with all the trimmings. "New York Strips... *get it?*" Frank elbowed me in the ribs. I quietly laughed at his silly steak humor. "My lady's quite the cook, isn't she, boys?" Michael, already several mouthfuls deep into the succulent feast, happily agreed: "Mmmph!" (Albeit, with his mouth full.) Frank and his wife seemed to make up the storybook married couple that you never seemed to get to see in all the old tales: the ones actually *in the middle of* living "happily ever after". He complimented her cooking and doted on her sweet smile, pulling her close for a tender kiss every time he thought we weren't looking, and she looked up to him with the utmost respect, seeing to it that after he was indoors that he didn't have a thing in the world to tend to - not his meals, not his warm hearth, nor any other comfort that one could imagine made a house into a home. I didn't think it was *possible* for Frank to love anything more than his land, but it was overwhelmingly obvious that he loved this woman with all his heart. And she went out of her way not to betray his love, making sure we (his guests) were in full view of her deference to his every desire. He was her loving king, and she was his respectful queen.

It actually hurt my heart a bit to think that his sons - who had been raised in the warm glow of this couple's happy hearts and in the ways of the mountains - could ever choose lives for themselves that involved doing anything else. But alas, as long as I had lived, that always seemed to be the ways of Fathers and sons... their life passions were never quite the same. "When I become a parent," I thought to myself. "I'll have to remember not to be hurt or insulted if I have a son that doesn't take up my Fatherly mantle." Despite my brave inner monologue, I truly hoped that I'd never have to endure such a heartache.

We finished the meal, and retired to the comfy leather couches in front of the fireplace, which had an empty wrought-iron grate behind some modified andirons that were made to be inserted into the stone beneath them. We talked all afternoon and into the evening about life on the farm and ranch, and specifically about what was necessary to properly take care of the hundred or so head of excellent cattle I would be getting as a part of the deal. Frank seemed almost to be infinitely knowledgeable about the whole she-bang, and delivered every fact, operation, and anecdote so clearly that even *Michael* didn't have any questions left when we were done.

His wife (whose name was *Mimi*, we finally discovered - and were surprised we had gone so long without knowing it!), whenever she wasn't lying across Frank's manly chest, was up making sure our drinks were always full and that the huge plate of cookies she'd put out never went completely bare. Every single time she'd sit back down, too, Frank would hug her so close that you knew he never wanted to let her go - and her contented smile from ear to ear let us know that Mimi was more at ease being in his arms than in any other place in the world. It seemed like they would make the very *best* of neighbors for me, if nothing else.

Once I'd noticed that there was no longer any light coming in the windows from outside, Frank graciously offered to take us back to town to our hotel. "Then again," he added. "You're more than welcome to just spend the night *here* and we can go sign the sale papers in the mornin'. I guarantee that those couches are just as comf'table to sleep on as a feather bed. I made them all *myself*, after all." "Of *course* you did, you big bear!" I joked.

"And you boys wouldn't want to miss out on my delicious homemade Belgian waffles in the mornin', with fresh whipped butter and maple syrup, would you?" Mimi offered. I looked over at Michael, whose eyes - even though he was full - were feverishly hoping that I'd choose Mimi's waffles over the continental *nothing* that our dinky hotel offered.

"We'd be honored to stay over and join you for breakfast!" I announced. "But you're sure it's no trouble?"

"Oh, no trouble at all!" Mimi reassured me. "It'll be nice to have some extra conversation at the table since all the cattle hands are out grazing the herd this weekend." One thing you could definitely say about Frank's wife: she was the *perfect* hostess, and loved *every* opportunity to serve.

We awoke in the morning to Mimi already bustling around in the kitchen, and the sweet smells wafting over from her waffle iron. Frank was already at the head of his table, enjoying a fresh cup of coffee and shooting goo-goo eyes over at Mimi, as if they were teenagers in love. With one more hearty meal under our belts, Frank drove us all into town in a truck even bigger than Jim-Bob's, although he drove it with such precision that the thin mountain trails seemed wider somehow. A few hours and a trip to the local bank later, the papers were signed and the land of my future castle and kingdom... was **mine**!

25

I managed to buy the horse (who I renamed "Freedom" - the horse didn't complain) from Frank that I had ridden the day I met him, and got to where I could make the ride back and forth between town and the furthest edges of my property in a single hour. Michael had taken to staying in town at the hotel (which I continued to pay Helen for - once a week), because my saddle wasn't really *made* for two, and the one time he *did* try to ride up to my land with me, he said it felt too "Brokeback-y". It was his homomisandristic way of saying it made his ass hurt - and his dick uncomfortable. I didn't care; I was glad to be rid of him with *that* attitude. He mainly went back and forth between the hotel and The Rusty Hoof, sleeping with whatever bar tramps would have him. The last time I visited the room, he'd even gotten himself a PS3 to whittle away a few hours every now and then. He told me that as soon as I had a place made on my land suitable enough for someone to stay, that he'd be more than happy to come and help me out with any work I needed done. I wasn't exactly holding my breath for that (after all, Michael was more of a party guy than anything else).

Frank went ahead and recommended a few good ranch hands to tend to the cattle on my property. "They're good boys," he said - talking about the *men* who were practically my same age. "Never had trouble, laziness, or thievin' from a one of 'em, and they're already used to that herd. I've had 'em doing some fence mending and chores over t' my place during the sale hiatus 'cuz I wasn't sure the new owner would want 'em, but we trust each other - so I know you'll do right by 'em and they'll never let you down. I give you my word." These were the kind of words I'd always imagined that **real men** spoke to one another, and I promised myself to my dying day that my word would be my bond *just like Frank's*. Honor would **not** die on *my* watch!

The ranch hands were even better than Frank had boasted, and each already had his own horse (which was lucky for me - considering I only had Freedom for myself). Oddly enough, even though I had yet to build a place for *myself* to stay, the corral and stables already had a ranch hand bunk house attached, so the "boys" had beds, trunks for their stuff, a bathroom, a small kitchen, and even a little TV corner, powered by some solar cells Frank had attached to the roof.

I told myself that I really needed to Google how Frank did those things with the solar power and water collection tanks for the bathroom and sinks, but then I remembered: I *didn't **have*** internet! The realization hit me like a ton of bricks. For the first time in weeks, I went to check the internet, and it just *wasn't there*. Frank had Wi-Fi at his cabin, but that was a half a day's ride from the spot I'd picked out to set up a temporary residence while I erected my castle keep. (Also, I didn't want to make a *pest* of myself, even though I knew that neither Frank nor Mimi would ever let on if I was.) All my romanticized ideas of setting up a small log cabin and living off the land were beginning to come apart at the seams. I swallowed my pride and realized that I'd have to go ahead and ask Frank to help set up what I had neither the know-how nor the materials to accomplish.

He was more than willing to help, of course, and one week into September, my little cabin was finally set up. I went ahead and had my own personal T1 line installed for my computer nook, and the look on the technician's face that installed the final portion of it was priceless. You could walk across my *entire cabin* in a good thirty feet, and I had a horse tied up outside next to a tanning rack that had a buckskin currently stretched out on it from the last bowhunting trip Frank had gone with me on... so needless to say, I didn't look like a millionaire - much less a guy who personally needed an internet connection fast enough to support a medium-sized *company*. What can I say? I hate slow internet.

After I'd set up my P.O. Box in town at the post office, I began slowly getting all the things I'd need for my soon-to-be empire: hatchets, axes, cutter mattocks, railroad picks, shovels, sledgehammers, woodworking hand tools, masonry chisels and bits - *you name it*. I was determined that there would be nothing in my kingdom that *could* be done, that I couldn't do. I began felling my own trees and replanting twice what I had harvested. I began to plane and shape my own wood. I found a cliff face that I could chisel out solid stone from that I could then mason into smooth, castle-quality stone blocks. I began making my own charcoal, and when I found a small vein of iron on my land, I set up a small forge so that I could fire my own steel.

Everything was starting to come together, but it was going too slowly. Winter was too close at hand to begin erecting a castle, even if I'd already had the workers in place (which I didn't). My research had warned me against stonemasonry in cold weather, as the mortar would be more susceptible to cracking... and the *last* thing I wanted to do was make a flawed or weak keep (as that was to be the centermost foundation of my castle).

I decided to put my castle engineering research and practical application on hold for the winter, and instead bunked up with the ranch hands in one of the spare beds. I began learning all that I could about the care, common illnesses, and shoeing of horses from the collective years of experience that the ranch hands had. I even got Michael to reluctantly join me ("I guess I could. It's getting boring here in town anyway," he said.); and Frank set about teaching him to ride - which he never fully caught onto, if you ask me.

All the winter nights served to help me glean every possible useful tidbit of information about my own cattle that I might need to know from the ranch hands, and with how well I kept them fed and how tall we kept our campfires, they were perfectly happy telling me everything they'd ever known or experienced with my cattle. Whenever I'd feel like my brain was about to explode from all the new things I was learning, I'd further challenge it by taking a trip over to Frank's place to learn how to properly raise vegetables and herbs from Mimi, or how to fashion leather crafts and furnishings from Frank. Our Christmas was even had there, and Michael somehow got drunk enough to deal with the fact that there weren't any women from town there for him. I was content enough to know the joy and camaraderie of this new mountain-man brotherhood... and that the spring (and the building of my castle in earnest) would soon be upon us.

26

Early spring turned into middle spring and passed on into late spring with no sign of the snow melting around the altitudes at which I had initially planned to build my castle. I consulted with Frank, of course, who said that (had I asked him - which he *really* hadn't expected me to do) he would have told me that the higher-up altitudes around these parts seldom melted for more than a month at a time. "Honestly, your visit to buy my land couldn't have *been* more opportune for this area. It was really the best time of the year."

The news didn't dissuade me entirely, but I knew - much like a swimsuit photographer waiting for the sun's "golden hour" - that the building of my keep would have to be precisely executed by absolute professionals, or else it would never happen *at all*. Also, I had to take into account the possibility that if I sincerely wanted the keep at that altitude, then I would have to consider making it either *smaller* than I'd originally intended, or construct it in a *modular* fashion (so that I could add onto it year by year, but it would never *actually* be "incomplete"). In any corporate conundrum like this, a COO would likely just throw more workers at the project, hoping that the increase in manpower would lessen the time necessary for completion. However, I knew that the amount of stone-block masons competent enough to work on a *castle* scale (or with any similar experience) was not just in short supply in *America*, but the whole world over... so I just didn't *have* that option. It was something (like the realization that my "millions" in prize money from the year before wasn't anywhere *near* two hundred) that seemed to be another supernatural road block, hindering my progress toward my dream. I decided, regardless, to press onward with the keep construction at the mountain height that I truly wanted, and began contacting all the American professional stonemasons that I could (as I didn't really want to pay the international flight/housing fees of professionals from overseas).

As with most professionals, they were not immediately available, and even *with* my increased buying power, their professional integrity kept them from leaving the jobs in which they were currently engaged. I could respect that (In fact, it probably meant that they would be all the less likely to ever leave *my* job once they'd begun work on it.). So, I made arrangements for all 24 of my most-wanted stonemasons to meet and begin work on my castle in late June. Frank reassured me that the snows (if any) around that time of the year generally did not "stick", so it should be a safe bet that I could start building then. I decided to spend the majority of my time (in the three months I had left to wait) getting to know every corner of my lowlands, and also getting a proper feel for hand-quarrying the local stone that I was so keen on using in my future keep.

As it turned out, even *one* good facing stone block took me nearly half of an *entire work day* to separate from its source mountain and craft into what I considered respectable. Taking into account that these stonemasons would not just have to *quarry* the blocks, but also *place* them (for the keep construction), I was sincerely hoping that they worked at a faster pace than I did.

On an unusually warm day in late April, I found myself wanting to get away from the quarry for a while and set out once again to get to know my lowlands. There was a particularly thick section of woods (about halfway between town and my future keep site) that I had always merely circumvented - rather than ride through - on my trips into town. Michael was too hung over that morning for even my cattle hands to make him stir, so I left him behind. I had just finished crafting a high-carbon steel longsword the month before (using an Ulfberht Viking sword PBS special as a guide) and was rather proud of how it ended up turning out... so I had had Frank help me craft a special saddle sheath so that I could take it with me on my rides. It made me feel like I was just one step closer to fulfilling my medieval goals.

So, as I was trotting Freedom through the thick woods, I would intermittently swipe at thin tree branches or whatever underbrush I could reach that might potentially obstruct the path I was making. It was nearly noon by the time I figured I'd made it halfway into the thick woods (which, by this time, I was thinking of calling "The Endless Wood"). The forest was so thick with yew trees where I was that I could hardly make out the sun at times. I shuddered to think how eerily The Endless Wood (decided to definitely stick with that) would be at night. A small break in the overhead tree canopy revealed a thin, dark plume of smoke that could only have been coming from a campfire ahead. As the entirety of The Endless Wood (I really like saying that now!) was on my land, and as exactly *none* of my cattle hands should've been on *this* side of the central mountain range that ran through my land, I had to assume that whoever was in my forest was trespassing there.

"Whoa, Freedom," I quietly urged my horse. I dismounted more slowly than I probably ever have (It felt like I was *crawling* off of the horse.), and gently eased my longsword from the saddle sheath. I wasn't taking any chances with a trespasser... it could be some hippie that had wandered too far from the nearby park's borders or it could be some kind of ax-murdering psycho that only *hunted* such hippies... but I wouldn't know for sure until I was already too close for comfort. In any case, it couldn't hurt to be armed. I'd never crept so quietly in the woods before. All the tracker stories that my Native cattle hand had told heretofore were starting to come back to me...

I moved only with the rustling of the wind. I brushed potential noises (dry leaves, twigs, and debris) to the side with my foot before moving each trepidatious step. I couldn't do much to mask my own scent (which I'm guessing was mostly quarry-work B.O., horse-back sweat, and leather) at this point, and moving downwind would make more noise than just continuing a short space to the trespasser, so I decided to chance that he was perhaps cooking something powerfully fragrant over the fire smoke I'd seen. Before I knew it, I rounded a particularly wide, old yew tree to see my target: a man sitting on a fallen tree in a tiny clearing, with a green hiking backpack propped up against the tree beside him, poking at his fire with a stick. I slowed my movement by half, creeping toward him with my sword leading the way. Without even turning around, he spoke: "Please don't stab me, Kai - I promise I mean you no harm."

27

I almost dropped my sword, I was so stunned. "How did he...?" I began to think. "How did I know your name?" he smiled as he turned to face me, bringing his legs to the other side of the fallen tree. This time, I dropped my sword. The fumbling I ending up doing to pick it back up would've made the Three Stooges proud. Flustered, all I could manage to answer was: "Yeah."

"I have to apologize for that. It really was discourteous of me," he extended his hand in greeting, and out of habit, I bent forward to shake it. "But when I hear the thoughts of someone sneaking up on me that's afraid I might pose some kind of threat, I kind of instinctually search his head for a name his friends might call him to put him at ease." I blinked several times in a row, unable to immediately process what he'd said. "Did you just say...?" I began.

He rose up from his seat. "Sorry; let me start again. The name's Jonathan Kylfing Sagebrecht, but most people just call me Kyle. Uh oh..." he seemed to retract into his own thoughts. "I could foresee that being a problem - if people call you Kai, and people call me Kyle - well, *that* could get confusing. Oh wait... people are calling you Mr. Hunter these days, aren't they? Damn - it is just so much easier to read *old* memories than new ones..."

"*WHOA!*" I stopped him. He seemed barely phased by my outburst. "Are you telling me that you can *read minds*?" I was flabbergasted, but also wasn't entirely sure that I believed him. "Oh... yes. I can," he admitted. "And to answer your question you had on the way over here - what am I doing on your property - well, to be honest, I didn't yet *know* it was your property. I've been coming up here to the... oh, you're gonna call it The Endless Wood? Nice."

"Would you *PLEASE* stop reading my mind while you're talking?!?" I yelled, convinced that that was what he (indeed) was doing.

"Sorry, Kai... uh, Mr. Hunter... my mind just works way too quickly to keep it on just one thing at a time. I don't mean anything by it, but I was hoping you'd understand. Anyway, so I've been coming up here to get away from town for quite some time now - ever since it was Mr. Meyer's land, and *he* didn't really ever wander into The Endless Wood. (As you can see, it's kind of overgrown.) I think *maybe* he was planning on farming it for lumber at one point, but..."

"Could you *focus*, Kyle?" I asked impatiently. "Oh! Yeah... sorry. So, I just come up here to get away from town because no matter how hard I push myself, I can never read any minds up here but wildlife, and I don't speak bird or squirrel or bear, so it's generally pretty calming. I only really seem to jump into overdrive around other *people*. I'd say it's a defense mechanism, but once I get started, it's hard to..."

"Stop. Yeah, I get it." Just *listening* to Kyle was exhausting; he spoke so quickly (apparently, when anxious) that it reminded me of that old cartoon mouse - what was his name? - *Little Blabbermouse!* That's it. "Look... what do you say I just sheathe my sword in my belt here for a second... and then maybe we can talk like friends for a bit, instead of jabber-jaw mice, hmm?" I grinned, amused at both the speed and prowess of his mind.

"Sure, yeah. 'Shut up, Kyle!' Yeah, I get it. People generally can't take me for too long even if they *do* believe me." I took him by the shoulders and sat him back down on the fallen tree where I then joined him. "Oh, I believe you. There're probably plenty of things in this world I *don't* understand, and honestly, I'd like to find out more about them," I earnestly revealed. "So why don't we just sit down here and take it easy, okay?"

His eyes squinted for a few seconds. "Advisor to a Royal Court? Wow - you really *do* believe me! Huh... well, I gotta say, at least your plans for me don't have anything to do with winning the lottery or seeing if a girlfriend is cheatin' on you or somethin'." Kyle really must've been concentrating (if he was right that old memories were easier to read than new ones), because I'd only had that thought for a fraction of a second when he latched onto it. It was really hard to stay in the moment when you had someone around that could read your thoughts.

"Exactly," he said, as if he'd read the narrative I just expounded to you (which, incidentally, was what I was also thinking at the time). "That's why I ended up talking so quickly. People could never verbalize thoughts they had fast enough, and it was just easier for me to respond to their thoughts before they spoke them (if they were even *meaning* to). As it turns out, most folks are never too keen to have you know what they're thinking, so I'm somewhat of a social pariah back in town." He flashed a toothy, uneasy grin.

"I've got an idea, Kyle," I was struck by inspiration. "Why don't you un-flex whatever brain muscle makes you predisposed to reading minds (as you can tell I have no intention to hurt you), and then pass me a fire-pokin' stick so we can just chat a bit? How's that sound?" He squinted again, and then his whole head seemed to relax at once. "Cool," he uttered his first non-rapid word in minutes. "I suppose we're the only people within a crow's flight from here. It couldn't hurt to chat a bit, as you say."

From then until sunset, we spoke like just a random couple of dudes... *way* calmer than I had previously thought Kyle capable of. We took turns grabbing nearby branches to keep the fire going, and even went through two or three different fire-pokin' sticks. Kyle had apparently set up a little "private eye" business in town, and was making enough to survive, but nowhere *near* what someone of his talents *should* have been making. It just so happened that Kyle had discovered his gift for mind-reading late in life: he was in his mid-20s, his parents had both died as a result of probably the town's only *ever* auto accident, and the town's benevolence turned to indifference *far* sooner than had he still been a child. He'd never really studied anything, so he had taken to reading old plays and poetry from the library (and was, in fact, the author of the bathroom-stall poem I'd admired earlier!). He didn't own a car, so poverty had basically kept him from being able to advance himself in the world - or even move *away*... until *I* came, that is.

28

Kyle never went back to reading my mind (or if he did, he didn't mention it), so I felt like he trusted me. His way of thinking was almost as childlike as it was complex. He seemed to immediately understand all points of ingress to any argument or problem, and (better) he also always had several simple solutions prepared. His innocent manner kept him from holding back any answers - even if they would possibly be taken as offensive or silly to the average person - and he was so forthright that he seemed incapable of guile. Needless to say, I revisited my idea of his being my Royal Advisor more than once during our afternoon of conversation. Once the sun was setting, I asked Kyle if he'd like to join me for some "grub" back at my cabin (which I had been missing, anyway).

"Oh yeah! I guess I must've lost track of the time. I probably would've hiked back to *town* by now if you hadn't have shown up."

"Yeah, my bad," I apologized. "Let me make it up to you with some smoked deer jerky, a nice *inside* fire, and my one good bearskin blanket." He looked at me quizzically. "You're not hittin' on me, are you?" If he'd have read my mind, he'd have *known* I wasn't. "No, you dum-dum. I'm just saying that if you stay the night in my freakin' tiny cabin, you won't have to sleep directly on the awesome wood floors (that I personally installed)."

"Oh. Cool. So did you say... *smoked deer jerky?*" his stomach grumbled, betraying his hunger - that he'd *also* forgotten to tend to all day. "God dang right!" I was *proud* of the few deer kills I'd gotten, and the jerky Frank had helped me make from them was particularly tasty. "Sweeeeet," he said through his teeth.

I managed to fit him and his hiking pack onto Freedom (who had been happily chewing all day on some of the shorter grasses where I tied him) with me, and we were back to my cabin (in the foothills of the mountain that I was preparing for my keep construction) before the darkness truly settled on the land. We probably ate through a pound of smoked deer jerky apiece (about half of my cabin stash) as we talked on into the night. For someone a year my junior who had never even left the remote mountain town in which he was born, he was quite the intriguing little man (Yes; he was shorter, and quite a bit skinnier than I.). Most of his deeply-held ideals and convictions had been gleaned from Shakespeare, which made him very well suited to the task of *being* my Royal Advisor in my future medieval kingdom.

"So what do you say, Kyle? I know we've just met, our acquaintance has been kinda superficial, and my *keep* isn't even built yet, but I feel like I can trust you. Would you like to be my Royal Advisor?" He smiled serenely. "You know what, Mr. Hunter (*ahem*, **Kai**)? I think the team of Kai and Kyle could be something really awesome for this little mountain here in the middle of nowhere. Would you still be feeding me... maybe even give me my own room in the keep?" he warily asked.

"*Are you kiddin'?!?*" I reacted as if his wants were preposterously meager. "Not only will you have your own *quarters* in the keep and access to the *finest* Royal foods, but I'll pay you **two** gold coins every month - exactly **twice** what any average worker in the kingdom will make!" I continued sheepishly, "You know... once the Royal smelter and mint has been set up properly."

"Man... you've really thought this whole thing through, haven't you? It's like you were *born* to run a medieval kingdom." It felt nicely to hear someone verbalize what I'd always thought.

"I **know**, right?" my eyes were wide with excitement, and I could tell that he was sharing in it. "So what do you say, Kyle?"

He stood up straightly and as tall as he could, placing his fists against his waist like Superman in the 50s. "I say you've got yourself an advisor, your majesty!" he beamed. I hadn't even begun to think of myself in a Kingly manner, but I've got to be honest... it felt *well* to be addressed in such a manner. I was (finally) truly **important** in someone else's eyes. All at once, I desperately wanted to return the favor, and racked my brain to come up with an honorific that could be applied to a Royal Advisor in everyday speech. I think Kyle could read that I was straining to come up with such a word, so he offered some suggestions: "Your thoughtship? Your wiseness? Your prominence?"

"Wait!" I stopped him. "What was that last one?"

"Your prominence?"

"Yeeeeaaaaahhhh," my mind coiled around the word like a greedy dragon's tail around a pile of gold. "I don't even think that's ever been used before! You see? This is why you're the perfect choice to be my advisor... *your prominence*," I winked at him.

"Hey, I like that," he agreed as he sat back down on the bearskin blanket I'd stretched out on the floor for him. The fire in the stone fireplace had burned down to red glowing embers at this point, and both of our minds seemed to disengage at once: settling us into peaceful slumber.

I dreamed of my future castle that night. I was seated on a golden throne whose cushions were covered with deerskins that had been dyed a deep, rich red. My golden crown looked really cool - it had spikes on it that angled outwards and then inwards toward the top. I don't remember what my clothes looked like (probably a deerskin tunic and leggings or something), but I was wearing a thick, brown bearskin that was fastened to my shoulders with opal-cut rubies set in latches of gold, with a heavy, braided golden chain that draped across my chest - running from one shoulder to the other. I was presiding over a session of Court (it seemed) and though many people were there, the only person I *distinctly* remember was Kyle, who stood by my side (even though he had a cool [smaller] chair as well) and would bend down to advise me from time to time. Oddly, though it was bureaucratic, it wasn't boring.

29

The next morning, I went to introduce Kyle to Michael and my cattle hands. Unfortunately, Michael had woken from his hangover late the previous afternoon, and persuaded one of the cattle hands to give him a ride back into town, where I could only guess he was back to his old distractions. Having Kyle there with me sort of softened the blow, however, and I decided to just take him over to Frank's place and see if he could spare an afternoon (and a horse, which I'd buy) to teach Kyle how to ride properly. I was hoping that Kyle could then tag along for a few days with my cattle hands and get to know that operation about as well as I did. Kyle had no problem with the plan, and when we got to Frank's place, it turned out that he had both the time to instruct my new advisor, and one spare horse left (which I promised him double payment for).

The perusal of my empty wallet convinced me that I needed to take a ride into town, so I left Kyle with Frank (who agreed to guide him back to the bunk house after the lesson) and spurred Freedom toward town. After a quick stop at the local bank for a relatively sizable withdrawal and a trip to the hardware store for some sharpening stones and extra flints, I headed over to the hotel, where Helen had installed a cool little hitching post for Freedom as a Christmas present to me. She'd even added a little brass label to it ("For Freedom!"), which I thought was nice.

"Hey, Mr. Hunter!" she greeted me. "I knew I'd see *you* before too long after Michael dragged his behind back into his old room last night."

"Yeah, I never want you to think I expect him to stay here for free, you little minx," I did some shameless flirting (which both Helen and I could enjoy guilt-free, as she was *way* too old for me). "Oh, I know you're good for it, Mr. Hunter. Besides, if you weren't, it would still be kinda fun to kick that city gigolo out on his perky little ass." I cringed a bit to imagine that Helen had been admiring Michael's ass.

"Gigolo, huh?" I chuckled. "Has he been having more bar skanks back to his room already?" She slapped my hand that had been resting on the counter. "C'mon now, Mr. Hunter... those girls are *locals* here, after all," she chided.

"Sorry, Helen," I apologized. She leaned in like she was telling me a secret: "But yeah, they're skanks. He had one in there last night for about an hour before she left - reapplyin' her lipstick like I couldn't *see* her as plain as day. He might be glad to see you, but it's pretty early for him, you know... considerin' it's before noon and all."

"You're probably right," I took out my newly-filled wallet. "Here... that's another couple of months' payment on the room at that reduced rate you gave me." I didn't want her to think I was shorting her, but also wanted to maintain the cheaper rate. "And I certainly do appreciate it, Helen."

"Oh sure Mr. Hunter; you're a nice fella, so I don't mind helpin' you out until you get that castle in the mountain all built and what-not. Just promise you'll have me up there for a fancy feast once your dinin' hall is all set up."

"You got it, sweetheart. Now, let me go check on Michael and make sure he's not smothering under a pile of floozy under-drawers."

"Oh, *you*!" she waved me off playfully. I used my spare key to unlock the room, went to open it, and was stopped shortly by the door chain. A low groan came from inside, followed by: "*See*, Helen? *That's* why I can't just *lock* my door! You can't just barge in here anytime you..." Michael had gathered up the bed's comforter around him and groggily made his way to the door, only to halt his tirade abruptly when he caught sight of me. "Oh, it's just you," he closed the door enough to undo the chain and then shuffled back to the bed and collapsed face-first into it.

"Nice to see you *too*, princess," I'd hoped he'd be a bit more enthusiastic to receive the man that was paying for his room *into* said room, but I was finding out that it was a bit much to expect of Mr. Party-all-the-time.

"Fuck you," he lazily breathed into his pillow. Then, as if he suddenly remembered that I was the one financing the whole operation, he flipped over in bed. "*Oh!* I'm out of cash. Can I get a few more hundred for the month?" I couldn't help but feel a bit used. "Yeah... I don't think you've really been pulling your weight *that* well with the cattle these days."

"Oh, come *on*... it's your fault I'm out here in the middle of BFE in the *first* place!" Nice to know that the ***adventure*** was now something that was my *fault*. I was definitely beginning to sour on the idea of having Michael as my ride-along. "Well, you know, I could always pay your airfare back to New York if you don't like being here."

He quickly realized the sweet deal he had going, and did the barest minimum of damage control. "Nooooo, that's not it. You know I get bored easily, Kai. I guess I just thought your whole castle and shit would've been *built* by now."

I felt like I was channeling Liz Lemon. "Yeah. Doesn't happen overnight."

He knew he had to make his attitude up to me. "Look, I'm sorry, bro. Why don't we just go get a couple of steaks and hang out here in town tonight? Cool?" It was probably the best I could expect from him, so I accepted. "All right, fine. *But no hoes!* Got it?" He made an X with his finger over his chest, "Cross my heart!"

As we enjoyed our filets (in the *main* room of Meyer's steak house this time), we laughed and joked about old times in NYC, and it became clear to me that Michael (in his own way) was pining for home. He really *was* out of his element here, and the pickings, though easy, were relatively slim - and he was a man that needed to be challenged. Also, I had a feeling that even if the castle had already been erected, that he'd be a fish out of water *there* as well.

30

When we got back to the hotel, I went ahead and made sure to put a small tub of water and a bucket of feed out for Freedom and covered him up with a few warm blankets, as it was far too late to try riding back to my property. I even caught Helen (who obviously liked Freedom far more than she let on) walking out of the hotel lobby with one of those wide brushes you generally see rich folks brushing show horses with. She quickly hid it behind her back and acted like she was outside to look at the stars ("Nice night out tonight, huh, Mr. Hunter?"). I didn't mind; Freedom seemed to like the old biddy, too.

I went back inside and started getting ready for bed, as my body had gotten used to a schedule where I only stayed up a few hours past sunset. Michael, on the other hand, seemed like he was just warming up - like the steak had been a long-awaited breakfast that he'd needed to start his day (even though it was quite clearly *night*).

"Come on, bro... what are you doin'?" Michael clearly had an issue with me calling it a night. "I've been telling this hot little brunette at the Hoof all about you - real wingman stuff - you woulda been proud! Let's go!" His rallying cries fell on deaf ears. "Sorry, Michael, I can't. I gotta get back to the land early tomorrow and see how Kyle's day with Frank..."

And it hit me... I'd gone this whole time without even ***mentioning*** the mind-reading advisor I now had in my employ! My first instinct (which, thankfully, I quelled) was to immediately spill everything and tell Michael all about Kyle. Then I had a more prudent thought: "Why not just use Kyle to see how serious Michael is about staying here with me? Does he expect to be some lazy hanger-on *forever*, or does he ever intend on pulling his weight?" Honestly, I was afraid that I already *knew* the answer to ***both*** questions, but I'd feel like a paranoid jackass if I was the *only* person that knew it. I still wasn't sure (even if it *could* be proven that he would be a jerk) that I could be the guy to send my oldest friend packing. It was one of those things I guess I was just hoping that Fate or Karma would take care of *for* me.

"Who's Kyle?" Michael asked. I hurried to think of a lie close enough to the truth to be believable. "A new hand I hired for the cattle - I just wanted to make sure he was all settled. I'll be riding out early to the bunk house before they leave for the day. Plus, my body's already on *my* land's time - I'd be no good as a wingman or anything *else* (for that matter) tonight."

"Dude - *lame*!" he was unimpressed. "But whatever - just don't put the chain on. If I bring some bitch home tonight, I don't want to end up just makin' out in the hallway because you can't go without *locking* everything in sight." He was right about that - there was never a deadbolt, chain, or any other door lock that I didn't usually end up securing before I went to bed. It was just old NYC habit: better safe than sorry - and *robbed*.

"Good luck, bro-ham!" I wished him well before my head hit the pillow. He bumped his chest with his fist twice and shot me the sideways peace sign before he hit the lights and left.

I didn't bother hoping that he'd accompany me back to my land in the morning, because I knew I'd be there for hours before he'd even be *up* - skank jackpot or not. I normally sleep like a rock, so I wasn't sure whether or not Michael had brought anyone back to the room when I woke up. Looking over at his bed didn't help to clear up the mystery either, as it just looked like a mountain of disheveled blankets and clothes. I wasn't intrigued enough to investigate further, so I just got my saddle from Helen's office, untied Freedom, and set off for home.

As I rode around The Endless Wood, I thought about how much quicker the ride from town would be if I were just to cut a nice, straight path through it. Once the engineering concerns of my kingdom turned to thoroughfares, all those yew trees would no doubt make for some fine source material for bows for the tower guards. I found that I now often thought about the bare basics of things: what things were made of... what raw materials went into making what... what skills were necessary for accomplishing greater, more complex things. I felt like any King worth his salt would absolutely *need* to be well-educated about common things such as these. In fact, if there were common things that *could* be done (while I still had the youth, strength, and presence of mind to do them), I wanted to be able to do them **all**. I've never understood how supervisors or managers or even *CEOs* could get away with knowing any less than how to do **everything** that the people beneath them did. I was certain that at some idyllic point in America's industrial history, things were like that - but not anymore.

And I felt it was my destiny to *change* that.

I arrived back at the bunk house after sunrise, but before the sun had gotten up enough courage to poke its head over the mountain peaks to the east of my land and flood the valley with light. Even so, all the cattle hands had already gotten up (like they were supposed to do) and had taken the herd up to feed on the east peak lands. I was happy that they had served me so well over the months that they'd been with me, and decided to leave them all a $20 bill inside each of their trunks. It wasn't much - maybe a few rounds of beers at the Rusty Hoof - but I'd always wanted to be the kind of boss that did random kind things for the men that worked for him. Their refrigerators and freezers were always full, their pay was always plentiful, and there was always plenty of wood for their fires. I wanted to give every single man nothing but good incentives for loyalty and hard work, so that I could expect 100% from *them*... just like I expected it of myself.

I went ahead and rode over to Frank's place, but since he was off enjoying a ride through his land, I left the double payment for Kyle's horse (that I'd promised him the day before) with Mimi. We exchanged a few pleasantries over a delicious pot of coffee she'd made, and while I had hoped to see Frank before I left, I knew I had work to do. I had decided that I needed my keep to be built on (or carved out of) solid rock. It seemed like a decent idea to me, even back in Sunday School when we used to sing a song about the parable Jesus told about the man that built his house on the rock (as opposed to the sand - which is just a silly engineering idea on its face). So, I set off to outline the base of the keep, hoping to dig down to bedrock at each corner.

31

I picked up my best shovel and railroad pick from the storage shed I'd built off of the cabin, and headed over to the planned keep base (It was near the cliff face where I had spent about a week and a half chiseling out demo stone blocks so the masons would have an idea of the *least* of what I expected. All twenty blocks I'd made were still there, too.). It occurred to me that though I had picked out the site, I hadn't really done too much planning of the actual construction yet - which, considering the keep was the cornerstone of the whole castle (and ultimately, my whole medieval *dream*), seemed like a pretty major, ridiculous oversight. I spent a while there at the cliff arguing with myself over how much room I actually needed (not *too* much, but enough to be impressive by itself)... whether or not I wanted the keep to contain a barracks, smithy, or feasting hall (I didn't.)... and which way I wanted the front entrance to face.

Seriously - the last thing was a genuine concern of mine. One of the things Kyle had talked with me about the night before last was the Chinese idea of Wu Xing, which I then had to Google. I immediately fell in love with it, and saw many ways in which it could seamlessly integrate with medieval living. My first favorite things about Wu Xing were the ideas of yin and yang, and how cardinal directions were assigned cosmological masculinity or femininity with Feng Shui. I wanted to be able to see the sun rise from my sleeping chambers, but I also wanted the entrance to the keep *itself* to open to the south (the most masculine direction). Fortunately, the solid mountain (and cliff face) was behind me to the north, so the entrance wasn't a problem... and the first sunlight that hit my land was after the sun had risen over a mountain ridge so far to the east that it was on federal park land, so that seemed fine as well.

I found what seemed to be the greatest, most central mass of solid rock of the cliff behind me and set that as my northernmost middle point. I used my yard pole to measure 8 lengths to the east, then 16 to the south, 16 to the west, 16 more back up to the north, and the final 8 back to the small hole I dug where I began. I'm no numerologist or whatever, but the idea that my outer keep wall would begin after eight eights, just sounded like double infinity to me (eights on their sides - which I thought was impressive). Plus, Kyle had said that Chinese folks thought of 8 as a lucky number, and most Americans think 3 is a lucky number, so since a yard is made up of three feet... well, you get the idea. My mind just thought of a lot of different cool things while I was really just dragging a shovel through the snow to make a square that I wanted to build my keep wall outside of.

I spent most of the morning digging downward into the outline - through the snow, through the dirt, all the way to the bedrock beneath. As I suspected, the closer I was to the cliff, the more likely it was that I arrived at the bedrock layer sooner. By the time I took a break to sit down and eat some deer jerky from Freedom's saddle bag, I was down to bedrock pretty much everywhere except the southern end of the square, which seemed to go down pretty sharply (as *just* dirt) about three yards away from its edge. I snacked on the jerky, looking upward at the cliff, which seemed to loom menacingly over my head. I knew it'd make one *helluva* solid wall.

I got to thinking, though: "You know, no one would ever think that such a solid thing could ever hide a secret back room... maybe I could chisel one out and then set up a fake wall in front of it before the builders got here!" The more I ate, the more I convinced myself that I could *totally* do something like that, even with my admittedly limited expertise.

By the time I was full enough to go back to work, I had worked myself up to superhero levels of confidence - for absolutely no reason. I grasped the railroad pick like I was lifting Excalibur from "the stone" (Really - no one was there to see it, but it was quite the over-dramatic moment... like *soap opera* style overacting.), sauntered up to the center of the cliff like it was the bad guy I'd been training for months just to knock on his ass, swung the pick backward like I expected to bring down the whole mountain with my first strike... and then swung. *SHTINK!*

"Great," I thought. "Now the pick is stuck." The pick sunk into the solid rock wall more easily than picks generally do. It actually reminded me of the ease with which Mr. Miyagi stuck that cork on the end of that weird "fishing spear on a pulley" thing for Daniel in *Karate Kid II*. I knew that I'd never be able to pull an embedded railroad pick out of solid rock, but the stubborn portion of my manliness didn't allow me to release my grip on the tool until I'd tried. Instinctively, I pulled downward instead of backward (which *shouldn't* have worked), and the cliff wall before me began to shatter and splinter away like a tall stained glass window breaking from the bottom upwards. I jumped back, tripped over my carelessly-placed shovel, and tumbled into the depression at the southern end of my bedrock square.

When I regained my footing, I looked up to see the last bit of the fragile cliff facade falling away from the actual mountain. What remained was an archway - easily seven feet tall - that had been meticulously, *expertly* carved into the cliff. The small alcove behind the archway removed all doubts I had about this being some undiscovered cave entrance. Freedom pulled at the log he was tied to, excited by the energy coming from the alcove... which I was beginning to feel as well. Still, I approached cautiously. I've seen too many movies to not feel like this was some kind of trap (and *far* too coincidental, considering I'd been thinking about making exactly such a little room there).

The alcove was far darker than it should have been, seeing as how it was in the direct path of the noonday sun. As I crossed the threshold into it, stone braziers (that I hadn't been able to see prior) lit up with a *Foosh!*. The oddly-burning silvery-yellow flames reminded me of the first sunrise I'd seen when I came to town. They also cast an ominous light onto the two stone pedestals against the back wall of the alcove. The pedestal on the right had a thick, leather-bound tome floating above it. A seal set in the middle of the tome looked like a gold and silver taijitu (without the dots). Taking into account the weird braziers to the sides of the pedestals, I figured I'd let the whole floating thing slide. However, what **really** caught my attention was floating above the *left* pedestal: a large, rotating crystal that shimmered unnaturally, with all the colors of the rainbow.

32

Now, I grew up in the eighties. As such, I had read more than my fair share of *Choose Your Own Adventure*-type books. These two items magically floating in front of me seemed to be one of those "Here is where the path forever diverges!" kind of decisions. All the same, I was inexplicably drawn toward the crystal. The closer I came to it, the brighter and longer the shimmer rays seemed to emanate from it... as if it were reaching out to me.

I extended both hands for it reverently, and when I grasped it, the shimmer rays retracted into the crystal in the blink of an eye, and I felt an invisible energy unlike anything I'd ever experienced or heard of surge through my arms and whip around inside my body before contracting into a ball in my very center. And then it was gone... I couldn't feel anything else.

Well... not *really*.

You know that feeling you get when your parents tell you that you can do *anything*, and you're finally old enough to *believe* you're capable of such things? The psychic glow (which is the only way I can describe it) left inside me afterwards felt like someone had put a whole *galaxy's* worth of that same potential inside of me. It really *is* hard to describe it to someone that has never experienced something similar... like trying to describe how snow and icicles feel to someone that's never set foot outside of a desert.

When the glare from the flash wore off, I looked back down at the crystal. It looked like just a multi-faceted prism, and was almost entirely transparent. It was just *blank* - no energy zipping around inside of it, no glow, no shimmer rays... nothing. I set it gently back down on its pedestal and looked to the right, expecting to see that the tome had vanished or some such predictable CYOA nonsense. Fortunately, it was still floating there, patiently waiting its turn. I plucked it from the air, and both braziers went out at once.

"Well, crap," I muttered. "I can't read this thing in the *dark*!" (The unnatural darkness had prevailed against the noonday sun in the alcove - without the lights from the magical braziers to fight against it.) I stepped out into the brightness of the day, and saw Freedom anxiously stamping at the ground. "It's okay, boy," I went to calm him and stroke his neck. A powerful spark leapt from my hand to the horse with a *Shtack!* like I'd just given Freedom the biggest shuffling-across-a-shag-rug-on-a-winter-morning static shock of all *time*. I grimaced, fearful that the shock would have sent him into a wild rage, but against all sensible odds, it actually *quieted* him. I looked, dumbstruck, at Freedom. His head just slowly bobbed and his eyes seemed to say, "No, no - I get it now, bro. You're cool." (As an aside - I have no idea why Freedom's voice in my head sounded so much like Michael's.)

I allowed my focus to return to the thick leather tome, whose taijitu-like symbol seemed to throw off a quick lens flare, like a bad J.J. Abrams movie. I figured it was just the gold and silver catching a beam of the noonday sun. Whatever was within it, this book was calling to me.

When I opened the stiff, leather cover, exposing its pages to sunlight for the first time (in who knew **how** long), the top of the front page blazed in flame like someone had lit a fuse or cracked open a road flare. It startled me, and I dropped the book. I looked over at Freedom who was shaking his head like, "You dummy."

"Pffft! What do *you* know? You're just a horse!" I reacted as if the horse had actually spoken to me. Since the flare-up only lasted about a second, I bent down to pick up the book. I went to dust off where it would have been burnt, only there were no ashes to remove! Where I could've sworn the flames were bursting from was replaced with elegant, gilded lettering. Well - *numbering*, actually - and where the numbers were placed was actually part of the first sentence in the book, which I decided to read. I sat down on the log that Freedom was tied to, and as I began reading, he continued eating the short grasses around the log.

I read: "I must admit that when I began the journey out from our home 370 years ago, that I had little hope of carrying out the continuance of your legacy, Master William. But, as you (quite likely) sit there reading these words (in whatever language you now speak -

thanks to that emblem you had me place in the cover),..." I flipped the cover back over to the gold and silver taijitu, and thought briefly about removing it to see what language this thing was *originally* written in, but considered that it was entirely possible that I'd not be able to *undo* such a reckless act and decided against it. "...you have no doubt led your future self - by whatever means - back to this instructional book."

"Future self?" my expression twisted in denial. "Well, my name isn't William, but I hope he doesn't mind if I read his book. Or the book that this guy wrote for him, or whatever." I allowed myself the brief reverie on how much that I personally had been through in order to *be* the person reading this book, and how cool it would be if the book actually *was* written for me.

"I know you would have been ashamed of me had I not taken the triple precautions that you generally afforded yourself in life, so once I've finished this introduction, found an appropriately remote cliff in the west in which to hide your crystal and magic tome, and erdemanced a cave into it, I will: protect the cliff with the amnesia amulet (armed with the day-fuse) you gave me so that anyone not of your lineage approaching it will forget that they saw it, shatter the orb that you said releases the Shade that will shroud your crystal and tome from all but your spirit or its first male descendant, and then mask the entrance to the cave with that terrain-match hardening paint you gave me." My jaw dropped open like that kid in *The Neverending Story* when he started reading the part about himself. However, I was already super into *this* book, so I didn't freak out and jump off my log or anything.

"I truly hope you make it here someday. You know how young I was when I first took my leave of you to cross this land to get here, and I've overcome daunting odds to do so. Had the western tribes not been so gracious to this old warrior in their lands, I doubt I would have made it this far. But my strength and my journey are at an end. Good fortune to you, old friend."

33

I looked back at the cave, which was now lit like any other thing that the noonday sun struck. Apparently, this shade that William's old friend referred to in his introduction had nothing magical left to obscure - and had just dissipated. The weight of the tome's words only pressed upon my mind for a moment, before I realized that it *couldn't* have been 370 years since they were written... not if I was supposed to have been the *first* male descendant of this old man's even *older* friend William!

But other things weighed upon my thoughts as well. This friend referenced a "future self" in a time when such things (as far as *I* knew) were unheard of. He wrote of crystals, orbs, magic, and amulets...

"Amulets!" I had an epiphany. "If this book is for real, then that cave should have some kind of amulet in it somewhere, right?" I was impressed at my own thought process. I bolted up from the log and rushed back into the cave. As well-lit as it now was, it was easy to see the intricate carvings that had been made on both of the pedestals therein. I imagined it would be what Natives would carve in stone if they'd been influenced by King James-era Brits... or vice versa. I searched the small niche of a cave entirely, and had almost given up hope when I turned to leave and saw the amulet I was searching for - hanging right above the exit. Even with the sun streaming in, the lip of the archway had kept its hiding place naturally shaded. "*Man...* William's friend thought of *everything*!"

I plucked the amulet from the peg upon which it hung. "Hmmm..." I thought. "If this thing is really wired to protect anything from anyone's memory other than my Dad or me, and its sphere of influence is big enough to mask the presence of an entire *cliff*, then perhaps it should hang in my treasury someday." I rubbed my hands together like a villain that had just tied a Canadian lass to a train track. "But it's got to be tested," I declared aloud. "Right, Freedom?" He nodded his head once. Freedom seemed to almost *get* what I was saying on some level now. For whatever reason, it didn't really surprise me.

I calculated about how much of a spherical area that would've had to have been affected in order to mask the whole cliff, and then went into my lowlands, spending the rest of the afternoon dragging my shovel in the earth to make a circle as wide as the sphere's diameter. The next day, I forged the iron and shaped the wood necessary to make a small wooden chest, and then rode through the night to get to town. I was so excited to test the amulet, that I only slept two hours at the hotel, before waking Michael up to accompany me to the bank, where I withdrew $1,000 in twenties. He asked me what was up, and I told him I was going to test him, with the prize being the bankroll I now held in my hands. That was enough to entice him to ride with me ("Brokeback-y" or *not*!) back onto my lands. Once I made it back to the circle, I tied Freedom up by a tree on one side of the circle and told Michael to stay there. I then took the wad of twenties out of Freedom's saddlebag and marched all the way to the center of the circle, where I had placed the wooden chest. After depositing the money therein, I then continued to the other side of the circle, where I had hidden the amnesia amulet in a hollowed stump. I then walked back to the center of the circle and opened the chest, placing the amulet on top of the wad of cash. I closed the lid, stood erect, and with a smile said, "Now, Michael, if you can find where I put the money, you may have it."

Michael scoffed, "This is the stupidest game of hide-and-seek ever. How do you expect me to not know that you put that thousand dollars in that silly chest by your feet?" I grinned, "You want it? Come and get it!"

"Pffft!" he exhaled as he began toward the chest. He was exactly three strides into the circle before an odd look came over him. "Kai..." he began. "Wasn't there...? What am I?" He scratched his head like my Mom used to do when she'd come into a room about a second after she'd forgotten *why* she'd come into the room. I got his attention, "Michael! I think you left something back in Freedom's saddlebag." "Oh, okay!" he said, as if I'd just reminded him of what he'd forgotten. When he'd gotten back to Freedom (and out of the circle), I tried again.

"Hey Michael, don't forget... I put your room key in this chest over here!" I snickered.

"Well, why would you do *that*, you asshole?!?" It was as I suspected - he'd completely forgotten about the *money* as well! "It was just a joke, dude. I really just wanted you to come see this chest I made. I'd bring it over *there*, but it's pretty *heavy*, so..."

"Fine; I'll come to you, Mr. Important," he acquiesced. Three strides later, I could see his mind was in a fog once again. That was all the proof I needed. I went ahead and hid the amulet back in the hollow stump and crossed the field to the chest again. Removing the money, I waved it over at Michael. "See this? *This* little discovery is gonna pay for our steaks tonight, old buddy!" Michael's face lit up, "Sweet!" After pondering for a moment he said, "I wonder if there are any *other* little treasure chests on your property!" He'd probably been playing too many RPGs on his PS3. "Nah," I dismissed the idea, then lied: "I've already been to every corner of my land, and that was the only one I found." "Aw, man... here I was hoping we could have a treasure hunt or something," he pouted like a child.

I consoled him later by giving him the change after I'd left a considerable tip for our server at Meyer's. "Awesome, bro! Thanks!" he exulted. "I gotta admit, I'd already kinda blown through the last little bit you gave me, so this is great." I was gobsmacked. "*Dude* - I gave you $200 only two *days* ago, and you've been *with* me all of today!!"

"Yeah... about that... I'd already pretty much exhausted the town's supply of ***non***-working girls, so..." he reluctantly admitted. "*DUDE!!*" I yelled (demonstrating the full range of the word's usage). "You are officially *cut off* until June, so you'd better find a *job* if you want to keep employing the services of working girls." I shook my head, "Your PUA brethren would be *so* disappointed in you."

34

I stayed in a separate room in the hotel that night so that Michael would feel the full brunt of being "cut off". He didn't seem like it had adversely affected him very much at Meyer's, as he didn't accompany me back to the hotel, but chose instead to head to the Hoof for his favorite opiate... sex with loose bitches. I didn't take offense... there was just too much waiting for me back at my land, my home. I determined then and there that I would no longer visit Michael when I came into town. In fact, if he was *ever* to find a place in my kingdom, he'd have to make his way back there on his own *and* pull his weight (considering all the work that had yet to be done). On my way out of town the next morning, I revealed to Helen that the last payment (also, only through June) that I'd made on Michael's room was going to *be* the last payment she'd receive on his behalf from me. I made her promise not to tell Michael that his room wasn't paid for until the money was fully exhausted, and she happily agreed. Apparently, Michael had long since worn out his welcome.

I honestly hoped that the next time I saw Michael that he'd be contrite and remorseful, but I had a sneaking suspicion that he'd only find his way to my lands in order to ask for more money. "If he does," I told myself. "I'm going to send him back home. I can't be expected to pay for him to *party* for the rest of his life. I was hoping he'd be a full *partner* on this whole medieval kingdom thing, but he's just not cut out for it, I guess."

I made my way back to the bunk house, as I hadn't seen my cattle hands (or Kyle) for long enough that I was curious as to what was going on with them. By the time I arrived, they had all headed out to graze the herd (as expected), so I went ahead and pressed on to catch up to them. Their path in the snow was easy to follow into the lowlands, and I overtook them by noon. Kyle was the first to notice me, and took off from the other hands at a flat-out gallop. Once he'd made his way alongside of me, he excitedly engaged me before I could even say "Hi!".

"Hey, Kai! Oh man, I'm *so* glad you showed up today! Old Bob was telling me all about displaced abomasa today and then I told him about one of your cows that didn't seem to be eating very much, and sure enough, she'd given birth to a bull calf about 4 weeks ago. I got out my stethoscope that I got on our last trip into town and listened for the ping sound Bob told me about and sure enough, she had it! I was like, 'So why don't we just eat her, then? She's gonna die anyway!' Right? And Bob was all, 'Well, we'll have to see what the boss man has to say about *that*. He might want to have Frank's vet do some surgery on her or something.' And then I was like, 'Man, I hope he shows up today so we can ask him!' and then **BAM**... here you are!" It was actually refreshing to hear the rush of words from Kyle's mouth again. His enthusiasm was always infectious, and I couldn't help but chuckle.

"Let me talk to Bob for a second first, okay Kyle?" I smiled. "Oh sure - awesome," he really *was* just like a kid sometimes. I consulted with Old Bob (the most experienced of my cattle hands) and he verified everything Kyle had told me. "I tell you, Mr. Hunter... that flappy-jawed man over there could talk the ears off a *deaf* woman, but he's like a damn *sponge* when it comes to learnin' about these cattle," Bob seemed moderately impressed with Kyle.

"So what do you think about the cow, then?" I asked. "Well sir, the bull calf she had a while back was her seventh one, and most cows only ever really have about eight in their whole lifetime, so I'd say it would be a decent enough time to cull her." Death in the cattle community was a given, as they were with us mainly for their meat, hides, and milk (for cheese production). It wasn't that we didn't think they were *cute* or anything, but all the same - we didn't *name* them. "Will the bull calf still be tended to?" I wanted to make sure. "Oh yes sir, Mr. Hunter. We've got some colostrum and milk formulas back at the corral, and it would be a good opportunity for ol' motor-mouth over there to see what it's like to tend to an orphaned calf." "Great," I agreed on the course of action. "Just bring the brain and hide of the cow up to my cabin afterwards so I can tan it, and you fellas can go ahead and enjoy all the meat you can get from her." Old Bob tipped his hat to me, "I sure do appreciate it, Mr. Hunter. You're mighty kind, as always."

As I began to canter away, I heard Bob deliver the news to a few of the other cattle hands nearby, who whooped in excitement at the prospect of the fine steaks they'd be enjoying in the days to come. Kyle made his way to my side once again, "So you gave us the meat, huh? Thanks, Kai."

"No problem, Kyle. You guys have been working quite well up here, and I certainly do appreciate it," I looked over my shoulder at him. "And I hope you've been learning a lot by working with these men, too." "Oh, *definitely*! They're just *full* of information - inside and out, if you know what I mean," he winked. I knew he was referring to his mind-reading capabilities, but I wouldn't have minded if he'd have taken a liking to any of the men, either. They were all fine, strong specimens of men, to be sure. I doubt a *one* of them ever came back from town without their needs being willingly satisfied... whether it was doe-eyed hussies or snazzy-dressed man-whores that fulfilled those needs.

"Have you guys come in contact with any ranch hands of Frank's lately, or seen Frank at all while you were tending the herd?" I hadn't seen Mr. Meyer in long enough that I was curious about his well-being. "Nope... can't say as we have. It's been all campfires, herdin', watchin', and learnin' the whole time *I've* been up here. That, and this one time I found a wild blueberry bush that Running Bear said he could make some blueberry wine from... but I think he just ate 'em when I wasn't looking." I laughed. Kyle was so much fun to listen to.

"All right; well, keep up the good work and be sure to come visit me up at the cabin in a week. I think I'll have a surprise for you by then," I wasn't sure whether or not I was going to show him the book I'd found yet, but I wanted at least a week to peruse it first. "Okay, cool. I'll be sure not to read your mind so you can keep whatever it is a surprise for me!" he flashed a toothy grin. I reminded him not to tell the other hands about his power, and he assured me it was still a secret. With everything neatly taken care of, I spurred Freedom back toward the cabin.

35

I woke up the next morning to the first sunrise of May, stretching my arms to the ceiling in a comfortable yawn. This week was all about getting to know this "magic" book (and any connection it might have to the blank crystal I'd kept), and I'd hung the amnesia amulet over the doorpost to ensure my total privacy. I reopened the tome (turning past the introductory note that I'd already read) and began reading where the style of the lettering suggested a different handwriting and author. "Perhaps this is where William *originally* began writing, and his friend had just taken advantage of the blank page prior for his note," I postulated. It seems I was right.

"The end of this life is drawing nigh, future William, and I sometimes wonder how I managed to find the crystal all those times before. I only wish that my mortal frame could hold all the memories of the lives of my past, but it seems that such remembrances are not in God's plan for us. (As you should know the Truth of the world and the stars, the God you may have heard of - or may even serve - is very likely not the *Highest* God who created him [or her, if you now live in the Grecian isles or the Indies].)

"Alas, my talents have once again shown through my terrestrial veil like the sun through a length of fine silk. Though my candle has burned low to its end, my fame has continued and enlarged itself. As Prospero shall no doubt be seen to be my farewell from the stage, I must admit that it was rather the irony that his magic was at an end, and I desperately needed an escape so that I could focus all the more on mine. I have managed to use all the power I could muster in my rather aged form to create a doppelganger of myself - a double who may continue in my footsteps, but will no doubt need assistance to do so. I sincerely hope that my ruse is not immediately discovered, as I suspect that it may be. If all goes as planned, I shall continue under cover of night to the Godspeed, which is bound for Virginia. I shall shear the hair from my head to hide my identity and work to protect the ship from what natural perils I can.

"I sleep with naught but the clothes on my back and my pack clutched to my chest, in which I keep the great crystal, this journal, and what dried victuals yet remain of my original store of them. Though a great deal of my power is still recovering day by day (after creating my double), I'm still able to maintain a small charge-bolt as I slumber (to protect my few goods from the would-be thieves aboard this creaky, wooden casket that passes for a ship), and able to do a bit of clandestine Sorcery and Pyromancy to maintain the purity of my water supply - as it seems the water all non-crew passengers are given is a bit brackish. When my shipmate Smith reckoned that we were within a week's journey from landing at Virginia, there came a dreadful storm on the horizon that surely would have been the death of us all. I quickly climbed atop the center mast (so as to hide my actions from as many as possible below) and cut a path for our three ships through the darkest of the clouds with probably the most forceful Aeromancy I've ever used. Captain Gosnold recounted that God himself had smiled upon his 'dear Godspeed', and I didn't bother to correct the misconception. The act has drained all my magic reserves, and I shall have to remain vigilant at night now, as I am unable to maintain the resting charge-bolt.

"When we first made land in Virginia, we fell under attack from the natives, and quickly retreated to the ships. We set out to sea a horizon away from the natives (so that they'd think we fled back across the ocean) and instead continued north along the Virginia coast. When we found a river deep enough for our ships' drafts, we sailed in and made land again. The natives here were more welcoming than the ones from before, and we discovered that where we disembarked was called 'Kecoughtan' in their tongue. After only a week, I am inclined to adopt these natives' lifestyle. Truly, it is one that is more in tune with the magical aria of the earth itself, and they give to the land as much as they take from it. It is a balance that would have made my former Cathay life's personage proud. It wasn't long before the council of Captains began sending scouting parties up the river (which they arrogantly named after James the King, despite the natives telling them it was named for their tribal confederacy - Powhatan) and found an island that met the requirements for settlement they'd been given from the Virginia Company. I bade a reluctant farewell to the natives of Kecoughtan, and chose to continue with my fellow countrymen because I completely understood their tongue (and had yet to learn the tongue of the natives). We had no sooner set foot on the island (which they'd also named for the King!) than the council directed that we begin to fortify it against 'the Spanish and the savages'. As this was the prevailing mindset of the rest of the crew, I began to sour on the attitudes of my countrymen. I knew that it was only natural for a people in a land of their own to vehemently defend it against invaders set on claiming it as theirs.

"Sure enough, their designs for the land were glaringly apparent to the upriver natives, who attacked within the month. After we managed to survive that onslaught (and I did my best to attend to the wounded), the council began drawing up plans for a triangular fort made from whole tree logs, with watchtower bulwarks at each point. I knew that enterprise would be labor-intensive, and that the 'labor' would mostly be made up of men like me. Considering I did not espouse their incursive agenda (and did not look forward to weeks of felling trees), I stole away from the encampment under cover of night, making my way back downriver along its bank to the welcoming natives of Kecoughtan. I knew that my countrymen would discover my absence, but I also knew that the incipient native threat was too great for them to pursue just one lone deserter." An arrow from the following pointed toward the paragraphs over it: "I have made a point (now that I am established at Kecoughtan) to chronicle these previous adventures that I have not been able to enter into this journal heretofore."

My mind stopped to put two and two together. This book really *did* seem to be more of an actual *journal* (now that William had mentioned it) than the instructive "book of magic" that I had imagined it would be. I took a break from reading the tome to look up on the internet what actually happened at Jamestown (a name that I remembered from elementary history classes), only to discover that (other than no mentions of a particular man named *William*) everything that was written in the tome was actual **history**... not just the fanciful, fictionalized reimagining of it for the amusement of this particular writer. If this tome indeed *was* a book of magic, it was *also* a historical **treasure** the likes of which had not been discovered for centuries!

36

Treasure or not, I knew that this family heirloom was *never* to be afforded a place of repose in some dusty old museum - let *alone* to be surrendered to the meticulous scrutiny of a team of the government agents that would *definitely* be interested in it. No - just as that wonderful crystal had housed a treasure of magics that I had yet to understand, this tome contained the record of possibly the most intriguing man I'd ever heard of in history. Also, some of the words (even though they were *supposed* to have been perfectly translated) were unfamiliar to me: "erdemanced"... "Pyromancy"... "Aeromancy". I reasoned that perhaps these were some sort of proper names or verbs for disciplines of magic that it would be a crime against magic to wrest into the common jargon that I'd come to know as English. I was mostly correct.

The history of this man William fascinated me, and I pored over the first chapter of the tome for hours, checking it all against the internet, and finding it to be factual every time. For the next few years of his life, William became an active member of the Native community there in coastal Virginia, ingratiating himself to every Native he came in contact with, and even teaching them certain low-level forms of a magic he called "Wodemancy". It was obvious (to me) that he very much preferred their free and natural way of communal life to the one he'd come from, with its oppressive and often prudish laws. He began to see the people of his homeland as the invaders that they truly were, and the Natives as the kind of kindred spirits that he'd only ever known in the theatres of London. Also, though he never outright *said* it, I began to suspect that this "William" was actually *William Shakespeare*.

The idea didn't stand up to the standard of recorded history as I'd always been taught, but then again, *a lot* of things in the tome didn't match up to the things I'd been taught in school as a kid. For instance, once the Kecoughtan Natives introduced William to Wahunsenacawh (the Chief of the Powhatan tribal confederacy, that the other Brits just lazily called "Chief Powhatan") and he had won the Chief's trust, the Chief revealed to William a "great sickness" on a *national* scale that had wiped out the *vast majority* of the Natives of North America before the colonists ever arrived. I looked it up online and found out that that was just the *end* of a centuries-long tale of Native badassery; apparently, the Natives had been kicking the *shit* out of fucking **Vikings** in the northeast before that national plague, since as far back as the 11th century! Needless to say, if armored rape-and-pillage machines like *Vikings* were no match for a country full of Natives, no amount of cloth-wearing, gunpowder-toting Brits would've been able to stand a *chance* against them at full capacity. Historically speaking, even in their plague-weakened state, the Natives were *still* quite a challenging match for all the European invaders.

The fact that America (such as it is) exists at all - peopled by *White immigrants*, no less - is just a testament to the fickle nature of existence. I couldn't help but wonder what windfall of fortune the *next* group of people to take over my birth-land of America (in the centuries to come) would have to thank for *their* continental dominance... and wondered what kind of fanciful historical fictions they'd "educate" into *their* children to account for their unearned successes.

I continued my reading into the amazing history of my "forefather" William to find that after he'd been accepted as the only White adjutant to the Powhatan confederacy, that they assisted him in moving further north, filling the office of a Native ambassador, as he explored expansive lands that were entirely new to him - and fiercely *fantastic* in comparison to his former urbane British life. Word of this White man's Native loyalty spread among all the east coast tribes he came in contact with, to the extent that his reputation as a wise man and shaman began to precede him.

Years later, he decided to settle down in New Amsterdam and took to assisting a man named Juan Rodriguez, who was a local beaver trapper and fur trader. William would assist him (even though he had a somewhat *limited* knowledge of Portuguese), facilitating trade with the Lenape tribe of Natives along the Muhheakantuck, which is called the Hudson River these days. William *so* helped Juan, in fact, that he was given his own cabin outside of Fort Nassau (to be closer to the fur trading post *in* the fort) when Juan set up a fancier house in southern New Amsterdam. William didn't mind, though, as the cabin was closer to the Natives that he loved so well. In fact, he was hoping to bring the leadership of the Algonquian tribes (mainly, the Mahican and Lenape) closer together, but was hindered by the constant invasions of the Mohawks from the north.

The journal became almost confusing to read at this point, as it seemed that for *years*, *everybody* was at war with *everybody*. The Mohawks fought the Mahicans for control of the upper Hudson in order to (most seemed to say) keep a steady supply of the European trade goods coming that they'd become dependent on. (As a matriarchal society, the Mohawks were more prone to both violence *and* dependence on goods that they couldn't make - sort of the first basic "welfare state", if you will.) The French fought the Dutch for the right to trade furs with the various tribes along the Hudson River valley, and so they could distribute guns to (or keep them *from*) whatever Native tribes they so pleased. As if nature itself also felt the upheaval of the time, flooding was common in the area as well. Needless to say, it was a hell of a time to be a New Yorker (or *New Amsterdam-er*, as William still was). By the time the Dutch West India Company came en masse to force all the private traders out of the territory (to make room for the "proper" *Dutch* settler/trader families), William had had enough. He gathered up his "fortune" that he'd managed to amass (about 300 guldens, some odd duiten, and a few impressive lengths of black wampum [in case he needed to trade with the Natives in his travels]), and headed further northeast with a few notable friends he'd made among the Mahicans.

The journal ended after he arrived and settled down in what he called "mountains full of the most oddly shaped rock formations I've ever seen". From that point on, it seemed his magical prowess was at its peak, but his body was near total exhaustion from advanced age. As he was nearing his end, he determined to split his time between teaching a young Mahican student (and devoted disciple - whom he called "Khuhkoke Mo-Quau-Pauw") how to "erdemance" and between chronicling his practically encyclopedic knowledge of magic into the tome I now held in my hands.

37

I was relieved to learn that the tome was not just a *journal*, and was what the "friend" from the introduction of the book (apparently, "Mo-Quau-Pauw") had identified it as: an "instructional book"/"magic tome". I sincerely hoped that the "instructional" part was about *magic* (and not *how to get along with Natives* [should I ever discover how to time-travel]), and that the "magic" part was not merely its ability to *hover* above hidden stone pedestals. Personally, I sleep much better when there are mysteries yet to be resolved and I was feeling drowsily *anyway*, so I went ahead and stopped reading for the day at what appeared to be the last "historical" chapter.

That night, I dreamed that I was aboard the *Godspeed* in the midst of the Atlantic, and waves higher than Brooklyn brownstones were all about us, threatening to capsize us, drown us, and even dash us against the two other wooden ships nearby. I wiped the foamy brine sprays from my eyes, and managed to make it to the central mast of the ship through pitches and rolls of easily more than thirty degrees, almost as if my boots were held to the deck with an otherworldly force. Though the dark, foreboding skies nearly blacked out the sun completely, I was able to see myself pull at the air beside the surface of the main mast with one hand, drawing out a peg hold as surely as if I had commanded it to grow to my perfect mental specifications. I repeated the action all the way up the treacherous column, thrashing to and fro in the mighty sea, and made my way against all odds to the middle of the yard across the topsail. Using the same otherworldly force as before to bind one hand to the main mast, I flailed about, seemingly directionless. Nonetheless, I saw myself strike out at the black air clutching a free line that I'd apparently been able to sense amid the violent din of the sea. Instinctually, I pulled the line through the now inky blackness and saw the finger of the hand that held it draw circles in the air. The line, as if a cobra responding to an expert snake charmer, wound its way around my belly and the mast behind me - binding me fast to the main mast and freeing my hands for what they had yet to do.

I bent my head downwards and saw my eyelids close, but my outstretched hands still felt the sting of the briny spray and the icy winds against them... and even *more* so, with nothing else on which to focus. At first, I allowed my hands to move with the wind, like a jib in a leeward gale. But then suddenly - sharply - I called a mystical force from what seemed to be behind me, carried it quickly (like an invisible ball of energy) over my head, and then flung it forward. From that point onward, I stared intently forward, seemingly some sort of psychic conduit through which a very focused torrent of east wind blew toward the bow of the ship. Not only did the wind all around me seem to propel us forward like some sort of jet engine, but the wind split the sky like Moses at the Red Sea. The clouds rolled back from before us, stealing away over separate horizons like guilty things, and the sea calmed within minutes.

The great surge of power began to drain from my body, and I felt myself growing limp, as the line began falling away from around me. I managed to climb back down the mast (pushing the magical peg formations back in along the way) before I collapsed with fatigue to the deck. I could see the crew mulling about, looking dumbfounded at the sky and the warming rays of sunlight that now caressed our cheeks like a long lost lover. As my eyelids began to close, I saw a man in a captain's uniform emerge from the aft cabin behind me, drop to his knees, and thank the "Lord for smiling upon my dear Godspeed".

I awoke with a start, back safe in my cabin at the keep construction site. I felt my hands all over my chest in disbelief, half surprised that I was not drenched in the water of the sea (although, technically, my *pillow* was drenched in *sweat*). It was the most immersive, realistic dream I'd ever had in my *life*, and I couldn't help but think that that cave, the crystal, the book, the amulet... ***something*** among all those magical things I'd stumbled upon was responsible for this! I gathered all three of the items I had together to see if any of them had physically altered in any way, or bore any new markings or something. (I wasn't exactly sure *what* I was looking for.) Nothing seemed to be different.

"Huh," I muttered, unimpressed with the commonality of my findings. I reopened the book to where I'd left off, having marked my place with a smoothed cedar bookmark that I had to remove from the last book I was reading before this one: *Dandy in the Underworld*. I turned the page expectantly, remembering that on the other side was perhaps the end of the journal (and familial history lessons) and perhaps the beginning of my training in *magic*. I closed my eyes as the vellum came to rest with its previously-turned brethren, revealing what was next to come...

I opened my eyes for the big surprise... blank pages. "Ugh!" I grumbled, having worked myself all up to uncover the pages William had left between sections. "You're such an idiot," I told myself, turning the next page with decidedly less ceremony. The next section appeared to be a relief print from a woodcut that William had apparently carved *just* to make the page fancier. In fact, all the writing from this point onward was decidedly more elegant, as if William had slowed down, taking his time to write, making sure that he'd be penning a manual that would stand the trials of the ages. I took that as a *good* sign.

The relief print was simply the word: "Artifacts". He continued, "I find that I sometimes forget the importance of the few magical items that I have gathered over my past few lifetimes (that I have been fortunate enough to recover); so I am leaving you a list, future William, of the things that my disciple shall be taking with him (including this tome) to a hiding place (that I have taught him to wisely discern) where they should safely remain until you unearth them. I will do my best to sketch each item (though I am truly no artist) and leave a full reckoning of every use and benefit that I can still recall for these most valuable of treasures."

"*This* oughta be good!" I jubilated, practically salivating as I turned the page.

38

The very first entry had to do with a quill that was enchanted to write down, perfectly describing, whatever the holder thought of. Apparently, one could even bind the quill to one's hand while *sleeping*, and it would still drag the slumbering body with it to an open page once a dream had begun playing in the sleeper's mind. (I couldn't help musing that perhaps this was how *A Midsummer Night's Dream* was written.) The quill was apparently an immeasurable treasure to a writer (which I'm not, of course), and I could imagine how closing one's eyes to write would make the whole enterprise less taxing, but I had been reading most of the entry before I had noticed it was crossed out with a single line. On the bottom right of the entry (where the cross-line ended), there was scrawled a note "Regrettably, lost during the ocean voyage."

I considered the possibility that William had begun the list of Artifacts *before* he had fled England, but that didn't make enough sense to me. The only other option is that he was perhaps *bragging* to his future self about once owning the magical quill, leaving yet another breadcrumb to follow should his next life have any questions as to the identity of the former one. At this point, my money was decidedly on William *Shakespeare*, but I purposed in my mind not to get too haughty over the fact that I might be a direct descendant of his. (*Squee!*) Sorry. I guess I thought you should know, dear reader, that as I wrote that, I giggled in my head like a girl. Anyhoo, I also like to think that some years later, the magical quill - still no worse for the wear - washed up onshore near the feet of Virginia's Edgar Allan Poe. It's too bad that it didn't do half the good for *that* poor man in *his* lifetime that it did for William.

The next entry was a picture (of an item I'd come to know *very* well) beneath which was written the name "Amnesia Amulet". I had to attribute the "amnesia" portion of the translation to the taijitu, as the word was not likely coined until the scientific study of it in the (much later) 19th century. More than likely, William had actually named this Artifact the "Forgotten Amulet", but I figured I'd defer to the taijitu on this one for now.

As I read, I discovered that the amnesic nature of the amulet was actually just a centuries-old enchantment that William had applied to the *already*-powerful Artifact with the help of a cambion spirit who went by the name of "Ambrosius". Apparently, William was the spirit's *keeper*, and though the lifelong bond they had formed was a *strong* one, it took nearly all of Ambrosius' spiritual influence among the lesser gods of the time to induce them to agree to release enough psychic power to enchant the amulet for *just* William and his firstborn son. It was well worth the effort, according to William (as it helped to keep his presence hidden from the more war-inclined Mohawks and the expansion-happy Dutch of the time), but it also proved to be problematic, as Mo-Quau-Pauw would be unable to find William's home quite often. William found a way around that with the help of another spirit he kept (a western gold dragon spirit named "Ieldran"), who would conjure simple "day fuses" for him - which appeared to be casings of magical wax that would envelop the amulet, only to dissolve away (if not covered with burlap) within a day's time - allowing the enchantment to regain its effect on the surrounding environment.

It seemed relentlessly complex, but after reading it over again several times, I felt like I understood William's explanation. What I *still* failed to understand is how I could *possibly* be his firstborn son (as the text about the amulet seemed to imply), considering that he'd written those words *well* over 370 years ago. And considering that I now believed him to be Shakespeare, his firstborn son would have been *Hamnet* (not *me*) - and that boy died way back in 1596! It seemed either insanely optimistic or just flat-out *stupid* to make a provision for a son that no longer existed, but I knew that William was far from senile by the coherent nature of his writings at the time. It was just one of those things that made me wonder if maybe he'd made some sort of mistake in his magic, that would've allowed for a distant cousin or kin of some long-forgotten line to find and manipulate his treasure. It just **bothered** *me*, all right? That's how my mind works!

Nonetheless, the *true* power of the amulet was its use as a supernatural memory *recovery* device. According to his notes, after his first death... "*WHOA!*" I stopped reading. ***First** death?!?* Was William about to lay some proof of *reincarnation* on me, or was he just a highlander or some other crazy kind of immortal?? Truth be told, I suppose I should've *expected* as much, considering all of his talk concerning the "future William". Things were beginning to add up. So, as I was saying (and William was *writing*), after his first death (which he didn't provide the details of), he was zipping around the skies and the space above Earth for many years (as a spirit, of course) before he settled in to marvel at the interesting things being done by the Egyptians of the time. Of course, *being* a spirit, he could see the gods and spirits influencing and interacting with humans as clearly as if they *themselves* were humans, albeit generally *flying* and with a telltale red aura outlining them. The two busiest gods of the time that he observed were Shai (the god of destiny) and Renenutet (the goddess who assigned babies their secret, psychic names). Renenutet interested him most of all, as he saw her not only provide these new births with the secret spiritual identifiers by which they'd be known in that world *and* the afterlife, but he also watched her guide spirits that were *already* thusly identified (about half the time) into families and lives more commensurate with what they had earned in their previous lives. It was the first spiritual example of active Karma that he'd ever witnessed, and it fascinated him.

Not only *that*, but he learned of the true story of the Yahweh crystal, listening to Jewish caravans that would pass through the city capital. He worked out how the crystal was linked to his Mother Lilith, and how he was actually a demi-god, born from an early relationship of hers with Dionysus (before he was particularly well-represented with worshippers). He spent the next hundred years befriending and assisting Renenutet, so at the end of them he could ask a favor of her and be born into a boy in a community where magic was revered (so that he could continue what he had begun practicing in his first life), close to a great crystal containing the magic potential of his former life. She managed to talk Shai into it, and they each spent about a year recovering William's energies, which had dissipated to quite a few remote locations in the Universe. Bargains were struck, loyalties were created, and more than a few followers of some gods in far-off galaxies were disappointed at having to relinquish the supernatural abilities they'd been given, but Shai was quite the smooth talker, as it turned out. So once they all met back on our Earth, they directed a Chinese temple acolyte (with the approval of the Chinese god of magic, Xuan Wu) to hide William's great crystal in a cave in the western mountains of ancient China, safeguarding it until William could be born into a local magic-friendly family. Considering the western cave, I mused that history *did indeed* tend to repeat itself.

When it came time to assign William's spirit identity (which he never actually mentioned - basically why I can only refer to him *as* William) to a new baby, Renenutet warned him that the rebirth process would generally strip the child of all his past life's memories, as our minds would only ever truly remember (even as an *adult*) about 20-30 years worth of memories at any given time. It *enraged* him, and he began to tell off Renenutet in probably one of the most ill-advised tirades against a goddess of all time. When the form of her head began to shift into that of a fire-breathing cobra, he knew that his spirit was in danger of actual *oblivion*, so he quickly back-pedaled, calming both himself and Renenutet in just the nick of time.

After about a year of apologizing, she again agreed to make sure that he was born into the magic-friendly Chinese lineage they'd found for him. "Still," he reasoned. "If I could not have found a way to retain my past memories at will, it would have been possible that I would have never lived up to my magical potential... and that would have been truly tragic." That is when he began influencing (under the watchful eye, and with the direct [amused] assistance, of Xuan Wu) the same temple acolyte to craft the amulet, with the sole purpose of being able to *remember* the greatness of his past, a thing that is *impossible* for normal human beings. It was no small feat to craft such a powerful, one-of-a-kind Artifact, much less indirectly guide a mere *human's* hands to do the work *for* you (as spirits do not generally move things in the physical realm). Xuan Wu gave greatly of his magics to enable the creation of the amulet, and made William promise *every day* to always honor the elements, and devote himself to mastering them - which he definitely did.

The creation and crafting of the amulet to exacting spiritual and magical specifications took three whole generations of temple acolytes to accomplish. The dictation of the odd written manual accompanying it - in the ancient language that William had spoken in the time of Lilith (which the acolytes did *not* speak [so that the next William *alone* would be able to read it]) - took the remainder of nearly three *thousand* years. The temple followers, as a result, were viewed either as holy men of the highest order... or outright *madmen*. When William finally returned to Renenutet for his rebirth, she had almost forgotten the bargain they'd struck. After reminiscing and laughing about their former universal scavenger hunt, she agreed to have him born into a prominent home in the Chinese community he'd been spiritually influencing for so long. His new family name would be Zhuge, and to defiantly prove that she was still in control of his fate, Renenutet had him born in the home of a family of temple followers so far *east* in China that Xuan Wu had to guide his fate back toward the *west* to rediscover his ancient and powerful amulet.

39

Fortunately for William (named Zhuge Liang at birth), by the time he'd settled down a bit on the farm he worked in the area called Wolong Gang, he had the kind of time for personal reflection that tends to lead to boredom and longing for adventure. He tried for years to satiate his inner desire to know more (that stemmed from his soul being one of a powerful magic user) by staying up nights reading and studying the intellectual writings of the day, hoping to fill the void inside. Of course, considering he would generally be *farming* all day, by the time he'd settled in to read the latest from Xu Shu or peruse old writings of Guan Zhong, he'd find himself nodding off like a fat suburbanite watching Conan O'Brien and snoring in a recliner.

I found the taijitu (which - I would later find out in the Artifacts section - was officially called the "Taijitic Seal") to be extremely helpful for this particular section, because I have **never** been able to read Mandarin, and get the distinct impression that *ancient* Mandarin would be that much *more* difficult to understand. "I recall working to bring in a crop of rice (a cross-bred strain that always cooked up with a pleasant taste, a savory aroma, and a general fatness to the grain) when I saw an old friend from the temple approaching. He bowed in respect, and I returned his bow. 'Master Zhuge,' he said. 'How fortunate it is that I find you here in the Wolong district. I thought my passage through Nanyang would be dreadfully lonely, as yours is the first familiar face I have seen!'

"I smiled serenely, as that is the face my friend best knew. 'It is good to see you as well, Master Sima. And how is Mr. Good today?' He answered with a wry grin, 'Well.' I grasped him about the shoulders in happy friendship and temple brotherhood. 'Does temple life still agree with you, or have you truly become the hermit that I hear tell of?' I asked, in order to finally learn the truth of it. 'Oh, no!' he denied, breaking my grasp and looking wildly about for anyone within earshot. As we were at the western end of the field, there was no one nearby, so I smirked as he drew me in closely to whisper, 'All right, yes. But don't tell anyone, okay? You get far more rice as a servant of the Xuan Wu temple than you do as just some common beggar.' As wise as Sima

Hui was, I often wondered why he would choose the life of a wanderer rather than to serve in the temple or (as seemed to be his calling) as the advisor to a great lord. Out of respect, I decided never to ask him about it. 'Good Master Sima, you shall not beg in the streets of Nanyang tonight! You shall join my brothers and me at our humble cottage, and I shall not hear a word of disagreement from you.' He smiled gratefully and bowed, responding only: 'Good.' The dinner was the most exciting one I could remember in quite some time. It was not simply my older brother Jin complaining about some tool breaking while I secretly hoped for my rice to be done earlier than usual... it was a dinner where I hoped the steaming bowl of rice would be forever full, so that I might drink in the tales that Hui brought from his journey from the temple in the east. He said that there was set to be a harvest moon festival near the main mountain temple in the west soon, and that they were going to have the first public trial of the Xuan Wu amulet in over a decade.

"I remembered how they used to tell us as children how one day a greater man than normal men would one day touch the amulet and release its knowledge, translating the west temple scrolls for all to see. Many charlatans had come to the temple throughout the centuries (as public trials of the Xuan Wu amulet used to be an annual event) and had made it so that the temple abbot restricted the annual trials to only committed acolytes of the temple order. But as the old abbot had recently died, the new abbot had decided to send an invitation to all the temples and districts across all of China, inviting people to come out and offer gifts, touch the amulet, and celebrate the harvest moon.

"Hui's eyes lit up as he told of it: 'It will truly be a gathering like none other in our lifetimes! Considering you had not heard of it, Liang, I hope that upon this happy news, you will decide to accompany me as I continue the short space to the western Xuan Wu temple.' He bowed his head, extending his clasped hands toward me in entreaty. I cast a quick glance across the table at Jin, my eyes begging for leave from the remainder of the harvest work so that I might accompany my old friend for the last part of his trek. His eyes rebuked me, but he nodded his consent all the same. 'I shall be honored to journey with you, my friend and temple brother. We shall make the preparations after dinner so we may depart with all haste in the morning.' As was his way, he replied, 'Yes. Good.'"

Liang continued to write of their sojourn that began on the following morning, and how he joked with his friend Hui along the way, each posing riddles to one another more difficult than the last. When they reached the temple, it took them three whole days to work their way with the crowds toward the inner sanctum where the amulet was kept. Liang had brought gifts of rice for the temple as offerings to Xuan Wu so that he and Hui would each have a chance to briefly touch the amulet. When Liang got to the pillow set before the amulet's altar, he kneeled quickly, trying to be as courteous as possible to the long line waiting behind him outside for their turn. He bowed, reaching forward to touch the amulet only with his right hand, intending to brush the top of it, and move hastily on.

What he couldn't have expected was the blast of energy that froze his hand in place, as five select years that explained the origin of the amulet, his life among the gods, his former life as the son of Lilith and Dionysus, and the language that he *then* knew (that was written in the Xuan Wu scrolls) streamed into his mind, replacing his memories of early childhood. The abbot recounted to him once he returned to normal that "streams of yellow fire" seemed to leap from the amulet into his widened eyes, and his head was thrown backward for a full minute. Liang replied, "But I remember years...!" The people waiting outside were only able to see the brilliant yellow light within the inner sanctum (due to the angle of the steps outside) but the ones closest to Zhuge Liang, the abbot, and the amulet began to whisper reverently of what had happened. As the crowd around the temple began to hear of the light and draw closer to the entrance, they found Liang inside, already reading the first scroll that the abbot had handed him. He looked up at the abbot and declared, "These were written for me." He turned to address the people. "I shall now be called Kongming... I am the Sleeping Dragon!"

40

I stopped reading to look up Zhuge Liang (as I did most things) on the internet, and though the story of the amulet didn't seem to be there, the rest of it checked out. I had to assume that once Kongming claimed the Xuan Wu amulet as his own, that would have then deflated *centuries* of the small temple's self-importance... which couldn't have been popular right away. The only logical solution would have been for the temple's abbot to surrender the Xuan Wu scrolls and amulet to Kongming as if they never had any real religious importance (because honestly, *they didn't*) and then redouble the temple's efforts to focus on the service of Xuan Wu. Since the tome said that Kongming then stayed in the temple (or the nearby cave where his crystal was kept) from then until the time Liu Bei came to beseech him for his help years later, common sense would say that that no doubt softened the blow of the loss of the temple treasures.

I went to read more, but I'd read so much on that second day that "the spirit" was only *slightly* more willing than "the flesh" was actually capable of. I succumbed to sleep within minutes. My eyes opened in yet another vivid dream, only this time I wasn't being tossed to and fro aboard some transatlantic wooden casket, but instead I found myself kneeling on a satiny, red pillow - seated on my raised heels. My hands were clasped in front of me, with the amnesia amulet draped over the top of them. I wore long robes, whose ample material hung down from my wrists. It seemed as if I was looking through the amulet at a seated statue of a portly Chinese man with a long black goatee. I didn't recognize him, but he had a golden sword in his right hand, two golden dragons across his chest, and he seemed to point toward the heavens with his left hand. I thought it rather odd that he seemed to be stepping on both a snake *and* a turtle as well. I guessed that he was the Chinese god of reptiles or something.

As I knelt there, I could hear myself praying over and over again in what I assumed was Mandarin. (Incidentally, I don't *speak* Mandarin, so the dream wasn't exactly helpful. Also, I'm pretty sure the signs next to the seated man said who he was supposed to be, but I don't *read* Mandarin, either!) It wasn't long before the temple in which

I was praying began growing suddenly and unnaturally dark - kind of like the end of *Mortal Kombat*, only less foreboding. I saw a figure outlined in red rise as if he were the statue, standing up... only the statue remained where it was. I could only assume that it was the spirit of whatever man (or *god*, I was beginning to think) was there represented. The red spirit clasped his hands together at the top of his stomach and nodded his head in greeting. The nod was so small, however, that I somehow knew that this spirit thought of himself as *incredibly* more important than I. He spoke to me in what sounded like Mandarin (How I wish the Taijitic Seal could be applied to *dreams*!) and then I saw another spirit appear to his left. This spirit nodded slightly lower and his hands were clasped higher on his chest, so I figured that he must be the spirit of a man, albeit an important one. He said something in a friendly voice, like a Japanese senpai giving instructions to his kōhai, and then formed a ceremonial-looking sign with his hands. He spoke only a few words after that before throwing his head back and breathing what appeared to be a stream of black flames out of his mouth, which fell upon the amnesia amulet, and then were promptly absorbed.

I awoke with a start to find that it was the third day, and hurriedly turned pages in the tome to see if Kongming had ever had any similar things happen in his life. Sure enough, I hadn't gotten to that point yet, but it was in the final explanation of the amulet's powers. It seems that Kongming had managed to work out the fact that the memories of his childhood (that he could no longer recall) had been replaced with the "new" selected memories of his past life (and afterlife). Realizing that with the proper magic, the amulet could be used as conduit through which he could better *know* himself and his magics, he at once knew that he'd never be able to contain the *entirety* of that helpful information in his human mind. So, Kongming prayed in the Xuan Wu temple (and boy, did I feel idiotic for not recognizing *him*!) for a week straight, taking breaks only briefly to eat and relieve himself, petitioning the god to allow him the first-ever "mulligan". At the end of the week, Xuan Wu appeared to Kongming while he prayed, and introduced him to Ji Dan, the Duke of Zhou - the "god of dreams". The Duke explained to Kongming that because he had promised Xuan Wu to maintain and master the magics of the elements, then he (the

Duke) would be willing to grant him a spiritual favor. He told Kongming that he (and any firstborn sons he'd ever sire) would be allowed to see parts of his past for free - without having to pay the mental sacrifice of other years of memory and knowledge. The Duke then spoke a supernatural incantation, breathing magical fire onto the amulet to seal it in. Kongming then began keeping a journal of his dreams in order that he might remember his past without sacrificing his present or personal history.

Remembering that Chinese books are often written from (what we call in "the West") the back to the front, I excitedly turned to the end of the tome, and sure enough... there were all of Kongming's entries, flipped around for my western eyes to be able to read them! Considering I was more into discovering all the powers of the Artifacts, I just left the entries for later, determined to press onward and find out the powers (if any) behind the book and crystal, maybe even discovering some overlooked Artifacts that might still be on my land.

Still, it was somewhat encouraging to discover that both Kongming *and* William had made preparations for their firstborn sons (or the *spirit* of whosoever the first son *was*) to be able to personally share in their powers and personal histories. It made me lament my own personal situation, as I never really knew my Father. My Mother had said that he was "...a wonderful, intelligent, *magical* man," and for the first time, I reflected on her statement as something *other* than romantic fancy. He had taken violently ill with a dreadful malady not long after I'd been born, and the doctors in the mid-80s hadn't the slightest clue what it was - they said that they'd never encountered something so foreign and aggressive before. It was a pathogen the likes of which they'd never seen - not AIDS, not tuberculosis, not *anything* they'd either known before or even *heard* of. They even tested him for *cancer* and the tests revealed nothing more than they already knew... it wasn't cancer. All they knew was that he was going to rapidly, painfully die, consumed with the illness. He used the last week of his life telling my Mom repeatedly to "Make sure that my son discovers his destiny!" And to think, before all this, I just thought his admonitions were the ramblings of a mind that had come up through the hippy 70s.

41

I pensively mulled over the possibility that William may have indeed been zipping around the afterlife for hundreds of years before entering a new human body, taking on a new life. (I mean, before he went from being Lilith's son to being Zhuge Liang, there passed at **least** a couple of *thousand* years, so a few *hundred* seemed entirely reasonable!) It filled me with a sense of belonging and purpose - that I might have in me the spirit of the firstborn son of *any* of these great men... or even the same spirit that had passed through **all** of their firstborn sons throughout history!

I was stirred from my reverie by the faint cries I heard from outside my cabin. It was Kyle, and he was calling out for me. I hurriedly put on some jeans (as the sleep pants I'd been bumming around the cabin wearing would have been insufficient for outside), a thick plaid shirt, a light jacket, and some snow-proof boots (just to be on the safe side). As I emerged from my cabin, I saw Kyle astride his horse - just outside of what I'd previously figured was the range of the amnesia amulet (which, by the way, I'd decided by then to call "The Amulet of the Forgotten", hoping that *that* translation would speak more to what the Artifact actually dealt with).

Kyle's eyes widened as he caught sight of me, "Oh, thank God! I was out here, Kai... I don't know what to think. It's not good, I can tell you that. I felt like maybe I was hearing your thoughts and you were a ghost or something, but every time I rode toward your cabin, I wouldn't remember anything until I'd end up guiding my horse right back to here! I mean, I see your cabin, I hear what sounds like your thoughts inside, and then I get close and... oh my God, oh my God... I think I'm going crazy. It's like I can't reign in what my mind's thinking - I can't focus, I can't..."

"Whoa, Kyle!" I called out, crossing the Amulet's sphere of influence to close the gap between us. "Everything's gonna be okay. You're *fine*..." I used my most calming voice. As I got closer I could see that he was in tears. His mind was too quick, it seemed, for the Amulet's effect to fully sink in. What would have developed an apathetic fog in any *other* person's mind, just pushed Kyle into a mental *frenzy*, like someone grasping at roots and shrubs as they fall down the side of a mountain. I was instantly sorry that I'd not shared my plan of study with him.

"What?? *What* book? What... a crystal and a cave?!?" he instinctively read my mind as I made it to his horse's side. "Dude!" I stopped him. "You have *got* to stop reading my mind without asking! It's like..." I searched for an apropos simile. "...like eating all of my smoked jerky without even asking if you may have a bite!" He pouted like a child that had had its hand slapped for reaching for the last cookie. "But... *adventure!*" he murmured through his pout, and I couldn't help but laugh. I patted his knee, "Tell you what, your prominence..." (He smiled when I remembered the honorific I'd given him.) "You promise to stop reading my mind, and I'll go get my horse, and we'll talk all about it on a ride into town."

Kyle beamed his approval, and I couldn't help feeling like a Dad for a minute, even though he wasn't my son. Definitely, I at least felt like a *big brother*, even though I'd never had any siblings, either. I went back to the cabin, changed into some riding boots, left the crystal and tome inside (under the protection of the Amulet), saddled up Freedom, and rode out to where Kyle was still patiently waiting.

I did my best to explain my situation during the ride into town. Kyle listened intently, only interjecting every so often with "*Really?*" and "*Wow!*" (I swear, this man was like every kid I'd ever known - it was adorable.) He accepted it all by faith without the need of magical demonstration or anything (which was convenient, as I'd technically not *learned* any magic yet!) - *totally* different from the response I would've gotten had I told the average *New Yorker* about my last few days instead. I was overwhelmingly glad that I was living in the country, but in the very same thought, my old Brooklyn cynicism stormed in: "Yeah... that's why all those jackasses and hypocrites believe in *religion*, too... ***blind faith***!" As if to show my thought processes who was the boss, I told myself that I would use the rest of the week to *learn* real magic just so I could show Kyle.

"*Really?!?* You're gonna do ***magic***??" he piped up before realizing his mistake and covering his mouth with the hand that he *wasn't* holding the reigns with. "Hey! You promised!" I rebuked him. "Sorry, Kai. Sometimes I can't help myself when my mind wanders, and you'd gone a good little bit there without saying anything, so..."

"Just *no more*, okay?" I glared, flustered. "And you can't tell any of the other guys - check that, **anyone** - about this, okay? It's our secret - I know *your* magic and you know about *mine*, so it has to stay a secret just between us, all right?" "Okay!" he exuberantly nodded his head. "It's part of the solemn vow of your office as my *advisor*, get it?" I pushed to cement the idea of secrecy into his brain. "Yes *sir*, your majesty!" he winked.

"All right, just cool it with all that stuff while we're in town, okay?" I playfully punched his arm. He agreed, and then went on to tell me how his past week with the cattle hands had been. He had helped deliver two calves ("...and even a foal back at the corral!"), and had come to be called the "Birthing Charm" by Running Bear, my Native cattle hand. Old Bob had apparently told Kyle about every illness and danger to both cattle *and* horses in the mountains (which he could rattle off like it was *nothing*), and had Kyle had a way about him that made others think of him as "mature" *as well as* "brilliant", then I would've had no compunctions about making him my cattle foreman on the spot. Fortunately for both of us, Old Bob was all the foreman I needed, and Kyle was being groomed for something greater. I decided that it was time for Kyle to begin working at the construction site... so that he could get a good idea of what I would be expecting of the stone masons once they arrived next month. Plus, I'd need someone to direct things if I ever took ill. Kyle was excited to try a new job, and in the spirit of it, he introduced me to a little out-of-the-way Mexican restaurant in town that I'd never been to. I was glad; I was tired of steaks.

42

We managed to come into town, eat, and even check in at the hotel without seeing Michael - which I thought was fortunate, considering I didn't really want to explain who Kyle was or why I was dining with him instead of Michael. (For a friend, he was pretty possessive.) By the time we were checking in, Helen informed me that Michael had been sequestered in his room that day (probably playing PS3), and had only an hour ago gotten pizza delivered from the little place in town that made pizzas and subs. I thanked her for the update with a little "20-dollar handshake", and when she saw what I'd done, she reacted with her typical: "Oh, *you*!"

I got Kyle his own room and gave him a couple hundred dollars, encouraging him to "order *whatever*" he wanted. While he didn't end up ordering a lady of the evening back to his room, he *did* manage to charge up an impressive list of Spanktravision viewing, according to Helen (Her loose lips would've sunk a whole *fleet* of ships!), who tattled on him the next morning as I checked us out. I rolled my eyes at her to further emphasize the unimportance of his healthy personal sexual appetite, and we both laughed as we untied our horses to leave.

When we approached the Endless Wood on our return trip, I mentioned, "You know, Kyle... something's gnawin' at me. You said you wrote the poem on the wall behind the stall in the Hoof, right?"

"Heh... 'wall behind the stall'," he chuckled at the rhyme. "Oh... yeah! That was me."

"So why does it sound exactly *nothing* like you normally do? I mean, I'm not saying that you lack the capacity to write something of that *depth*, but as someone who's done a bit of acting, I've gotta say: it doesn't really sound like your 'voice', you know what I mean?" He knew exactly what I meant. "Yeah - I used to get told that at the Rusty Hoof all the time. Apparently, I'm a lot more insightful and introspective when I'm drunk." "I would've said *morose*, but yeah... insightful," I agreed. "So why do you suppose that is?"

"I don't know," he answered glibly. "I guess *everybody's* different when they're drunk. I know I'd rather be a *philosopher* when I'm drunk than a brawler, a loud-mouth, or a wife-beater. Makes better sense, wouldn't you say?" *There* was that insight that I almost never got to see! I smiled warmly, "I absolutely agree." I pursued it a bit further, "You know, you may not need *alcohol* to slow your senses long enough for you to be outwardly brilliant..."

"You don't think so?" he seemed surprised. "Of course not," I reassured him. "In fact, if the life of an Advisor in a Royal Court isn't enough to slow you down a pace or two, perhaps I'll find a way for *magic* to focus your laser, as it were." "Cooooool," he gushed. Truth be told, I hoped it wouldn't have to come to that. Too often had I seen examples of the victims of a society that was predisposed to prescribe drugs to slow down a boy's natural youthful vigor, when all he really needed was for it to be *run* out of him. That was one of the drawbacks to being a boy (or even a *man*) in America... your natural strengths were always demonized or otherwise handicapped when they should've been *encouraged* and allowed to fully develop.

I had a friend back in Brooklyn who had a *brilliant* son that he was raising to be his "Number Two" (as he said), and this boy could only really properly be held in check by my friend, who had mastered the "Daddy Evil Eye" that all good Fathers know. He'd spank him when he needed it as well, but he always used it as a *teaching* opportunity, and never did it in a *rage* (like his *wife* was prone to do when she couldn't make the boy settle down by *yelling* at him). And before they'd leave the room where the boy had been spanked, my friend would make sure to look his son in the eyes, make certain that he understood what he'd done wrongly, and how "Daddy only spanks you because *I love you*, and I want you to turn out *better* than all those bratty little kids out there these days." By the time this boy was five years old, his Dad hardly ever had to spank him at all, and he was busily training the boy to climb trees, have stick swordfights, and other boyhood things. Unfortunately for the boy, my friend's wife had decided (around that time) that her marriage vows were more like polite *suggestions*, and she began cheating on him under the guise of going out with "girlfriends from work". By the time she'd alienated my friend enough that his life was unbearably *miserable*, he was forced to move back in with his parents (as he was unemployed), hoping that she'd change her belligerent ways in his absence. That's all the window she needed to swoop in for the kill with a divorce, and because she didn't admit to cheating on him until *after* the divorce, the corrupt American courts took my friend's son away from him and gave him to his mom, who hadn't the slightest *clue* how to properly raise him. When his son slid back into his wild, boyish ways, she ended up putting the boy on Ritalin because she was too *lazy* (not to mention ill-equipped) to do the proper amount of parenting that the boy needed. I haven't spoken to that friend since a long time before I won the lottery, but the last time I did, he relayed how his ex-wife had shacked up with the man she'd been cheating on him with, and how they'd moved out of New York so that my friend (lacking a car or any decent job prospects) would be *incapable* of visiting his son.

It was just another textbook example of how a bitch in a westernized society had *ruined* a perfectly good and innocent boy, decimating a good man's life in the process... and I did **not** want to have to do anything even *remotely* like that to reign in Kyle. I just *knew* that I'd be able to find him enough work, studies, and training to put his agile, brilliant mind to work. I wanted him to aspire to be the kind of advisor that Kongming had been to Liu Bei, because I knew that he had a similar, natural gift.

When we arrived back at my cabin, I knew that it just wouldn't be proper for him to have to crash on my *floor* every night, so I decided that during the construction of the keep, it'd be a great idea for my advisor to have an adjacent cabin to mine. So, after I moved the Amulet back to the alcove, I discovered that Kyle was so receptive to the whole idea that he *jumped* at the chance to fell trees and shape logs for the rest of the day with me to start making his cabin's walls and flooring. I had to admit - it would be nice to have a friend and compatriot so close that I wouldn't have to saddle my horse and ride to be able to converse with him.

43

We were fortunate that some early May cloud cover that was threatening to turn stormy just passed us over instead that night, as I had never purchased any tarps or anything from the hardware store in town. (More often than I'd care to admit, I've been rather short-sighted when it comes to the "total picture" of construction.) As we enjoyed a roaring fire in the fireplace and some "town food" from the refrigerator, I filled Kyle in on the remainder of the history written in the tome, as he was the most trustworthy person (other than Frank, who had his *own* stuff going on) I knew, and he could read my mind *anyway* if he wanted to. He sat transfixed like a kid hearing a bedtime story, and once I was done he piped up, "Do you have the tome *here*?"

"Yes, Kyle, but you have to remember that this is the *most important secret* we share - you cannot tell **anyone** about this book! If you do, you'll not only stop being my *advisor*... you'll stop being my *friend*." I wanted to fully emphasize the importance of his secrecy, as it was more than just a book of magic; it was literally my family history. "Oh, I **promise**, your majesty! Your friendship is the best gift I've ever received in my whole *life*, and I wouldn't want anything to get in the way of that or remove it or jeopardize it or *anything*!" His sincerity was evident, with not a trace of irony (or any *other* sarcasm) in his delivery. "I mean... and I hope this isn't overstepping my advisor-ly boundaries or anything... but you're like the big brother I never had. I know we haven't known each other that long, but I feel like we were meant to do great things - like **family**." I felt a tear welling up in my eye from the wellspring of genuine emotion from this man, and I grasped him close to me in the biggest bear hug I'd ever given anyone. "You **are** my family, Kyle!" I tearfully pledged. "From now until the end of time, your spirit and mine will strive toward the same goals of honor and justice... you are my *brother*!" He hugged me back as strongly as he knew how, "I could never ask for anything better in my entire life, Kai! Surely, whatever God runs this crazy world means for us to change it together!" I pulled back from him to see the tears streaming down his face as well. "Let's hope so, little brother." He smiled, "I like that name. I really like that."

I pulled the tome out from under my bed to show him the source of all the stories, and when he saw the shiny Taijitic Seal, his reaction of awe was instantaneous. He wiped the tears from his eyes (to get a better look at it), and I did the same with mine. "So *this* is the *tome*?" his wide eyes reminded me of the time I unwrapped and saw R.O.B. the Robot for the first time when I got the Deluxe Nintendo Entertainment System from my Mom so many Christmases ago. "Yep," I beamed with pride. "This is it." I opened it to the section on Artifacts so that he could see what I was talking about, as I had explained the Amulet of the Forgotten to him earlier. He pointed to the sketch of the Amulet and said, "Oh, is *that* what it looks like? Cool!" "Yeah; sorry you might never be able to see it up close and personal," I knew that was a distinct possibility. "Oh, that's okay - it's *your* necklace-thingy anyway. What's all this writing around it?" he squinted. "What... you can't read it?" I asked. "No, it's just like old Shakespeare writing," he traced his finger along the words. "I think it says, 'Amulet of Divinations Forgotten', or something like that. I don't know; I'd always read *updated* Shakespeare in the library."

"I'll be damned," I was only a *little* surprised at what I *thought* was going on, but I had to further test it. "What?" Kyle didn't catch on immediately. "Here; tell me what it says here in the back of the tome," I directed him, turning to the portion where Zhuge Liang had transcribed his dreams to remember his past. "Are you kidding?" he looked at the words like they were hieroglyphs. "I can't read Chinese!" "How do you know it's Chinese?" I ribbed him. "Well, that's just what I call *all* writing that looks like that! Heck, it could be Japanese or Korean or Vietnamese; *I'd* never know!" I knew Kyle was too forthright to lie to me, so I skipped ahead in my Artifacts section reading to the part that covered the Taijitic Seal to confirm my suspicion that... "Yep! Here it is!" I pointed triumphantly at the page. "What? More old Shakespeare stuff?" he still couldn't quite make it out. "No, silly - it's the part dealing with the Taijitic Seal set into the front of the book. Apparently, while William was busy making sure no one but me or he could ever come close to the Amulet of the Forgotten, he was also enlisting the aid of an Egyptian djinn spirit to enchant this Taijitic Seal in a similar fashion so that no one but me or him would ever benefit from its effects. Jeez... he really did think of *everything*."

"You don't think it was cool that he knew all those spirits?" Kyle queried (I swear - like a child at story time.) "Oh yeah, of course. William seemed to keep different spirits with him that he got to know very well over the course of his lifetime, so that was actually pretty cool," I admitted. "So, did his magic attract them to him like a bug zapper, or was he only able to talk to 'em because he *was* so magical, or what? How does that work?" His curiosity really was a boon sometimes, as I'd not even questioned the origin of William's spirit keeping heretofore. "I honestly don't know, Kyle. I guess that's something I'll have to find out as I continue my studies into this bad boy here," I joked, carelessly slapping the pages. He let out a long, stretchy yawn and agreed, "Yeah - you really *do* need to study that some more! I want to see some *magic* tomorrow." Then he snapped his fingers, "*Hey!* I've got it! Seeing as how you've already shown me what I need to be doing with my cabin walls and flooring, why don't I just work by myself tomorrow on that, and you can get back to studying? I'll just come get you when I need help with the roofing and what-not!" "Sounds like a plan, little brother!" He grinned widely, and I tossed a couple large logs behind the fireplace andirons to make sure we'd have a decent supply of heat during the night. With the Amulet of the Forgotten hanging back in the alcove, I even had a relaxed, dreamless night - sleeping "in" for the first time that week.

By the time I got up, Kyle had already left my cabin to begin working on his own, and had even rolled up the bearskin blanket he'd slept on and placed it back near the foot of my bed. It wasn't long after I got out the tome to begin the fifth day of my studying (after my somewhat truant *fourth* day) that my stomach starting grumbling with hunger. As I got out the skillet to cook some bacon and eggs, it occurred to me, "Hey... I don't see any dirty dishes here. Did Kyle start work without *breakfast*?" My first instinct was to open the drawer where I kept the bear jerky we'd been snacking on the night before - and that instinct was correct. That little buster had absconded with the whole bag! "Well, at least I won't have to worry about feeding him," I thought. After a little breakfast for myself, I settled back into bed to start reading again.

44

Kongming's journal of dreams was my main focus that day, as I deduced that perhaps the first "rebirth" lifetime of William's spirit would be the one in which he most vehemently sought out the wisdom and skills he had previously attained. As the historical record of Kongming maintains that he was an unparalleled genius in his time, preternaturally inclined to realms of the highest intellect, I assumed (of course) that it would have been the result of having kept his vow to Xuan Wu and mastering the elements of which that god was the overseer. "If a mind can master the *supernatural*, then what challenges can the mere *natural* pose, right?" I rhetorically asked myself.

Liang's first dreams led him to discover and diagram the interactions of the five Chinese elements (as displayed in Wu Xing: Fire, Earth, Metal, Water, and Wood), but it looked as if later magic circles he drew contained two *additional* elements - spiritual elements (that the gods made his pre-rebirth self promise to keep secret) that were more revered at the beginning of time than they were in ancient China: Air and Lightning. He had even accurately completed the circle of creation and destruction (how the elements interacted). It was the perfect relationship of the elements: an intuitive diagram of how they all were fitly joined together. And - *finally* - I began to understand what William had been talking about before, as Kongming had listed the names of the magic disciplines beside each element... a master of: Fire would be a Pyromancer, Earth would be an Erdemancer, Metal would be a Metamancer, Lightning would be an Electromancer, Water would be an Aquamancer, Wood would be a Wodemancer, and Air would be an Aeromancer. They were all disciplines in a school of magic that he called "Elemental".

Although he set out to master *all* of the elements, it seemed his greatest strengths of all were in Metamancy and Electromancy. In fact, when he commissioned the forging of the Taijitic Seal, he directed that it be made of pure gold and silver to *symbolize* his strengths. It may have even begun as a vanity project, for he wrote: "The Emperor has the Jade Seal to symbolize the power of his rule; I shall make the Taijitic Seal to emphasize the intellect of mine!" After he'd summoned a dragon spirit to help him enchant the Seal (making it a universal text translator), he would often hide the seal in his hand while holding scrolls open for others to read. What was *indecipherable* before (like the Xuan Wu scrolls) became *perfectly readable* in Kongming's hands. He was venerated in the temple closest to his mountain retreat as "the man who can make anything clear". As such, I was sincerely hoping that he could make the practice of these disciplines... these Arts... clear to *me* so that I might begin to master them *myself.*

I found myself flipping back and forth between the dream journal section and the life journal section to instruct myself in the Arts. It was like going back and forth between an 1828 Noah Webster dictionary and a Riverside Shakespeare copy of *Hamlet* - one perfectly *defines* the words, and one shows you how to perfectly *use* them. Like when I learned English back in high school, I was preoccupied with having the *definitions* of the Arts down before I set about attempting to *use* them. I wanted to be prepared for *everything*.

Unbeknownst to me, magic (I discovered - like *most* things) is generally a matter of exercise - and until you have mastered the small things, the greater ones are impossible. It would be like a kindergartener trying to bench press three hundred pounds. It's not going to happen for the little tyke. Even if he *could* get the weight up, he wouldn't be able to *control* it and one or more muscle group(s) would give out, making him drop the weight on himself and cave in his own chest cavity - or it would fall off-balance and dent the floor. For a non-weight-lifting example, imagine you turned on the water pressure to a fire hose with no fireman on the other end of the hose to control it. It would flail wildly about, damaging everything that a solid metal nozzle *could*... until some veteran fireman would shut off the water, shake his head, and probably mutter something about you being a "punk kid" as he shuffled back to the firemen's lounge.

So I started small. I pyromanced a small stream of flame from the fireplace. I erdemanced the dust out from under my bed. I metamanced a paperclip into the shape of a star. I electromanced a few sparks from my nearest empty outlet. I aquamanced a drop of water from the spigot. I wodemanced a few sprouts out of a potato. I aeromanced a tiny whirlwind that made the dust from under my bed dance across the floor. Amazingly, there was not a single Elemental Art that I was incapable of performing. It was just that my power in them was rather "less than impressive" at that point in time. All the same, I knew Kyle would never forgive me unless I showed him what little I could now do.

I could hear him chopping a tree that he meant to fell before I even opened my front door, so I knew he was actively engaged in his work. It gave me a devilish idea - *surprise* him. I snuck slowly up on him as he hacked away at a respectably sizable tree. I crouched behind a nearby shrub, thinking over all the things I could do that would possibly be supernatural enough to shock and amaze him. By the time I noticed he'd stopped chopping the tree, he was standing directly over me. "You *know* your thoughts are the loudest things *in* this forest, right?" he smirked. "Damn!" the jig was up. "But *magic*, right? That's cool - show me some stuff, huh?" his enthusiasm made me forget my disappointment in not being able to surprise him. Considering we were surrounded by nature, I decided the easiest thing to show him would be Wodemancy. I had him back against a tree that had a vine growing up the side of it. I told him, "Now close your eyes and only open them when I tell you, okay?" "You got it, big brother!" he cheerfully chirped. I wodemanced tiny offshoots of the vine around the tree on both sides until they had curled around his sleeved forearms like so many green bracelets. I then wodemanced the shoot roots into the tree bark as firmly as I could before calling out, "Okay, open your eyes!"

"What? What am I looking at?" he stepped away from the tree with little effort, uprooting the vine restraints that I thought would've *surely* given him more trouble than *that*. I dejectedly pointed at his arms and he finally looked down at his sleeves to see what vines still remained. "Oh neat!" he observed, before twisting his expression in confusion. "You tried to tie me to a *tree*?" "Meh," I mumbled. "Doesn't matter - it didn't *work*." "No," he agreed. "But it was still pretty cool." I smiled a defeated smile, "Thanks, little bro." He patted my shoulder, "No problem, big brother."

45

He agreed that it was more important (for the moment) that I concentrate on my burgeoning Elemental magic skills, as he had read something similar about writers - that if, after having been struck by inspiration, they waited to *act* on it - their inner muse shriveled within them (often costing them the magic of their next story). He settled the matter for me (as the most prolific poet between the two of us) that writing was close enough in nature to magic, so I didn't argue. It truly seemed that the extra exertion of felling trees and shaping wood all morning had made him exponentially more "advisor-ly", so I allowed *his prominence* to get back to work... and returned to my cabin to study and exercise my disciplines.

I spent the rest of the day exercising not the *amount* of any given element that I could control, but rather the *sphere of influence* in which I could control it. If I could aquamance a cubic inch of water (making it levitate), I'd spread that same inch over a line drawn on my counter a foot long, and then attempt to aquamance all the individual water droplets at once. I tried to exert my energies in different directions at once, but would end up dropping the water, as my concentration was not yet strong enough. The only elements that seemed to come quicker to me were (strangely enough) the same ones that my ancestor Kongming had had little trouble mastering. Granted, I was nowhere near *mastery*, but the same exercise I'd attempted with the water came *much* more quickly to me, as I electromanced the capricious sparks of electricity from my open outlet. Before the end of the day, I was also able to (I know it doesn't sound like much.) metamance three separate (and rather bulky) butter knives - as well as melt/shift their structures until I could make them into forks or spoons. No, I didn't use very much imagination to do that, but hey... I was just starting out. It may take no more than a mustard seed's worth of *faith* to move a mountain (or so Jesus used to say), but if you want to do that with *magic*, I figured it would probably take a ***lifetime***'s worth of magic exercise.

The point I would make is that magic (or at least *Elemental* magic) isn't intuitive. It's not like acting or writing or music or massage, where you either have a talent or gift or feel for it - or you just *don't*. It really is all about the rudimentary elements of things... about doing things over and over from as many different perspectives and in as many different intensities as you can fathom (Of course, one could argue that *that* is the way in which it's intuitive, but I'm trying to make a point here. Bug off.) until you've completely mastered it. See, a good massage therapist instinctively knows what should feel well on another person because he has a gift for internalization - he knows what would feel good to him, and how to properly translate it to another body's reception of his touch. It's what I would call an "ethereal inner ear". Elemental magic, on the other hand, is completely different. You practice and practice, taking note of what *didn't* work (or didn't work as *well* as a different time) and keep focusing your psychic aim until you're hitting a bulls-eye every time. Once you hit your target from *one* metaphorical direction, you see how many *other* directions you can hit it from. Then you make the target *move*. It's one of those slow buildups that explains (to me) why magic isn't as prevalent in modern society anymore. No one wants to *practice* to become good; they just hope they're *talented*.

And it's not as simple a repetition as weight lifting (considering I mentioned that before), in that - as any scientist should tell you - it takes a different kind of effort to flex one's *mind* than it does to flex one's *muscles*. The psychic energies that control magic are more akin to: the comfortable shiver you get on a cold morning when you stand in front of a fireplace and begin to get warm, the feeling of dread you get as a child when you've broken something important (knowing you'll get a spanking for it), the half-poisoned euphoria you feel after drinking a *liiiiittle* too much, that justified superiority that rocks your essence after you've listened to someone say how bad you are for a while before you drop an incomparable verbal **bomb** of something awful *they've* done, the foreboding fear you have while walking through someplace dark and silent that you've never been before, and the inner peace you feel standing in your special place when the world is still and the birds chirp like a heavenly choral accompaniment to the warm breeze. They are **all** *of that* - the things you feel but cannot define, the things that can control your mind but don't physically bind you, the things that make life beautiful, dreadful, passionate, and uncertain. And needless to say, most people can never focus sufficiently to control their psychic energies long enough to even converse with a spirit, let *alone* levitate balls of fire.

Anyway, I wanted you - the reader - to know what I had found out on just day one of my serious magic practice. Also, I hope you'll bear in mind that generally one's potential for magic is limited by birth, not passed down (in the form of an entire *lineage* worth of lifetimes) through great crystals. So some people may focus on the Arts for their entire lives, only to accomplish tiny things like I've done here on my first day. It doesn't mean I'm better than you as a *person*, but I *did* have much more of an advantage than you to begin with. It's like those trust fund asshole kids of rich people who inherit millions that they never had to earn when compared to the struggling but hard-working children of the lower rungs of society that have to not only fight for every bit of headway they make but have to do so with no ancestral advantages whatsoever. Just because they had more to begin with doesn't always mean they'll use it wisely, and just remember: when the revolution comes, we *outnumber* them about a million to one! And in case you haven't noticed, I'm nothing like the hypothetical rich jerkwad kids I mentioned. In fact, my magical abilities would leave me better suited to *lead* the underprivileged people that I grew up with against the machinating aristocracies of the rich, who've historically profited from our misery.

Back to the story, though - I had just tucked the tome away out of sight under my bed and was done practicing magic for the day when I heard a knock at my cabin door. I wondered why the hell Kyle would bother knocking, when it hit me... *he wouldn't*! I immediately thought that it was Frank, come to share my hearth and hospitality for a bit, as such a visit was long overdue. I got up from the floor, dusted myself off, and called out, "Be right there!" before mentally doing a facepalm (as that's generally what a guy says after he's been caught masturbating). I crossed quickly to my door and opened it to reveal not Frank, but Running Bear - one of my faithful cattle hands. His gaze rose to meet mine. "Could we talk, Mr. Hunter?"

46

"Yes, Running Bear; come on in," I welcomed him. I was about to close the door behind him when Kyle came running up to the doorway. "Are you all right?" he asked once he'd caught his breath. "Of course I am, Kyle," I answered, amused. "Why wouldn't I be?" He propped himself up against the door frame, and saw Running Bear standing inside waiting. "Sorry," he waved over my shoulder at my guest. "I just thought I sensed some fearful anxiety in you a bit back there." His voice was lowered, but I still thought that Running Bear might have been within earshot, so I gave him the wide-eyed, "Hey, be careful what you say!"-look. It was then that I saw his axe in his right hand, and realized he had run from wherever he was chopping wood to potentially put his *life* on the line to save me from some unknown danger!

"Well, as you can see, it's just Running Bear here, so why don't you come inside and join us?" "Okay, thanks - I've still got some of that bag of bear jerky left in my pocket if you guys want some," Kyle cheerily offered. "Yeah, I noticed you swiped that this morning, you buster!" I chided him. He started to come in with the axe, and I motioned next to the door, "Just leave that out here - it'll be fine." I closed the door behind him and motioned toward the wooden chair in front of my computer table, "Have a seat, Running Bear." "Thank you, Mr. Hunter," he politely nodded. Kyle took his favorite spot - on the floor next to the fireplace - and began putting a few smaller logs on the fire, which had dwindled down to mostly red embers. I sat (as professionally as possible) on the edge of my bed across from my guest.

"I'm not great with pleasantries, so let me get right to the point," began Running Bear, in such casual English that (even though I'd heard him speak at small intervals *before*) I again realized that all those black-and-white cowboy and "Indian" movies over the years had prejudiced my expectations of Native speech.

"Sure," I agreed. "Go ahead."

"Mr. Hunter, I've experienced first-hand how active, engaged, and kind you are as a boss. You direct your men well, know how to delegate, know when to accede to a subordinate's opinion, and know to praise in public and rebuke in private." I admit that I was a bit surprised to hear it because, as a boss, you don't really get praised too often. I nodded acceptance of the remarks. "The only White man I'd ever worked for - before you - was Frank Meyer. And although he is a wise and generous man, you have outdone him. I want you to know that I recognized the seed of greatness in you (given your young age) even before... well..." he seemed reticent to continue. "Go on," I urged him.

"I've heard you speak before about how western women, raised in western societies with western ideologies were a plague on this land." It was true; I had. "Well, Mr. Hunter, I have a daughter - Flowering Bear Grass - who was not raised in such a reprehensible way as the western women. She is soft-spoken, supportive, respectful, industrious, honest, pleasant, and (if you will allow a Father to be proud) the most beautiful young lady in these mountains."

"She sounds like a wonderful lady," I admitted. "*Any* Father would be proud to have a daughter like that." "Indeed," he continued. "Her Mother set a fine example for her, and I have managed to shield her from any destructive western influences her whole life. It was particularly difficult on the family at home this past winter when her Mother caught RSV, but my daughter has always excelled in domestic things, and has borne the load of her Mother's work around the homestead without complaint." "I doubt you'll have any trouble finding a match for her among her many suitors, then," I posited.

"You would be surprised then, sir, for before I met you, I'd begun to think that there was not a single man anywhere near her age in all these mountains that also espoused the eastern ways as you do," he said, matter-of-factly. The look on my face must have revealed that I had begun to suspect he'd come to see if I'd *court* her - and that I was *not* looking for such a thing at present. "And I don't mean to suggest that you two would make an excellent match, Mr. Hunter, even though it's very obviously true. I have come only to ask if you would consider employing her services, for you see..." I listened. "...she has a *gift*." This drew me in; now I was listening *intensely*. "A gift?"

"Yes, Mr. Hunter. And I know it will probably sound like 'crazy shaman talk' to a man that grew up in the big city, but my daughter can see the future." The Brooklyn cynic exploded in my mind. "Then why not have her see the next big lottery numbers and retire, rich in the mountains?" He smiled a knowing smile, "Your government watches rich people, and we are very private. Besides, we are *happy* living a simple mountain life here. Wealth would not help us... in fact, *it could hurt us*. As you White guys say: 'If it ain't broke, don't fix it!', right?" It was an honest, believable answer - and one that my avaricious upbringing would have dismissed entirely if I had not come out here to these mountains and experienced that happy life for *myself*.

"True - we do say that a lot," I admitted. "But how exactly could I employ her? It wouldn't be proper for her to bunk up with the other guys back near the corral, and I lack the space *here* - even Kyle is busy felling trees to make a decent cabin for himself here." "Oh?" asked Running Bear, spurring me to remember that I'd not made it public cattle hand knowledge concerning Kyle's installation as my advisor. "Yes, he is to be my Royal Advisor." Kyle swept his hand outwardly in a Royal gesture. "My apologies, Mr. Hunter; I had not heard." "Oh no, the apology is mine to give; I've meant to tell you guys at the bunk house, but we've been so busy setting up his cabin that... well, anyway... isn't your daughter caring for her Mom at home? She's sick with... SPV or something?"

"No, sir; the RSV passed a couple of weeks ago, which is why I felt free enough to come and ask you this. You see, when you came out to see the herd and gave us the meat from that injured cow, my daughter was walking through the woods behind us to deliver a lunch to me that she'd made as a surprise. When she saw you and didn't recognize you, she instinctively did what she often does, and read your immediate future. It was then that she came to ask me about you."

47

My heart skipped a beat, and I looked over at Kyle, who had obviously been wondering the same thing: "Have our magic abilities been revealed to the outside world?" He was squinting ever so slightly, which meant that he was looking for recent memories, as (you will recall) they are the most closely guarded in the mind. Kyle's look softened in seconds and he asked, "So what was it that Flowering Bear Grass told you, Running Bear?" We both looked at him expectantly, though I was far more unsettled than Kyle.

"She did not tell me specifically, which I have learned not to take offense to," he recalled. "Often if I come to know the same future that she does, I am prone to over-react to prepare for it, which in turn changes the future for the worse. I have learned to just accept what she decides to tell me." I couldn't help but think that that last sentence was most often the case with *any* man listening to a woman, whether she can predict the future or *not*. "All right," my curiosity was stretched to the point of ultimate strength *(Engineering/metallurgy joke!)*. "So what *did* she tell you, Running Bear?"

"She said that you were destined for great and wonderful things, and that your lineage had prepared you for it for generations, much the same way Solomon built the temple that his Father David had designed." I must have thought it incredulous that a Native mountain girl would be so familiar with the Jamesian Old Testament account of Solomon's temple, for Running Bear saw it in my face. "Oh, she is well-read. She loves the stories of the Old Testament, *The Odyssey*, Grimm's Fairy Tales, *The Once and Future King*... all the fanciful western fables. Even so, she is very level-headed, and knows that they are *just* stories - no matter *how* entertaining." It occurred to me that he never stopped recommending his daughter's wifely capacities, but I decided to overlook it for the time being. "So... great and wonderful things, huh?"

"Oh yes! And she said that there was a man who could 'see beyond the skin' with you by your side. As you had already ridden off by that point, I didn't figure until tonight that it was *Kyle* she was referring to." We simultaneously looked at one another with a combination of trepidation and amusement - if there *is* such a thing. "So why would you think she would have a job waiting for her with me?" I didn't mean to be rude, but the question seemed to be a natural implication. "She knew that there was no such offer waiting, but she thinks that she can be of aid to you in the future, and as *I* know you to be a just and wise man, I wanted to present you with the offer from someone (myself) that I know you trust and are familiar with. I can see that you don't have any housing prepared for her (I mean, why *should* you have?), so I am prepared to take a few days off from herding to build one in a place you select as suitable... should you decide to employ my daughter."

"Even if you were not paid for the days you miss herding?" I had to test his resolve. "Yes, sir. I would use my own tools, tent, and hunting gear to supply the wood, shelter, and food for myself. All that matters to me is that my daughter has the chance to help a good man with great ideals." My heart was touched; here sat a good Father - sacrificial, hard working, loving. "You are a good man, Running Bear. Your love for Flowering Bear Grass and your honorable word of her gift is all the recommendation I require. If you agree to help my advisor Kyle finish his cabin first, I will search out an appropriate site for your daughter near here where she may assist me with her gift. I'm sure Kyle will help you build your daughter's cabin as well. I shall make sure you both are well fed and sheltered, and your herding pay will not suffer for your sacrifice."

He put his right fist over his heart and bowed his head. "Your graciousness is as boundless as the mountain sky; I shall forever be in your service, Mr. Hunter!" I laid my hand on his shoulder, "Your service honors me. Call me Kai." "Yes sir, Kai," he complied. Out of Running Bear's line of sight, Kyle pantomimed some hand magic to remind me the kind of things I'd been doing of late that *really* needed to remain a secret. "Oh yes," I looked back at Running Bear. "Your daughter will also have to swear to secrecy all the things she sees or experiences here. Will you be able to bear a few more secrets around your home?" Keeping his fist clasped to his chest, he vowed: "I swear that neither I nor my daughter shall *ever* betray your trust or your virtuous principles - and I know that she would tell you the same!" I placed my other hand on his other shoulder and looked directly into his eyes. "I trust that you will not. A good man is measured by the sum of his words *and* his deeds. May we *always* be good men in one another's sights." He smiled gratefully, "I could wish for nothing more, Mr. Hunter... I'm sorry; *Kai*." A manly hug ensued, and Kyle - either swept up in the moment, or unwilling to be left out - joined it from the outside.

The next morning, I sent Kyle and Running Bear off to get an additional set of tools for Running Bear, because I didn't want him dulling his *own* tools to make a residence for someone in *my* service. Fortunately, I had a couple hundred dollars left in a drawer to give them for the task. While they were gone, I went ahead and scouted out an area a good 200 yards away from Kyle and me (to give Flowering Bear Grass a significant amount of privacy, but also so she'd be within yelling distance should she be attacked by rogue wildlife or something). The area was mostly flat, about a stone's throw from a creek that could either be diverted for water or used as it was, and had plenty of young trees around it so she could chop her own firewood. Of course, thinking about firewood led me to thinking of woodstoves which led me to wonder if she was *good* at cooking or merely knew the rudimentary basics. My mind chose to believe the former so it could torment me with all the best home-cooked dishes my Mom used to make, forcing me relive those glorious sights and smells and salivate at the prospect of having a woman in my service with such capabilities. Granted, that wasn't to be the *purpose* of her service, but I couldn't help hoping that it might be a *bonus* thereof.

Once Kyle and Running Bear made it back, they had the majority of the afternoon left for working, and they made very good use of it. Kyle's cabin now had all four of its walls firmly up, and all that remained was to put a proper roof on it.

48

We all spent the night talking of things to come, and enjoying the two pizzas that Running Bear had deftly carried back to the cabin on horseback (Don't ask me how - I *still* don't know!). Afterward, we enjoyed an old bag of smoked beef jerky that I'd forgotten Frank had given me quite some time ago (Apparently, I'd covered the bag with a notebook or something.) I told them how I had scouted out a site for Flowering Bear Grass a "good little ways" away, and Running Bear seemed pleased. He thought my idea for a castle (which I'd somehow failed to mention around my cattle hands) was an interesting one, and knew that his daughter (with her love of the Arthurian legends) would be excited to see it being built up close.

It occurred to me for the first time that his daughter might not yet be of a consenting age (And while a couple of bachelors hanging out in the mountains with a teenage girl might be acceptable in *Native* cultures, it would *definitely* garner us sour reputations in the mostly-White town in which we did a majority of our business!), so I asked him how old she was. He said that she was about to turn 18 in June, and I breathed a sigh of relief. "You didn't think I'd let my daughter live so closely in your employ if she was a *young girl*, do you?" he asked, as the idea would have been as genuinely ridiculous to *him* as it was to *me*. "I apologize, Running Bear. My brain's still running on old notions I was given about Native people when I was growing up. You'll have to forgive me." "Yeah, I forgive you - it's a good thing you *asked*, too, or else I'd have had to scalp you," he shot back as dead-pan as Leslie Nielsen. Kyle and I shot each other a look before both looking back at him. "How," he imitated a terrible bigot's impersonation of an "injun". We all burst out in laughter for a good couple of minutes.

Running Bear had brought in his sleeping bag and pillow from his horse, and Kyle had taken some of the money he'd made while being a cattle hand to buy his own, so after I laid out my grizzly bear blanket for them, they each had nice, comfortable places to lie in front of the fire. Having bunked with him before, we both knew to expect Running Bear's loud snoring, but oddly enough, it ended up being *soothing* and we all had a great night's sleep. In the morning, after a nice breakfast of bacon and eggs, I let Kyle and Running Bear get to work on Kyle's cabin's roof and I went hunting to see if I could get us some more meat (as we were running quite low). I got outfitted with my regular deerskin leather tunic and drawstring pants and covered my chest with a water-hardened boiled cow-leather cuirass that I'd been meaning to field test. Not wanting to bind myself up, but wanting some additional protection on my legs, I strapped on some connected leather cuisses and schynbalds, leaving my "silent sole" moccasins until last. I left my arms mostly just covered by the long sleeves of my tunic, but after I'd slipped on my archery gloves, I decided to also put on the boiled leather vambraces with the protruding bone shards I'd crafted for extra protection should any larger prey decide to charge. I slipped my strung bow and a sheaf of ten arrows into my quiver, strapped my Ulfberht sword to my waist along with my hatchet, and picked up my best ten-foot spear (that had a serrated iron tip that I was proud to have forged). After a quick trip to the nearby creek to smear some mud on my face, I was ready to go.

There was something very manly about the hunt... that tenseness in the air, not knowing whether the next thing to come into your sights would be a giant bear or merely a deer, rabbit, or squirrel. It felt affirming in the noblest sense that - no matter *how* well you outfitted yourself - there was always the chance that *you* could be the meal; the hunter as the prey. And here in the mountains, it wouldn't take too much, really. If you failed to notice a black bear at full charge until the last minute, or happened to get encircled by a pack of wolves on the hunt, your bravery would be remembered in the earth-nurturing footnote known as *animal crap*. And that was okay. The bear's speed could be stopped with a well-grounded spear, and even the bravest wolf in the pack wouldn't attempt to finish you off after seeing the alpha felled by your longsword. It was the circle of life - a game *always* played to the death.

I rounded the highest mountain on my property to a side on which I didn't often hunt, hoping that the numbers of prey there would be sufficient to get lucky and get a meaty kill right away. I followed a pathway that I'd only partially cleared before, continuing through the brush a bit at the end of it. Through a clearing in the trees, I noticed a small cave about halfway up the hill, and involuntarily tightened the grip on my spear. This would definitely be a hunting ground for bears. I heard a stream downhill through the thicker part of the trees, so I considered that it might be possible for a bear to be chasing some salmon fry there (as it was likely the season they would've been heading back to their native lake), so I eased my way downward. I was equally focused on not slipping and not making any noise, so I could only keep the barest minimum of attention toward the stream. Thankfully, the slope ended before the treeline did.

When I got to the last position in the forest with any cover before the stream, I looked out to see a small bear cub batting at the water. Now while cubs are cute in internet videos and the like, in the *wild* it means that you are "public enemy number one" to what is likely a very angry, protective mother sow. As quietly and motionlessly as I could, I scanned the waterline and then the treeline for the mama bear that I *knew* had to be there. Nothing.

I thought if perhaps I edged forward *juuust* a bit, I'd be able to see around a particularly thick tree to my right. At that exact moment, I saw the cub look up from the river to the hill above me, and I followed his gaze to see that the sow I'd been looking for was *barreling down the hill toward me!* I grabbed my spear with both hands and spun around, intent on impaling the bear on it with her own momentum. I misjudged my surroundings and whacked the spear on the tree I'd been trying to see around, and my arc of motion carried my hands straight forward and knocked the spear right out of my hands. The sow was a split second away from me, her gait preparing for the final death lunge onto me. I stumbled backwards over a stray branch, and her teeth missed my skull by *inches*. Fear had replaced my every instinct, and as I fell backwards, I instinctively drew my arms up over my head to protect it. Fortune favored me, and the sow fell - *heavily* - onto the bone shards protruding from my vambraces. Once we crashed together to the earth, she went to swipe at me as I was pinned beneath her. I repeatedly dug the long shards of the vambraces into her chest... and within minutes, she was dead.

49

I rolled from side to side painfully on my quiver (out of which had spilled my bow and the majority of my arrows in the fall) until I rocked the gigantic beast off of me. Once I regained my proper senses, I scanned every direction quickly to ensure the sow had no boar backup on the way down the hill. All was still, save for the gurgling of the stream behind me. Even the bear cub was long gone. "He's an orphan today," I declared morosely. "But in a year, he'll have prepared his revenge."

I set about crafting a makeshift stretcher sled from the younger trees near the waterline with my hatchet. It was a long job, and I had to keep on the lookout for area wolves, who would no doubt pick up the bloody scent of my hunting kill if the winds were unfavorable. Once I'd rolled the heavy bear sow onto the stretcher sled, I washed her blood off of me as best I could in the stream (not intending to make myself *too* much of a target for the long walk back to my cabin) and began the laborious uphill journey home. Hours later, Running Bear caught sight of me in the foothills and hurried down with Kyle to help bring the carcass up the rest of the way. We managed to work together skinning it and stored the unshredded portions of meat safely in my large floor freezer. After setting aside the suet for tallow and the brain for tanning, we buried everything we couldn't use about 300 yards west of camp. Running Bear made a huge outside fire and we dragged some folding stools out from my cabin to roast some arm and leg meat that didn't easily come off the bones. Kyle remarked, "Holy hell... we look like *cavemen*!" We laughed, because with us tearing away at meat on oversized bones, we definitely did.

It turned out that the meal was the first meal they'd eaten since they finished up the work on Kyle's roof that day. They hadn't installed any cisterns or solar electricity yet (which I'd have to help with), but it was such a decided step in the right direction for Kyle's true independence that it was cause for a decent helping of celebration. So, in the festive spirit, I pyromanced the fire a bit, causing small licks of flames to dance for us, spin in circles, and I even (during the course of it) learned how to adjust the heat of the little individual fireballs -

making floating, flickering lights of blue, white, yellow, orange, and red. "*Whoa!*" Running Bear's eyes grew wide. "There are spirits in the camp! They're dancing in the fire - *look!* Please tell me I'm not the only one seeing this, because this would be a helluva time for an acid flashback." I had forgotten that we had yet to reveal our magics to our Native friend. As badly as I wanted to reveal myself to him, my unfortunate past had taught me to keep my most inner circle of trust *as small as possible...* and I couldn't risk having to "out" Kyle (who was shooting me a "What the *hell* do you think you're **doing**??"-look) either. I had put myself in an awkward position, being the man that generally aspires to a lifestyle of complete honesty. For the moment, I chose to be deceptively specific with the truth.

"There's much magic on this mountain, Running Bear," I said (taking note of how Kyle's eyes breathed a sigh of relief that his *mouth* didn't dare to). "I only hope that - with your daughter's help - I might do justice to it and honor it, as your people have honored this land."

The answer pleased him, and he seemed to calm down, simply enjoying that (ostensibly) there were spirits in the camp that thought enough of us and the trials of our individual days to entertain us a bit with a light show. It made me wonder if the God of the Universe was enjoying *our* show, considering all he really *does* is watch, allowing the lesser gods that he made to cause enough havoc to make us little human ants *worth* watching. I don't think he bothers knowing the future, either - because that would make our "shows" (the *comedies* in particular) rather boring and predictable to watch. I mean, sure... every extreme now and then, he'll have to step in and prevent one of his lesser gods from screwing up an entire planet, but the gods that are *that* bloodthirsty are generally in other universes (and typically on supernatural probation for millennia at a time).

I believe one of them was Zargon, a really belligerent asshole god in Universe #453 that William had written about getting his Pyromancy magic back from (Shai had lied and told Zargon that William just needed to borrow the Art for a millennium, and that it didn't matter anyway because God had put that magic of his on "time out" for a few millennia the last time Zargon tried to burn the planet he was the most influential god on. *Talk about your butthead gods,* right?).

      Wait a second... where was I? Oh yeah! *God.* We entertain him. And while I thought I was dreadfully close to getting my "show"... um, "cancelled" that day... it was moderately humbling to think that of the hundreds of shows God can watch at the same time, that *I* might be one of his favorites. Of course, I'm just guessing. It's not like William ever wrote about talking to God *directly* - most of his accounts were second-hand stories from the other gods (whom I'd just have to *assume* had met/conversed with/knew the God of the Universe). Really, you've got to be pretty damn full of yourself to think God watches or listens to you in *particular*, let alone has *spoken* to you - considering William had met **gods** that had never had that opportunity. So I guess the whole thing wasn't that humbling after all. Maybe I'm just spiritually Narcissistic. Hell, I don't know.

      All I know is that the specific truth that I told Running Bear allowed me to practice my Pyromancy all the rest of the time we sat around the campfire, which wasn't long as it turned out; I was already mostly physically and mentally drained from fighting and killing the she-bear earlier that day. I ended the whole display with the tallest fire column I'd ever pyromanced - a blue pillar that I spun out of the center of the fire about six feet higher than its yellow flames. I managed to make it diffuse at its apex so that it ended up looking (for a split second) like a Las Vegas fountain spray. Kyle clapped, Running Bear cheered, and I even let out an "Ooooo!" (to make it seem like I was merely enjoying it as well - I'm a pretty decent actor). About a minute later, when Running Bear was convinced that the "spirits" were done showing off, we turned in for the night. And although Kyle's place was already sealed against the elements (and snakes and bugs - *you know*), they hadn't cut out any window holes (I hadn't bought any paned windows from town, either.), so I invited them to sleep another night in my cabin, which they did. In fact, Running Bear had had such a good time, that I think his snoring was even extra loud as a tribute.

50

The next day, I asked Kyle and Running Bear to work on what was to be Flowering Bear Grass's cabin while I went into town to get some of the smaller, more complicated metal and electronic parts that I'd need in order to complete Kyle's solar hookups (considering I couldn't exactly fire them in my *forge* just yet). Kyle suggested that they spend the morning making some smoked bear jerky *before* they settled in to work on the new cabin, and I couldn't argue with that! So I saddled up Freedom, slid my Ulfberht sword (that I'd decided to call "Justice" [while I was naming things after virtues and all]) into its saddle sheath, and rode into town. I was tying Freedom up at the hotel (and preparing for a nice walk to the hardware store) when Michael came out the front entrance.

"Hey, Michael - what's goin' on?" I asked, about a second before the smell hit me. He had been drinking - *heavily*. His clothes were disheveled and dirtier than I'd ever seen them, and his breath was rancid. It was nine in the morning, and he was carrying an unconcealed fifth of Jack in his hand. I assumed that things were not going well.

He literally swiveled his entire body to face me. "Weeelllll, look who it is! Mister fancy King man ridin' into town on his high horse. Yeahhh... too good for ol' Michael, huh?" He shuffled toward me, pointing with the hand holding the Jack, and I tried to evade any potential whiskey sloshes coming from the bottle.

"*Whoa*, man!" I tried to slow his advance. "What has *happened* to you?"

"*Me??*" pointing toward his chest with the Jack hand, he sloshed it all over himself. He didn't even notice. "Whass happen to *you*? Goin' round town with some new guy... new friend... don't need ol' Michael anymore. You big... jackass!" I knew he must've been talking about Kyle. I could see through the glass front doors that Helen had stopped watching TV and come out to the front desk to take in *this* debacle instead.

"Dude, that's just my friend Kyle. Besides, we can't have been into town any more than a couple of times, and I don't remember seeing you when we were here. How have you seen Kyle?" I was honestly curious.

"My friend Billy from the liquor store told me about 'im. Yeahhh - you're not the only person nat can make new frenss. Mister lucky... lucky money winner," he was circling the tank for sure. I could tell from my years of bouncing in NYC that he was going to pass out or throw up any minute; and since I'd known him for a few years, I knew there was a much stronger chance for the former.

"Look, Michael, I love you as a friend, and you *know* that." He rolled his eyes and scoffed. "But since we first got here, you seemed more like you were ready to party and help me *spend* that money, than in helping me work to set up my kingdom... which is *far* more important! I kept hoping you'd come around, but..." "*Oh yeah*; I *know*!" he interrupted. "Helen toll me *alll abow* yer lil' plan..." I shot a glare through the front doors at the desk, just quickly enough to see Helen guiltily ducking behind it. "...an' how yer gonna leave me high an' dry when June gess here. I guess ol' New Yorr Siddee Michael ain't enuff fer big ol' mountain Malachi," his eyes had drifted downward toward the sidewalk. No matter how generally unhelpful he'd proven himself for kingdom-building work, I couldn't help but feel a little sorry for him in his current state. I mean, he was coming back to the issue of friendship and abandonment *a **lot***, even fixating on it in his drunken state (and like the Romans used to say: "in vino veritas").

"Michael... look," I waited for his eyes to drift back up toward mine. "I'm sorry you found out that way. It was wrong for me to do you like that - I should've just come to you with my concerns. I really can't even remember why I didn't." I could tell that my quieted tone had calmed him somewhat.

"Yeah, 'cuz... I coul... I..." he was seconds from passing out. He sighed, "I juss miss my old buddy. It's juss me here... juss me..." He slumped forward and I caught him under his arms. The fifth slipped out of his hand, remarkably managing to fall upright on the sidewalk and not break. "I've got you, old friend," I reassured him.

I carried him inside to the front desk, where Helen was still crouched behind, hiding. "Gimme his spare key, blabbermouth," I curtly ordered her. She sheepishly rose and fetched the key for me. I got him to his room without too much trouble and laid him down on his bed. Once I rolled him on his side (so he wouldn't choke on his tongue or anything), I took his shoes off and covered up his legs. "Sleep it off, brother," I instructed my clearly unconscious friend. "We'll sort this all out after you wake up."

I headed back to the front desk, where Helen was already worrying about what to say to me. "Mr. Hunter, I'm sorry. I..." "Stop," I didn't have time for a garrulous apology. "What's done is done, Helen. I just can't trust you with secrets, that's all. I know that now. And I forgive you... because we do *business*." "Thank you, Mr. Hunter," she contritely offered.

"Here's what I want you to do *now* - and I know you'll do fine with it because it *requires* you to talk..." She listened acutely, intent on redeeming herself. "Whenever Michael wakes up, I want you to tell him that he has two options: he can fly first-class back to New York with $5,000 in his pocket *or* he can come and stay with me on my land. If he chooses the latter, I will never again offer him money that he does *not* have to *work* for, but he *will* have a home with me and a place in my kingdom. I want him to know that he's my friend, but I need him to grow up and act like a ***man*** to continue to be my *brother*." Helen had begun taking notes about halfway in, so I asked, "You got all that?" "Let's see..." she reviewed the notes. "First class and five thousand to New York or work on your land... no more money without work... he's your friend, but has to man up to be your brother." I was impressed at her shorthand skills. "Good work," I slapped a $100 on the desk. "Oh, *you*!" she chirped.

51

I stopped by the bank for a quick withdrawal and then headed over to pick up a pack's worth of supplies for Kyle's electrical setup. I figured if I could do nothing else, I could at least have his solar panels, lighting, and an outlet or two rigged up before sunset - barring any further setbacks. On my way back to camp, while riding around the Endless Wood (for the umpteenth time), I noticed a wild pig scurrying deeper into the trees as I approached. "Good," I told myself. "Hopefully there's a whole *drift* of them in there; you can never have too many sources of meat and hides for a kingdom!"

By the time I made it back to the camp, there was an old jeep parked outside of my cabin. "Well *that's* odd," I thought. "Especially considering there are no **roads** that lead onto my land!" It was true, and whatever thoughtless imbecile that *was* trespassing on my property had left muddy tracks through the light snow cover where the jeep had torn up the ground. I checked both my *and* Kyle's cabin before I thought to look out toward the build site for the culprit. I spotted a man dressed like a forest ranger and another man in a button up shirt, tie, glasses, and slacks talking *at* Kyle and Running Bear, pointing as one would when talking to dishonorable subordinates. "*Bureaucrats,*" I growled through gritted teeth.

Without even bothering to dismount, I grabbed my bear-hunting spear that was leaning against the cabin (as I had neglected to put it away from yesterday). I spurred Freedom down toward the men, and Kyle was the first to notice me. He ran to my horse's side, "Thank goodness you're here, Kai. These guys just came out of *nowhere* a little while ago, and..." "It's all right, Kyle. I'll handle this, but don't forget to do *your* thing while I do," I winked, signaling him to employ his magic skill while I dealt with the insolent intruders.

"Mr. Hunter, I presume," the man in the tie approached with a sneer.

"You presume a *lot*, don't you?" I shot back. "There are no roads onto my land because vehicles are not *welcome* here. And from the way I saw you talking to my men, I'd venture a guess that *neither are you*." The man was taken aback, probably because he was used to talking down to *others*, and not being talked down to *himself*. He adjusted his tie and pushed his glasses upward along the bridge of his nose, seeming to mentally collect his wits. "Yes, well... be that as it may, there seems to be..."

"You're not even going to *bother* introducing yourself, are you?" his condescension was quickly igniting my anger, and I led my horse closer to him as I spoke. "Who the fuck are *you* to come on *my* land uninvited, as if I should be **thankful** to have a little piss-ant *turd* like you tear up my ground with his jeep before being rude to me and my men?!?" He backed up, clearly as intimidated as I had intended to make him. Having been on the receiving end of this asshole's rudeness, Kyle and Running Bear were *clearly* enjoying this turn of events. With the last of his waning arrogance, he pulled a piece of paper from his shirt pocket and weakly pointed to it. "Look, I..."

I raised my spear in an instant, pointing it squarely at his chest. "Listen here, you duded up cur - you've got exactly *four seconds* to tell me who you are and why I shouldn't **run you through**!!" He dropped the paper, turned his face away and cowered, lifting his trembling arms in surrender. The man dressed like a ranger spoke up, approaching me carefully. "Whoa whoa whoa, Mr. Hunter! Please don't do anything rash. Ed didn't mean any harm... he's just not a... not a..." the fear was making him lose his vocabularic recall.

"People person?" I filled in the blank.

"Yes! That," the ranger began to recover, and took a deep breath. "Now, I'm Ranger Richard Crockett (although I'd prefer it if you called me 'Rick')... and the man at the end of your spear is Edward Ahgoh, the town Mayor." I glared at Edward. "Could you *please* stop pointing that at him, Mr. Hunter? I'm... I'm sorry about the jeep tracks; it's my jeep. We didn't know."

I pulled the spear back up to my side and Edward let out a sigh of relief. "All right, Rick. Now why are you two here?" Edward bent down to get the paper he dropped as Rick continued, "It's just that, well, I was out on patrol the other day when I spotted your tussle with that black bear from one of the park's peaks. I went to come down the mountain to speak to you *then*, but by the time I got there, you'd already gone." "*Really?*" I skeptically asked. "I was there a good *hour* or so making a sled stretcher out of trees I had to chop down in order to haul the bear away. You couldn't make the drive in that amount of time?" "Well, the roads toward your place run out about halfway down the peak, and I *walked* from there, but that's not really the point."

"Then *get* to it, Rick," I was losing my patience all over again. "The *point*..." Edward had regained his composure. "Is that you're not allowed to hunt wildlife in this county without a *license*, which Ranger Crockett here can attest that you've not applied for. And I can see (now that we're here) that you've put up several structures without stopping by the county seat to get the proper *building permits*, either. The citation I have here..."

"Let me get this straightly, Mayor Ed," I interrupted. "You want me to pay *you guys* for the privilege of hunting and building on *MY LAND*, and tore up the side of my mountain in your little fuckin' Jeep to come and charge me a *FEE* for not coming to that idiotic conclusion *beforehand*??" Ed tried the old stand-by: "But it's the *law*, Mr. Hunter!"

"*FUCK* your law, you greedy-ass, pencil-pushing bureaucrat! Laws like those were made by tiny little men like *you* who saw real men like *me* changing the world while they sat behind their cramped little desks, scheming on how they could get a piece of the money without having to put in a lick of the work! You and everything you stand for *disgust* me; now *get off my land* - and take your chicken-shit citation with you!" Realizing they were getting nowhere quickly, they trudged back toward their jeep dejectedly. Once he thought himself out of range, Ed shot back: "This isn't over, Hunter! You can't fight City Hall!" Without a second thought, I deftly launched my spear at him like a javelin and it pierced the ground between his feet. I roared with the gravel of manly defiance in my voice: "*TRY ME*."

52

My unwavering indomitability made the Mayor and his park Ranger lackey take off in their jeep with the kind of speed normally reserved for outrunning stampeding elephants, so I thought it sufficed to say that I'd made my point. The only real drawback was that it left a second, *deeper* set of tire tracks speeding away from the campsite to match the set they made when they arrived. I figured it was worth it.

Kyle and Running Bear left the work site, walking alongside my horse as I rode him back toward the main cabins. "That was quite an impressive throw, Kai!" "Thanks, Running Bear; I was aiming at his *nuts*, though." Kyle looked up at me, apalled. Running Bear just pointed and laughed that frat-boyish "*Ah!* You got me!"-laugh. "I'm so glad you get my kind of humor, Kai. Not everyone does," he admitted, with a hint of personal dissatisfaction with gentler comedy. "And who's to say *you're* not just getting *my* kind of humor?" I responded. "I *am* older than you by a couple of years, after all." "Touché," he grinned. "Besides, I could never argue with a mounted warrior with *that* kind of spear-throwing arm." Kyle broke in: "You guys *laugh*, but..."

"Pardon me, Kyle..." Running Bear continued. "But I just have to say that I've really never known anyone like you, Kai. Not even *Frank* has ever threatened the Mayor!" He went on, almost as an aside, "I mean, it's not like he *has* to - his son practically runs the town police force, and he's the richest man in these mountains - but they've always seemed like giants that would just stare one another down because they knew that they were equally matched." His revelation sent an involuntary chill down my spine, as I reached down to pluck my spear from the earth. "Did you say *evenly* matched?" He smiled and shook his head with the same amount of ignorant bliss as a child that'd just signed his "hero" Dad up for a charity cage match against Ken Shamrock.

Almost as if he heard the mental **gulp** I was thinking (Come to think of it, he probably *did!*), Kyle added: "That's not all, big brother. Ed's gonna..." He almost started saying outright what he had read in the Mayor's mind, but remembered that he was hiding his magic from

Running Bear. "I mean, *I heard* that the *last* time that someone threatened our Mayor Ed Ahgoh, he whipped the local huntsmen's club (of which he's a member) and the church (in which he's a *deacon*) into such a frenzy that they were ready to storm his house with a *lynch mob*!" Translating from Kyle's story that he had read Ed's mind to find that that was his *intent*, I was both aghast and impressed. "When was this?" Running Bear asked incredulously. "I've never heard anything like that." Yep; that was what Kyle read, all right. "Oh, it was over pretty quickly, man. You probably just didn't hear about it way up on the mountain because no one in town really talks about it after the *end* of it." I knew Kyle was leading me toward it, so I asked: "*What* end?" "Well apparently, Ed's plan from the beginning was to step in and be the 'cooler head' (as if he hadn't started it in the *first* place) and just propose that the mob instead *banish* the now-frightened man from town, after he'd put in a call to his cousin the *bank manager* to have a 'bank error' in the *entire town's* favor (that he and Ed would take the lion's share of, of course!)"

"That conniving son of a *bitch*!" I yelled. "***All** of that?*" "I know, *right*?" Kyle's eyes were wide, conveying the urgency of our preparation for the future throng.

"It's weird... you'd think I'd have heard of this," Running Bear shook his head.

"You couldn't have, Father," a female voice came from around the corner of my cabin. "Because it hasn't happened yet." Out stepped a beautiful young woman that I knew *had* to have been Flowering Bear Grass, with the kind of serene smile you'd expect someone to have that knew the future. "Forgive me for coming early, Father; my curiosity got the better of me again. I've been watching from beyond the trees since morning. I also should apologize for eating the lunch I packed for you, considering I meant for you to have it. When I saw you (and who I *thought* was the 'Mr. Hunter' you mentioned) eating fresh-smoked bear jerky, my stomach overwhelmed me and I ate."

He shook the cobwebs from his thoughts as he spoke: "You - you're forgiven, child, but... what do you mean 'it hasn't happened yet'?" I knew we were soon to be discovered, so I shot a look at Kyle that asked his permission to reveal him. He was reading *everyone's* mind at that point, so he nodded as nonchalantly as he could. "I owe you an apology as well, Running Bear. You've proclaimed your faithfulness to me and been an excellent working hand for as long as I've known you, but I chose to keep some things a secret from you about my advisor and me. Ultimately, it was *my* decision to do so... I... just didn't know how you would respond to knowing that we have... magics."

He looked as if I'd just said the most ridiculous sentence in the world. "*Me?* You wouldn't know how *I* would respond? The guy who told you about his daughter that can *see the fucking future*??" If I hadn't felt like a heel *before* that statement, I certainly did *after* it. I puffed out my lips as I exhaled, "**Pfffooo** Yeah. It's sounds even *stupider* now that I *really* think about it." Running Bear looked at me with the solemn, earnest eyes of a man three *times* his age and said, "You know, Mr. Hunter, I told you that my daughter saw greatness in you; and I've even seen some of that greatness for myself. But no man is an island, entire of himself... not even a King. I trust you enough to offer the gift of my *daughter* to you and to the virtues of your cause. I need to know that you can trust *me* enough to be in your *actual* inner circle of friends. I want to deal with you like a *brother*." He took a deep breath. "That is my peace."

I dismounted and grasped the man to myself. "I beg your forgiveness, brother of my spirit." I then moved backward, holding him by the shoulders. "I allowed my past dealings with lesser men to taint my vision of you, and it clouded my focus with undue distrust. You have indeed been loyal; I pledge to repay your loyalty in kind... *my brother*." He pulled me back in to a hug, slapping my back twice (*strongly*) with his large, working hands. "Let us speak no more of this," he spoke resolutely. "Mistakes are forgotten between brothers." "Agreed!" I consented.

"Um, guys...? Don't we have more *pressing* matters at hand?" Kyle broke up our conviviality. "True," Flowering Bear Grass concurred. "A mob shall be set against us tonight."

53

I quickly set my mind on defeating the imminent dangers that lay ahead, when the perfect idea (of how to stop a rabid mob) came to me: the *Amulet of the Forgotten*! I could set it in my cabin as an inner "keep" type of defense (as it was mentally crippling), which would make the campsite essentially impenetrable. As an "outer wall"/confusion tactic, I could attempt to wodemance a few acorns I'd bought into full-grown oaks (or at least saplings) along the path of the tracks that they would no doubt be trying to follow back to me. Hopefully, a few convenient patches of thorny brambles woven through those same trees would make vehicular progress nearly impossible, and make passage on foot treacherous. Lastly, considering I'd be dealing with small town hunters and members of a church willing to participate in a lynch mob, I was fairly certain that they'd be a religiously superstitious bunch. To that end, I planned to set a ladder up against the top of my cabin's roof and address them from it, ending an impassioned speech about the "judgment of gawd" coming down on them (and the Mayor) for their "unrighteousness".

In my past studies, I knew that the most prominent Christian example of Yahweh being on one's side was to set up an altar, dig a trench around it, cut up a bull to put on it, drench the whole thing in water, and then pyromance a conflagration from the sky to burn it all dry. "But..." I ruminated. "I'm not Elijah; so if I prepare all of that, it'll give away the fact that I knew they were coming, and I'm not ready to tip my hand like that." (That, and I really didn't see the point of wasting a *whole bull* for a silly show meant to sway religious zealots.) So, considering modern Christians often confuse the main judgment elements of Yahweh and Zeus (and considering I was better at Electromancy *anyway*), I decided my "show of supernatural favor" would be a lightning bolt or two. "*Then* we'll see who gets to act magnanimously, Mayor Ed!" I mused.

During the time I spent formulating a plan, Running Bear and Kyle went back and forth between themselves, trying to come up with possible defenses we might be able to employ, and generally disagreeing on the proper course of action. Flowering Bear Grass had been facing me, but her eyes had been fluttering millimeters above actually closing. I guessed (mentally) that perhaps she was looking into my personal future. Mere seconds later, she threw open her eyes and gasped as if she'd been confronted with a horrific ghost.

"What have you seen, my daughter?" Running Bear asked of her. Her gaze remained fixed on me - half in fear, half in awe. I wondered which one *I* was the cause of. "Your plan... the trees, the thorns, the necklace, the lightning... it all was working... but..." she looked as if she were delivering the worst news she'd ever given. "Go on," I urged her. "What happens?" She went on hesitantly: "You're shot in the heart from the darkness of the trees, far behind the mob crowd, over there." She pointed to a thick portion of woods to the northwest. "I saw the bullet exit through your back here," she pointed upward over her head to the southern edge of my cabin behind us. She'd definitely seen what I'd imagined, and the introduction of a sniper to the mix was a cunningly malevolent precaution on Edward's part.

I turned to Kyle, shocked that he hadn't mentioned such a thing. "What about the *sniper*, dude?" He stuttered, "I... I don't know, Kai. I guess he didn't think about it until *after* he left." I brought down my reaction intensity a few notches, as his explanation was entirely plausible.

"Wait... so you don't have the Sight?" Flowering Bear Grass asked Kyle. "You... read *minds*?" Her expression was such that I didn't know whether she was in awe of Kyle - or suddenly distrustful of him. I could tell that he didn't like the possibility that her tone may have been an accusatory one. "I never said I could see the future; why would you think that?"

"Okay, easy, you two. Full disclosure: we now know that you see people's futures, Kyle here can read minds, Running Bear is a master tracker, and my magics deal with the Elements. If anyone has *any* reservations about continuing..." "Hah. '*Reservations*'," Running Bear amusedly muttered to himself. I shook it off and continued: "...then I need to know *now*. Not a one of us will judge you. There will be dangerous people here tonight that are spoiling for a fight. If you aren't ready to lay down your lives for the freedom I fight for..." "Your *horse*?" Kyle interrupted, joining in with Running Bear's joking. "*No,* Kyle! I... *really? Now?* Could you just...?" I wasn't used to having my *Braveheart*-esque speeches cut short. Running Bear smiled and lay his hand on my shoulder. "Brother... we are with you. To the end." I looked to Kyle, who nodded his agreement, and then over to Flowering Bear Grass, who nodded as well.

"All right. Good," I said, determined. "Glad we've got that figured out. Flowering Bear Grass? Would I still get shot if I sent Kyle and Running Bear to guard that forest with their bows?" She faced me, her eyes fluttering for a few moments. "No, Mr. Hunter. You wouldn't. The mob would disperse after your lightning display." I had a dreadful thought: "What about Kyle and your Dad? What happens to them? Do they make it out all right?" She looked to her Father and read his immediate future as well. She told me what she saw while she foresaw it happening: "Father is the one that discovers the sniper... He draws his bow and tells him to put down the gun... Kyle comes up beside Father and draws his bow in support... The hunter looks up at them, and then goes to shoot anyway... Father looses an arrow that pierces his trigger hand, also - *Oh, nice **shot**, Father!* - jamming up behind the trigger... Kyle shoots an arrow..." She stopped to giggle. "...that shoots the sniper man in the butt!" "*Hey!*" Kyle protested. She continued, "By the time the man looks up, Father has notched another arrow aimed at his *head* at full draw! The man snaps the arrow shaft stuck in his trigger to release his hand and then puts both of his hands up in surrender... He reaches back to snap off the other shaft with his free hand... backs away slowly... and then takes off running, leaving his gun!" She opened her eyes, "You live; we win!!"

"Okay... one last check - does the future change because we now *know* it?" I had to be sure. She read me first and then her Dad again. "No, Mr. Hunter... we all still perform the same, thankfully." "Excellent," I concluded. "Well, I've got a lot of preparations to make. Kyle... Running Bear... you guys go ahead and do whatever you would have done to prepare. And remember, once the Amulet is in my cabin, give the whole campsite a *wiiide* berth. Let's go!"

54

I remounted Freedom, preparing to ride up to the cliff alcove, where I'd last put the Amulet of the Forgotten. Before I spurred my horse, Flowering Bear Grass put her hand on Freedom's neck and asked, "Mr. Hunter? Would it be okay if I came along with you?" I looked down at her and, with a tone of mild rebuke, asked: "Shouldn't you ask your *Father* first?" "*Oh!* I'm sorry," she realized her mistake. "I forgot myself." She turned to her Dad and asked, "Father? Would it be all right to accompany Mr. Hunter as he prepares?" her eyes begged him, as a daughter's eyes are wont to do. "If he says it's okay *and* if you don't get in the way, you may take my horse and ride along. I wasn't planning on using it to prepare anyway." She spun around, excited. "Well, Mr. Hunter? May I come along?" "Yes, you may," I answered. She jumped a bit, clapping her hands with glee. "And now that I've allowed it, I need you to check my future again and make sure that tonight *still* happens the way you saw before." I'd never been what you'd call a *careful* man, but one thing was for certain: *I didn't mess around when it came to my future.* She checked again (and was becoming quicker with the practice of doing so), and then opened her eyes. "Yes, sir! You still live!" "Awesome," I said decidedly. "Go ahead and saddle your Dad's horse and mount up! We've got a *lot* to do." I waved to Kyle and Running Bear, "Good luck, you guys... we'll be back in a little bit with the Amulet." They nodded their assent, and went to get their bows from inside my cabin where they'd left them.

Once Flowering Bear Grass was ready, I led the way as we rode up toward the cliff alcove. I warned her to stay back from where I was because the Amulet would disorient her, possibly making her forget where she was. She agreed without hesitation, as she had no reason to doubt me. After I recovered the Amulet from the alcove, I yelled out to her, "Go ahead and ride to the campsite before me! If Kyle or your Dad are still there, have them vacate to the site where we planned *your* cabin! They'll know where it is!" "Cool! Okay!" she yelled back.

I slipped the Amulet around my neck, musing that both Kongming *and* Shakespeare had, at one time, likely done the same. I rode back to the campsite at a languorous pace, giving the Native young woman enough time to carry out the fullest extent of my directions (and giving *me* enough time to fully think about the battle to come). When I arrived, the campsite was vacated. I carefully stashed the Amulet of the Forgotten under the bed with my family tome and the empty great crystal, covering them up with a fur blanket to make myself feel better about their security. Now that the inner "keep" was established, so to speak, I made my way down to the building site for Flowering Bear Grass' cabin. Once I arrived, I saw the young woman leaning forward in her Dad's saddle, watching Kyle and Running Bear taking turns firing practice shots into a wooden board that they'd covered in some leftover scraps of deer hide to make a target. Running Bear called his shot: "The dark-colored patch." It was the smallest of the strips of hide, with wider (lighter) strips on either side of it. He loosed his arrow and struck the dark patch - in the perfect center. "*Damn*, you're good!" Kyle was more complaining than complimenting. Running Bear good-naturedly slapped him on the back. "Don't feel badly, Kyle. At least you're hitting the *board* now!" Flowering Bear Grass snickered, but tried to hide it behind her hand.

"Good work, guys!" I reassured them. They all looked over their shoulders at me. "Now that we're all together again, I wanted to run something by you all that I was thinking about on the ride back here." "Okay, Kai... shoot!" Running Bear quipped. "Well, it's about our names. In all the war movies I've ever seen, when the heat of battle overtakes soldiers, they have short nicknames they can call each other to get help or attention from their comrades." They nodded and Kyle smiled in approval (He was already *ahead of me* - that mind-readin' so-and-so!). "So I was thinking... Kyle and I *already* have monosyllabic names that *we* could be called in such a situation; I was just hoping that you guys wouldn't mind going by R.B. and B.G. for just this one confrontation. Is that all right?"

"Hell, most of the other cattle hands occasionally call me R.B. *anyway*. I'm surprised it hasn't come up *before* now, to tell you the truth. You're more than welcome to call me that anytime you think my full name is too much of a mouthful, Kai. I don't mind." Running Bear then looked over at his daughter with what was likely his version of the

"Daddy Evil Eye" I mentioned before and told her, "You know, it's just a *courtesy* that Mr. Hunter is asking this of you. It would be improper not to comply." "Oh, I don't mind! It's always seemed to me like people felt more obligated (than anything) to call me by my whole name once they found out I'm of Native birth. B.G. will be a nice change of pace. I'd be happy to oblige you, Mr. Hunter!" she genuinely smiled. "Great!" I was relieved that they'd agreed, because my brain had been trying to talk me out of asking them, imagining for me the worst case scenario-type responses I was "definitely" going to receive. I *hate it* when my brain does that!

"So R.B., you and Kyle just keep on doing what you would've done anyway (Great shot, by the way!)..." "Thanks!" he grinned from ear to ear. "...and B.G. and I will head out so I can prepare some obstructions." I turned Freedom back toward the cabin and B.G. followed, making sure to stay outside of the Amulet radius I'd told her about. I got the Gambel Oak acorns (that I'd ordered online - hoping to *everything I loved* that they were viable) and then we followed the offending Jeep tracks down the mountain. A few hundred yards out from the campsite, the tracks cleared what was left of the treeline right before they zigzagged deep grooves into the open clearing. "That malicious **asshole**!" I couldn't help saying it - whether the tracks were a quick "Screw *you*, buddy!"-joyride or whether they served to easily mark in the snow how to return to the campsite, it was decidedly mean (considering the previous emphasis I'd put on their "tearing up the ground"). I knew that *there* was where I'd place the first five-acorn row.

As it turned out, wodemancing trees was *far* more psychically exhausting than growing sprouts from a spud. I'd liken it (mentally) to doing complex calculus, written as word problems... *in German*. Needless to say, it was helpful to have the encouraging cheers of B.G. there (I think I somehow recovered faster when she voiced her excitement!). After the trees were up, she handed me the section of goathead she'd plucked up during the ride here, and I made sure to shake out its seeds and wodemance them in *abundance* around my new oaks. I repeated the whole process a few more times around the area, and by the time the sun was setting, I was pretty exhausted. The job of obstruction done, we directed our horses back toward camp.

55

We passed the main campsite and headed down to where Kyle and R.B. had been practicing their archery. Apparently, at some point, R.B. had stopped removing his arrows from the target plank, because there was a cluster of five arrows shot in almost exactly the same spot on the darker hide area. There were two arrows at random in the lighter-hided areas, which I assumed were Kyle's. They both were sitting down at the edge of the cabin flooring they'd previously finished and watching what appeared to be a skinned deer roast over a makeshift fire pit they'd made from creek stones, a couple of Y shaped branches, and a long branch for a skewer. "That could probably use a turn, brother," R.B. told Kyle right before we came into the fire-light. "All right, all right..." Kyle grumbled as he got up to turn the meat.

"Let me help you with that," I rode into view and dismounted. "*Brother!!*" they cheered in unison at my arrival. I was happy that they were as comfortable as I was in making the inner circle of my future kingdom into a brotherhood. *The Prince* would tell us that it is "safer to be feared than loved", but for as much trouble as it generally is to retain the affections of a capricious populace, I think I'll always prefer the latter. "We knew you'd probably be hungry after all the magic you had to do, so we wanted to make sure there was food roasting when you got back!" Kyle exuberantly reported. "What's all this *we* stuff? *I* shot the deer!" R.B. balked. "Yeah, well *I* made the fire pit!" Kyle shot back. "*Easy*, brothers," I calmed them. "I thank you *both* for your efforts to prepare this fine meal. Let's just enjoy it and be glad of our future victories, okay?" I could see them mentally shake off the frustrations of the day in a single nod. I walked to the side of Running Bear's horse to offer my hand to Flowering Bear Grass to assist her in dismounting. She was surprised at the attention, but not offended (like most *western* women generally are at shows of gentlemanly courtesy). "Why *thank* you, kind sir!" she graciously accepted my assistance.

"Even a king can stoop to help a mere woman, ay brother?" R.B. laughed. "Don't ruin this, you clod!" I replied as she got down. "A real man should have no compunctions about offering his assistance to the weaker sex... *especially* when she has proven herself to be a *lady*." I gestured at B.G., and she pantomimed a curtsy to humorously "prove" my point. "Ladies are *rare* nowadays, brother, and they are to be recognized and appreciated in my kingdom to come." He uttered that half-groan that people do when they're "on the fence" in regard to a particular subject, so I went to pull him *completely* over to my side. "It doesn't mean that they will be allowed to undermine or supplant the natural authority of the *men*, but every real lady knows not to do that *already*, doesn't she?" "Yeah... I suppose you're right," he conceded. It was a small victory, but if Running Bear had any lingering experiential or cultural biases that would cause him to underappreciate the proper role of ladies in my future kingdom, I hoped to fully convince him over time. Like retaining the favor of a fickle populace, promoting the recognition and valuing of ladies seemed (to me) to be a delicate balance. Prize them too *highly*, and they become high-minded - thinking they *naturally* deserve things that are generally **earned** (like respect or wealth); prize them too *little*, and they become the subjects of derision.

We all enjoyed the fine meal of roasted deer meat, eating our fills in preparation for battle. The company and feasting renewed my spirit, and I felt relaxed and ready to showboat a little magic. Once we were all done eating, I took the leftover meat up to my cabin's freezer while everyone else washed their hands in the creek. By the time I got back, they had properly doused the fire coals and were ready for the next step. I had Flowering Bear Grass read my future quickly as a last-minute precaution (and to see about how long we had to prepare). She assured me that I still avoided being shot, and that the mob would arrive within the hour. I directed Kyle and Running Bear up to the northwestern woods (that B.G. had originally identified as the hideout of the sniper) to silently patrol them. They hastily agreed and were off. I told B.G. that she would be "safer hiding back here" at her future cabin's site, and gave her the blanket I had tied up behind my saddle for extra warmth. She tucked herself away behind a particularly wide red cedar, and I led Freedom and R.B.'s horse back up toward the campsite.

It seemed like I was waiting **forever** (once I'd gotten to the top of my roof and cleared away a thin layer of snow to have a decent waiting seat) for the lynch mob. That's the thing about lynch mobs -

they're *not at all* courteous. I took the time while I was waiting to behold the clear, starry mountain sky and meditated on how truly infinitesimal we are in the world... let *alone* the universe (or, to an even more grandiose scale, among **all** *the universes*)! You had to give the nihilists their due: on a relative scale, life is pretty pointless.

It wasn't long thereafter that I began to see the flashlights of a good dozen or more men thrashing through the woods west of the campsite. When I knew that they were close enough to see me (but far enough away to be outside the circle of influence of the Amulet), I stood up on the roof, wodemancing my wooden shingles to wrap around my feet, anchoring me well so that I didn't slip. "*STOP!*" I yelled out. "You are all *trespassing* on private property! **Leave** *at once!*" They could see that I was unarmed and laughed in unison. I heard the cocking of several rifles and shotguns they used to make a point of their superior firepower. I heard a random redneck shout, "We don' **need** yer permishun to be on our mountins, ya uppity city slicker!" "*Yeah!*" another agreed. "These here mountins are a gift frum **Gawd**!"

"Oh, I think you'll find that God wants **me** to have this land now!" I called out. "What do you say, God?" I cast my gaze skyward. "That's *blasphemy*!" cried a voice that I immediately recognized as Mayor Ed's. "**Is** *it, Ahgoh?* Or is it more heretical to lord oneself over a people too weak-minded to question your authority?" I countered. "Let's let God decide!" I roared as I pointed toward the night sky for dramatic effect. The lightning was not immediate, but the gathering of the clouds that blotted out the full moon *was*. I could see every armed man there gaping in awe at the sudden skyward change. I electromanced four thin bolts from the clouds in rapid succession along the ground in front of the mob, to deafening effect. Some stood staring at the smoldering holes before them; some just dropped their guns and flashlights and *ran*. I even heard one old guy yell out, "Gawd's pissed! Let's git outta here!" I aeromanced the clouds away enough to see Ed standing in the moonlight, livid, among the last men to retreat. It was obvious that he was waiting for the sniper's shot, but when it didn't happen, he silently skulked away.

56

I watched as the last of the flashlights disappeared over the furthest hill, and then wodemanced the wooden shingles back to normal, almost collapsing off of my roof with fatigue. It turns out psychically taxing activities (much like mental ones) are also *physically* taxing after a certain point. I made my way down my ladder, as weak-kneed as a weight lifter that had spent all day doing squats. I took the Amulet out from beneath my bed and spurred Freedom quickly toward the northern cliff, so that (once I'd returned it to the alcove) everyone would be able to stay in the campsite that night. After I got back to camp, I dragged my wooden chair out from my cabin to be near the fire pit. As I slumped down into it, Kyle and Running Bear returned to camp. "Great job, you guys," I faintly commended them. "Thanks, brother!" R.B. replied. "What should we do now?" Kyle asked.

All I really wanted to do was relax by a nice fire for a while, but directions were needed. "Okay... R.B.? Could you throw a few logs in the pit there; make us a decent fire?" "You got it, boss!" he shot me a two-finger salute. "Kyle, could you just go and get B.G.? She's down by her cabin site, hiding behind a red cedar." "Right away, *your majesty*!" Kyle definitely one-upped Running Bear's title with that one, but I was too tired to praise him. "And make sure you announce yourself, okay? I don't want her thinking one of those men from the mob got past us." "Good thinking, sire." "*All* right, all right... go on, *your prominence*," I jeered. He chuckled and headed down to bring back Flowering Bear Grass. It wasn't long before R.B. had stacked an impressive pile of logs in the campsite fire pit. I attempted to pyromance a small fireball to start the fire, but was weakened and could only manage a few flashes of flame.

Running Bear saw my predicament and pushed me gently backward in my chair. "Don't worry, Kai - I've got this." He produced a flare from his horse's saddlebag, struck it to light it up, and then placed it in the base of the fire pit. Within seconds, we had a tall, roaring fire. "So I guess all the balls of 'spirit light' around the fire the other night was you all along, huh brother?" "Yeah. Sorry again about not being up front with you about that," I apologized. "Oh no worries,

Kai. I'm just glad I'm on *your* team, you know? Mayor Ed's guys just looked like a bunch of scattering *roaches* when faced with the magic *you* were doling out tonight!" "Heh heh," I weakly laughed, feeling more physically drained than I'd ever been. "Incidentally, if you ever shake hands with a bearded White guy and he draws back from your grip in pain, swat him on his left butt cheek. If he howls at *that*, I'd say you're well within your rights to *kill* that asshole." I assumed he was referring to the sniper he'd no doubt shot in the hand (and Kyle had shot in the ass) during the fracas, and his subsequent miming of an arrow going into his right hand confirmed it.

Kyle and B.G. stepped forward into the light of the fire, and circled it to take seats on the wooden bench I'd carved out of a log on the other side. "So... everything went well, then?" B.G. inquired. "Hell, you should be the *least* surprised about that, daughter!" R.B. bellowed. "I know; I just like hearing it," she grinned as she reached out toward the fire. "*Mmmmm!* This is so nice and warm!" "Your Dad made it," I gave credit where it was due. "Thanks, Daddy!" she got up and hugged him. "You're welcome, baby girl." She turned toward me. "May I get some of the deer meat from your cabin for us, Mr. Hunter?" "Sure; that would be nice," I could feel my eyelids relaxing.

Before I knew it, she was pressing a roasting stick into my hand that had a generous hunk of meat on it. "Here... so you can warm it back up!" her cheerfulness was light and refreshing. "Thanks, B.G." "No problem, Mr. Hunter!" The warmth of the fire, the smells of the burning red cedar and the roasting savory meats, and the relaxed conversations of my compatriots were so serene that had we not personally experienced what we just *had* been through, you'd think nothing had happened at all. I fought with the very last of my strength to retain consciousness long enough to have B.G. read our futures again to let us know that we were out of harm's way for the night. And indeed we were.

The next morning, I awoke in my own bed though I seemed to remember falling asleep by the fire. Kyle recounted how he and Running Bear had borne me inside and put me to bed. They had given Flowering Bear Grass all the biggest blankets and had her sleep in

Kyle's mostly finished cabin, and then after bringing some fire inside there for her, they had done the same for themselves in my cabin, getting as comfortable as they could on my wooden floor. "That was nice of you guys; thanks!" "No problem, brother," Running Bear said. Kyle was busy frying up a heap of bacon and eggs over my wood stove, and the smell of it was absolutely revitalizing (even though I was still noticeably a bit "psychically sore"). As I put my feet over the side of the bed and stretched to greet the morning, there was a knock at the door. "Is it all right if I come in?" we could hear Flowering Bear Grass (who was apparently also now up) on the other side. Running Bear looked to me for approval, and I nodded. "Sure; come on in, sweetheart," R.B. revealed his softer morning side.

Over a delicious breakfast, I revealed a plan that I'd come up with to keep the kingdom from having to suffer any further assaults. Each day, B.G. would read our individual futures, ensuring that we would be out of harm's way. Kyle would accompany me on any future trips into town so that I could always tell if anyone we met was planning any further mischief. And finally, I would have to primarily focus on "working out" my magics on a daily basis in order to push them to their maximum capacities (perhaps even mastering the entirety of the Elemental school of the Art). Kyle and B.G. pledged themselves to the same goal, and Running Bear said that he would continue to do all that he could. I felt sorry for him because he didn't possess a magic as well. I would later learn of *every* individual's capacity for the Art; but at the time, I hadn't read far enough in the tome to have discovered such a thing. Kyle, R.B., and B.G. committed themselves for the rest of the day to attempting to finish B.G.'s cabin, and I decided (even in my half-weakened state, thanks to B.G.'s future assurance of safety) to head out a ways from camp and push my magics a bit more than maybe I would've felt comfortable with otherwise. I wodemanced a small wall of intertwined fir saplings, merely to see if such a thing were possible. Just as I began fully enjoying the task, nearby I heard: "*Malachi??*"

57

It was Michael. He'd come around the end of the tree wall where I'd begun. "What the... what the *hell* are you doing, man?" He had yet to find out that I had magic, and would probably be none too happy to discover that he was the *fourth* to know. "I heard some old drunk in town at the Hoof talking about how some man in the mountains had the lightning of *God* on his side and how he was gonna 'up and move outta this crazy town', and when I asked who he meant, he named *you*. What the hell *happened* here last night, dude? Don't tell me I walked about a fuckin' mile (after the cab driver was too scared to take me any further) just to find out that these damn mountains have turned my best friend of five years into some kind of *wizard*!"

I honestly didn't know what to say to him. Admittedly, I had been considering the very real possibility (for quite some time) that Michael was a genuinely lost cause. How could I *possibly* explain to him that my modern life had turned into some kind of Tolkien on the Ponderosa? "Bro..."

"Don't give me that shit, Malachi! You haven't thought of me as your '*bro*' for quite some time now!" Now that he was mostly sober, his thoughts came a lot more fluidly. "And what's this bullshit Helen told me this morning? Some crap about wanting me as some fuckin' *hired hand* (just so I can keep being your 'brother') or else you'll fly me out of town with a wad of cash? You've got *some damn nerve*, dude!" I could've sworn I worded it more eloquently than that, but I figured the spirit of it was lost in translation.

"Michael... just *listen* to me, all right?" His eyes darted all around as he took a deep breath. "Fine, Kai. *What?*" "We *have* been friends for over five years now. And when I was in New York, that was more *your* scene. But I was *your* wingman then, so we hung out where *you* generally wanted to be. *Admit it!*" "All right, fine. *So what?*"

"Well here in these mountains is *my* scene. This is where I feel *I* belong - where Destiny herself seems to whisper my name on the

wind." He was obviously not sharing my elation for nature. "*And?*"
"It's just that... well... I guess I expected you to be my wingman out
here. Not in some scuzzy bar or some loud club, but somewhere that
makes *me* happy. I thought that *maybe* we were close enough friends
that I could ask for some reciprocity in the friendship, that's all."

"Really? *That's* what all that shit was about?" his flippant,
condescending attitude was starting to grate on my nerves. "Look,
Michael - I don't know what you thought it would be out here. I didn't
fly us out here because I wanted NYC two-point-oh; I did it because
this life..." I pointed all around me with both hands. "...calls to me. I
thought we were good enough friends that you'd *understand* that, and
not just expect me to be your personal ATM-slash-free-ride meal ticket
in some wacky new locale!" "*Pffft!* Whatever." He, like most
Manhattanites, defaulted to feigned apathy when he was clearly in the
logical wrong. It was pretty irritating.

"You know, Michael, I didn't tell Helen to relay all that stuff
to you because I was hoping to *piss you off.* I really, sincerely wanted
to offer you a place in the new life and kingdom that I'm making here."
He rolled his eyes and crossed his arms. I didn't care; I was slogging
on until I'd made my point. "*I'm serious!* I want this to be a genuine
kingdom of truth and justice the likes of which there hardly *is* anymore.
I want a brotherhood citizenry that rules *itself* so that it hardly has any
need of further ruling. I want a place where peace can thrive because
man lives *with* nature, and not because he treads it underfoot." "*Really*,
Gandhi?"

"Yes *really*, jackass!" I was **done** with his sarcasm. "But this
kingdom won't be built by *money*. It'll be built with trust and
understanding and loyalty and *hard work*... and that's never really been
your thing, has it? Work." "Maybe not," I could tell I'd struck a nerve
with him. "Maybe my upper middle class family raised me to *enjoy* life
rather than just trudge my way through it... or **maybe** I party so hard
because at the end of the day, there's nothing left *to* life if I don't! I
don't *have* millions of dollars like you or even hundreds of *thousands*
like my cheap-ass Dad, who says he won't leave me any in his will! All
I have is liquor and sluts and a head full of crazy memories - and I don't

see how living like Maria von fuckin' *Trapp* is supposed to make life any better than that!"

"But don't you *see*, Michael? Life really *is* about more than that!" I gave reason one last try. "You're right," he said with a placid evil on his face. "Apparently, life is also about *magic* - like what I saw you doing with these trees, or what that not-so-crazy old drunk in town was talking about you doing last night. And I know what that kind of information is worth, '*brother*'. So I'm not leaving on a first class flight with some chump $5,000 consolation prize... *oh no*. You'll send me out of here first class with a *hundred* thousand dollars or I'll go back to New York and have the slimiest paparazzis out here crawling so far up your ass, every wrinkle of your colon will be front page news from here to *eternity*." I never imagined that such unmitigated, avaricious *gall* lived inside a man who would have ever *dared* to call himself my "friend", but when he flipped the script on me like that? *All bets were off*.

In less than a second, I had wodemanced thick fir trunks around his legs like wooden candy canes, planting him to the spot. "What the... *what the fuck??* **What are you doing?!?**" he panicked, struggling to free himself. "Now here's what I don't understand, Michael," I walked slowly and deliberately toward him. "I offered you a place at my side. You didn't want it? Fine; I wasn't gonna *make* you take it. Then you heard about and then *saw* me performing magic the likes of which you've seen abso-fucking-lutely *NO ONE* ever do in your *entire* lifetime, and you have the *balls* to think you can extort *ME*??" I cycled through elemental energies in my open hand to drive home the point, stopping on a sizable ball of searing blue flame. His eyes were wide with fear, his mouth agape in silent horror. "I gave you every chance to be as good of a friend to me as I *always* was to you, and you not only spit on that opportunity, but you want to *threaten* me like an *enemy*? Oh, you're *going* back to New York... but not with *one fucking penny* of my money. And if I hear that you've mentioned my magic to *anyone*, I will find you and burn your ungrateful carcass to drunken *cinders*!"

58

Michael had to have known I meant business, as I'm *positive* that he'd never seen me that angry before. And although it hurt me to have to speak so harshly to a man I'd been friends with for so long (prior), I couldn't afford to let him jeopardize the dream - this utopian society that I was building with the help of so many like-minded new friends. I didn't want to become the "villain" that threatens people in order to get things done, but he'd backed me into a corner... and even the most *docile* of beasts will bare their claws in such situations!

I left him planted into the ground while I walked over to Freedom, whom I'd tied up near the *original* treeline. I pulled all $700 of the money I had in my saddlebag out and brought it back to Michael, who was struggling against his wooden leg restraints. "Now here's seven hundred dollars," I slapped the money in his hand. "That's plenty enough money to get you back to New York and into the homes of any other family or friends you still haven't somehow alienated. If you're as clever as you *think* you are, you'll put me and this town to your rudder and never give *either* of us another waking thought." I wodemanced the fir trunks back into the ground, freeing him. He stumbled backward - silent - utterly flabbergasted at what had just happened.

We both turned to go our separate ways, but I looked back over my shoulder at Michael. "It didn't *have* to be this way, you know. But I'm a different person now; people really *count* on me. I just can't abide anyone that would threaten what I... what *we're* building here." I watched as his head dropped in regret. "Maybe we can find each other in *another* life," I whispered as he trudged back down the mountain. "But I think our time in *this* one is at an end."

I continued wodemancing the twisted wall of fir saplings for a while, but my heart just wasn't in it anymore. No one ever likes losing a friend, but there just comes some times in life when you realize that you're headed in two different directions and you have to let one go. Ships can't head in opposite ways at once if their refueling or mooring lines still bind them together. I just wished that I knew some kind of magic that could heal the wound left behind by a disingenuous friend.

After building and practicing our magics for days, our next visitor arrived in camp. It was Frank, and his look was not a reassuring one. He asked if he could speak with me alone, which invitation I accepted (after a "The future is fine."-nod from Flowering Bear Grass that we'd practiced for situations like these). Considering he was mounted, I saddled Freedom and rode out with him toward the foothills between our lands.

There was more than a comfortable amount of silence that passed between us, even given the crisp, clear weather and warm breeze. "You look troubled, Frank. What's on your mind?" "Well Malachi, I always like to warn my friends when trouble's a-brewin', but from what I heard, your situation is likely to put me square in the middle of a fence that I've got no mind to straddle. You see, my boy - that I hear you've met - has been given orders by the Mayor himself to come up in these mountains and arrest you by any means necessary. From what I understand, they're some trumped-up charges, but that don't rightly matter up here. Now, my boy knows we're friends, so he asked me if I'd come to you man-to-man and see if you wouldn't come into town *peaceable* so there wouldn't be any ruckus. I honestly think you're a good man, Malachi, so I doubt any of these charges would stick..." at this, he turned in his saddle to look me squarely in the eyes. "...but I also know what a *horse's ass* that Mr. Ed in town is, and I heard about the lynch mob he stirred up against you a while ago. Hell, he'd ride in here in a *tank* if it wasn't for him bein' a deacon and the word spreadin' through town like wildfire that you've got *God* on your side or somethin'."

"Heh heh," he clapped me on the shoulder. "I don't know how you pulled *that* one off, but I sure wish I coulda been there to see it." "Me too, Frank. Me too," I smiled warmly. "So let me ask you, then... what do *you* think I should do? I don't want to put your son in harm's way or risk having him lose his job just because Mayor Ed's got a wild hair up his ass for me." "I really wish I could tell ya, Malachi. Sometimes, there just ain't an easy solution for everything, but I'm sure if you think on it hard enough, you'll come up with somethin'." I pulled at the beard I'd begun growing, trying to come up with something apropos. "Any chance your son would give up his position as a

Deputy? Come work for *me*, maybe?" "Couldn't tell you - I only know he's right happy with what he's got there, and never really took a likin' to the mountain life that you and I love. Not to mention that if he left that post, Ed would probably fill it with some goon of *his* choosin', and then you wouldn't even have the *option* of a nice talk like this." "Yeah, I guess you're right. *Damn.*"

"Needless to say, if the bank in town is where you're still keepin' your money - with that warrant out for your arrest, you might as well be broke. 'Cuz there ain't any way you can walk *or* ride into town and get your money with that jackass's cousin bein' the bank manager." "*Shit,*" I thought to myself. I'd forgotten all about *that* little tidbit. My entire fortune *was* currently sitting in the town bank... the only accessible bank for many miles around these parts. And who knew *where* the town's post office's loyalties lay! My relative societal isolationism was to be put to the test *far* sooner than I had anticipated... and it was unsettling. I had planned (later) to put a million or two of my winnings into buying foreign gold (that the U.S. would [I'd *hope*] have no problem with me melting down in order to make a kingdom currency standard), but without access to a bank to facilitate the transaction (or a post office to deliver the treasure thereof), I was indeed up a fecal-themed creek without access to rowing equipment.

"What I need is a way to *depose* that tyrant!" I deliberated. "Without all the flak Ed's generating, I doubt this 'cousin' I've never even met would have the *balls* to oppose me on his own!" "That's probably true - he *is* kind of a *tiny* little man. But how do you reckon on keepin' my son out of the crossfire?" "You leave that to me, Frank," I told him. "I promise to do my *damnedest* to make sure your Deputy son ends up both blameless and unharmed." "I trust your word on that, friend. So should I send my son up to meet you?" "Not just yet, Frank," I grinned. "I'm planning a trip into town."

59

Frank and I parted ways and I rode quickly back to camp. Kyle and B.G. met me excitedly as I rode up and dismounted. They were eager to tell me of the advances they'd achieved since I'd instituted the regimen of daily magic practice several days ago. "I can see *two whole days* into the future now!" B.G. exulted. "Yeah; and I can read two people's minds at the same time now!" Kyle joined in. "Excellent, excellent work you two." I looked up to see Running Bear poking at the coals burning beneath a fresh kill he had roasting over the fire pit. "I still just shoot things with my bow," he said dejectedly. "*Hey* - we *all* need to eat!" I tried to encourage him. "I don't know what we'd *do* without your hunting skills!" "I know - it's just that since we finished building my daughter's cabin the other day, I've felt a little useless." I could *tell* he was a bit depressed. "Well I don't want you to feel *that* way, brother. Do you think you might feel better going back with the cattle hands for a few days?" "I don't want you to have to stop all *your* magic stuff because you've lost your main hunter, so you have to personally replace him," he reasoned.

"I don't think you'll have to worry about that, R.B. We might *all* have to put our magic on hold for a little while after what Frank just told me." "*Oh yeah!*" Kyle thought back. "I remember when he rode up that I was busy trying to read Running Bear and B.G. at the same time, so I didn't do him. Is it bad?" "Well, *it ain't good.* Apparently, scaring Mayor Ed and his gun-totin' church flunkies off the other day was just the *beginning* of our problems. Ahgoh has convinced the Sheriff to put out a warrant for my arrest on false charges." B.G. gasped. "*What?!?*" R.B. roared. "No!" Kyle yawped.

"Yep... and if the Sheriff wasn't so lazy that he gave pretty much *all* of his leg-work to Deputy Meyer, I might not have heard about it until he was knocking on my door." "But I don't get it - I would've been able to warn you!" B.G. pouted. "Don't look so wounded, B.G. I've had no prior beef with the good Deputy, so since you're mainly on the lookout for when one of us is *killed*, a trip into town with him might've slipped under your radar." She crossed her arms and looked off to the side, "I still would've *told* you." "That's good to know, because I told Frank (who I'm guessing will pass it along to his son) that I'm planning on going into town of my own volition. But much like how Nic Cage was able to save that chick at the end of *Next*, we're gonna need to spend all night (probably) going over the scenarios that allow me to walk into town tomorrow and then walk back *out* of town without getting shot, beaten, blind-sided, or (most importantly) incarcerated." I looked over to Kyle and Running Bear. "I'm gonna need the recommendations of my Advisor and my chief stealth expert as well. Are you guys up for it?"

"*YES!*" R.B. shouted, as he stood and struck the air with his fist. I think it was fair to say that he was feeling like a useful part of the team again. "Absolutely," Kyle answered with a fire in his eyes that I could tell was more than the mere reflection of the campfire. I turned back to Flowering Bear Grass. "Well, B.G.? You want to help me instigate a little mayhem for the cause of truth, justice, and our kingdom's way?" She flashed me a devilish grin, "*Hell yeah.*"

About an hour later, we were all in my cabin enjoying an inside fire and splitting the succulent meat that Running Bear had caught for us. I would adopt a plan, have B.G. read my future to the point of the plan failing, and then have Kyle and R.B. advise me on how to possibly improve the plan, before I'd decide on something new - starting the *whole* cycle over again.

"Okay, so I can't ride straight into town or else some gun club whack-job will overreact and shoot me." "Right," B.G. agreed. "And after I tied Freedom up outside town and circled around behind the hotel, Helen saw me through her window while she was on the phone, and then somehow the *whole town* knew." "Yep." "When I sent you around front of the hotel to distract her until I passed by, I was fine until I crossed the gap between the hotel and the shopping center." "Different gun nut; yeah." "So once I quickened my pace and wodemanced some tall cover shrubbery in the gap, I was fine until I crashed into the guy carrying the trash out of the back of the pizza place." "Mmm-hmm!" "If I quicken my pace even *more*, I end up coming out from behind the shopping center in full view of some shrieking church biddy, and if I slow it up so I don't crash *into* the guy, he ends up trying to *talk* to me and his manager (also gun club) comes out and catches me." Kyle exhaled a heavy sigh. "That town is a damn *minefield*!"

"Yeah, no kidding," R.B. concurred. "All right - how about I metamance the pizza place door lock until it's melted into an immovable solid? That could work, right?" "Let's see..." B.G. read my future quickly. "Yes! That works, and you're able to pass unseen behind the Post Office, but then there's a big gap between there and the main municipal building at the end of the street. You try to run for it, but Deputy Meyer spots you as he's coming out of the front. Let's see... *yep*. Jail." "I didn't talk my way out of it?" I asked, incredulously. "No - can't jeopardize losing what little money he makes... standing in the community... doesn't want to lose his house 'cuz of his wife and kid... blah, blah, blah. You get the picture." "*Damn*."

We went on like that for *hours* more, until I found the best way to enter town, make it to the Mayor, get him alone, threaten him with something perfect enough to have him call the Sheriff and rescind the warrant (without raising suspicions), leave him brooding for long enough to head to the bank and personally authorize a wire transfer of *all* of my fortune to purchase gold bricks from an online company that I arranged (beforehand) to pay *an entire brick* to deliver the rest of the gold to me on my land at specific mountain coordinates by *helicopter*, aeromance a dirt cloud as cover in the street when Ed finally changes his mind and sends men out after me, meet B.G. back where I'd tied up Freedom, and then pyromance an impressive wall of flame to cover our escape and deter vigilantes from following us. It sounds complicated, but by the time we'd worked it out to where we all *lived*, no one followed us, and everything went perfectly, we'd practiced it enough to perform it on *Broadway*. The next day, it all went off without a hitch, I arrived back on my land with the guaranteed delivery of the remainder of my fortune (in 99.99% pure *gold*, no less!), and managed to keep my promise to Frank as well that I wouldn't jeopardize his son's life or career. All in all, it was pretty fantastic. The best part of all was that *now* if Mayor Ed wanted to come for me, the only foot soldiers he could *possibly* recruit would be from an entire intimidated **town** that knew the kind of magics that I was capable of.

60

It wasn't until days later, when my 585 kilograms of gold bars was airlifted onto my property that I fully respected how wealthy I indeed was. When you have over half a *ton* of gold delivered to you almost as readily as a pizza, you get a whole new respect for who you are as an individual. I had done the math, too... that 585 kilograms would break down into over 18,800 troy ounces of gold once I'd forged a smelter and mint from surrounding iron deposits I'd found using my Erdemancy magic. Each newly-minted troy ounce gold coin (worth around $1,300 when I researched it) would be a month's wages in my new kingdom. So basically, I could easily pay the monthly wages of 15 worker citizens for *over a hundred years*. I wanted to somehow also ensure the money would be spent *in* my new kingdom so that all the gold didn't just naturally re-disperse itself all over the globe. I figured that there would always be things that people would prefer to *barter* for, and hoped that the money would just serve to mitigate any trades in which one party had more value (gold) than goods with which to trade. It wasn't a *perfect* system, but in my defense, the last real time I was thinking of it was way back when Michael was still in town and I hadn't discovered my own magical potential. To be perfectly honest, I'd *first* had thoughts of making gold currency as far back as NYC, though I hadn't even *begun* to work out the details until some of the more inactive times I enjoyed once I got to the mountains.

After I'd used my cabin's laptop to Skype the video proof of payment to the delivery liaison at the gold distributorship (somehow keeping from chortling when I broke open one of the crates to hand the stunned helo pilot a gold bar from the treasure stash that he *obviously* had no idea he was carrying), we all began unloading the bars until they were all properly stacked inside the cliff alcove (from which I'd previously moved the Amulet). Once we were done the surprisingly easy yet novel task, I did what Mo-Quau-Pauw only made it *appear* that he had done all those many years ago: erdemanced a giant slab of solid stone up from the earth at our feet to cover the entrance to the alcove. It displaced quite a bit of soil in the process, but I was able to balance the shifting until everything settled back into a nice round hill... onto which I had to wodemance some grasses, so that it wouldn't look like a huge mound of tilled-up dirt. Kyle (along with the others) was dazzled with the amount of power I now commanded, but complained after I was done: "*Awww!* I thought you were gonna leave it out so we could look at it! I've never even *seen* gold up close before, and now it's all encased in solid rock!" "No, he did the right thing, brother," R.B. admonished him. "Now none of us will be tempted to steal the gold and it's completely safe from all those jerks in town who probably *know* we have it, if the Mayor's cousin is as 'trustworthy' as his kin." "Yeah," B.G. added. "And you saw how easily Mr. Hunter raised that stone from the earth! I'll bet you he could push it back down *just* as easily."

"I know..." Kyle sulked. "I just wanted to look at it some more." I laughed and put my arm around his shoulder. "Don't worry, brother! You'll see it again. Remember, once the smelter and mint are up and running, you'll be being *paid* in that same shiny gold."

He seemed to take comfort in that fact, so we all went ahead and walked back to camp. As we walked, it became apparent that Running Bear had something on his mind. "Do you care if I ask what might seem like a silly question, brother?" "Of course not," I replied. "Go right ahead." "Well, I've heard you mention a kingdom more than once (and, trust me, I *believe* you can build one), but why are you still living in wooden cabins? Didn't you plan on making stone castles and what-not?" "Of *course*, R.B.! In fact, two dozen stone masons are set to arrive here in late June to begin the official work. I'm surprised I hadn't mentioned that." "You told *me!*" Kyle piped up. R.B. raised an eyebrow. "It was probably just that I was closer to having *just* planned that when I first met Kyle here, and all this craziness around here lately has kept my mind *elsewhere*... but yeah, it's set to begin next month."

"That's cool, I guess. What are you gonna name it? Every great kingdom should have a great *name*, right?" I stopped dead in my tracks, as stunned as when I heard that Ben Affleck had won an Oscar for - oh - *anything*. I couldn't believe, with all the detailed thought that I'd put into the construction, economy, and governance of my future kingdom, that I had failed to yet think of a *name* for it. "Would you like me to read ahead and see what we decide on?" B.G. offered. "*Don't you dare!!*" I snapped at her. "Sorry... I just don't want to spoil

the process." "Okay; my bad." "No, you're fine. Thanks for the offer."
I stood stroking my beard for a minute. "Well, what do you *want* to
name it?" Kyle asked. "I don't know," I pensively stared toward camp.
"I'll tell you the first name that popped into my *head*, though."
"What?" they all asked in unison. "*Shadowgate!*" I parted my hands in
front of me as if I were spreading a paper marquee in the air. "Wasn't
that the name of a kick-ass, medieval-themed NES adventure/puzzle
game from back in the day?" B.G. revealed a surprising nugget about
her that I would never have guessed. "Okay... A) You're all of what...
17? How do *you* know about old-school 'cart's? and B) ...It *was*?"
"Yes, it was, Mr. Hunter. And I'll have you know that I'm *quite* the
retro gamer. Where did you think I lived before here... *a tee-pee?*" To
be honest, the public school system and TV shows I was raised on had
taught me to think of *all* Natives as living in tee-pees. I hadn't even
challenged the brainwashing-installed prejudice in my head enough
(even after meeting Running Bear) to have erased that default! Of
course, I couldn't admit that: "**Pfff*!* No!" She looked unconvinced.
"Well, anyway... I guess it can't be Shadowgate." "I like the 'gate' part;
maybe you should keep that," R.B. offered. "Why do say that?" "Well,
like when we used to reach the back gate onto your grazing lands... it
was like a welcome mat. When you saw it, you knew you were home."
"I like that," I said. "How about something even *better* than just a
home?" B.G. excitedly asked. "Like what?" "Well, in the games I've
played, once your character dies, she has to resurrect, right? The places
where you do that are called 'res points'! So, how about 'Rezgate'?"
"It's getting there - but it still feels like it's missing something." "*I've
got it!*" Kyle yelled out. "Your name is Malachi, but we call you Kai.
Well, Kai sounds like 'Chi', the Greek letter 'X'! Why not 'X-rezgate'?
You know, like it's *yours*!" I chuckled, "I like the addition, Kyle, but I
think it can flow better." "How?" "We'll make the 'X' sound like a 'Z'
so the whole thing sounds like: '*ZAIR-ehz-gayt*', and just spell it 'X-e-r-
e-s-g-a-t-e'!" "Perfect!" they all agreed at once. And just like that, the
kingdom of Xeresgate was officially born.

61

Once we were back at camp, enjoying some more venison over a nice fire, Kyle had *another* thought that had not previously occurred to me (It truly *is* like they say: "The group is always smarter than the individual!"). "Hey big brother, if you can raise entire slabs of solid rock from the earth with your magic, why would you bother paying professional stonemasons to build your castle? Wouldn't it be easier to just... I don't know... do it yourself?" "You see?" I stood, with a leg of venison in one hand and a wooden cup of water sloshing in the other as I pointed at Kyle. "*This* is why he is my Royal Advisor!" He stood and took a bow. Running Bear asked, "Hey - considering we're all in your inner circle, do *we* have titles, too?" He was referring to himself and his underage daughter, both of whom had over-and-above proved their usefulness to the future Xeresgatian kingdom. "I don't see why not!" I admitted. "For you, Running Bear, your title will be... the 'Royal Covert Tactician'!" "*Noice!*" he accepted, pleased. "And Flowering Bear Grass, as you are yet to be of age, your title at 18 will be... the 'Royal Strategist'!" "But I'll be 18 next *month*," she protested. Running Bear stood, "*How dare you backtalk our King??*" She appeared to physically retreat inside of herself. While he wasn't wrong, Running Bear's application of the principle was too severe. "*Easy*, R.B. I forgive her." I spoke, turning my whole body toward her, "To address your concern, B.G., you shall come into your title when you are of proper age. Until then, you are still under your Father's auspices, and must remember to show *him* as much respect as you show *me*." "Yes sir," she humbly answered. "And R.B., remember the natural weakness of the woman and remind yourself to *love* her - even over and above what she's earned. Your kindness and concern will *free* her spirit to respect you as greatly as you deserve." "Yes, my brother," he bowed his head. "...my *King*."

It felt nicely to be revered as the King of a kingdom yet to be, but felt even *better* to be the arbiter of **peace** among these, my people. After cancelling with the stonemasons and promising them a gold coin (a month's wages) apiece - should they have lost any potential contracts while beholden to me - I set about quarrying the stones for my future keep with my Erdemancy. It was a constant psychic workout, and taught me to focus my magic until I made cuts through stone so precise that even modern engineers would (surely) say that they rivaled the thinnest of diamond-tipped blades. I had previously Googled how to make cement (and found a proper limestone deposit on my land, thank goodness) so that I might be able to make mortar for both a thin layer in my *outer* walls and to mix into concrete in the thick reinforced layer between that and my *inner* walls (Which inner walls - you will recall - were begun after an "inside" space of 16 x 16 yards). The project was *massive* for a first construction, even at what I had earlier thought to be a "conservative" space estimation. Before I was done with the first course of inner and outer walls (that, thankfully, had *one* wall made up entirely of the northern cliff) I had erdemanced *150* (1 x 1 x 2-foot) solid stone blocks with who only *knows* how much mortar layered thinly between! (I decided to use the twenty rough-hewn blocks I'd made previously for something *else*... perhaps the insulants around the small-scale smelter I had yet to metamance?) With the outline down, it amplified my faith in the dream: that I would make a utopian kingdom.

Meanwhile, after daily assuring us all of our death-free futures, Flowering Bear Grass began to work on her own precognition magic, wishing to expand her future-reading capabilities to be able to read multiple targets at once. She would consistently push herself to read further and further as well - by seconds, then minutes, then *hours*. I once asked her, "So B.G., doesn't being able to tell the future make your own life kind of *boring*? I mean, who *could* be a hardcore gamer if you already knew the end to every game?" Her answer surprised me, "I can't read myself." "*What?*" I was personally upset for having never noticed that she, indeed, *never read herself.* "Why not?" "I don't know, really. But I'd have to guess that it's like electricity: if you have the power source (me) and then a resistor (whoever I'm reading) to pass the voltage through, then there can be a proper flow of current (or, my magic). If I (as the power source) attempt to complete the circuit without a resistor, then nothing really happens except me overloading my *internal* 'resistance' and then I get a headache that gets worse and worse the longer I try to do it. I stopped trying about a year ago." "Wow," I was summarily impressed. "That's a damned good analogy!" "Yeah; I've watched a lot of *Sherlock*," she said with a nonchalant grin.

Kyle, on the other hand, had begun working on the *area of effect* of his mind-reading magic, attempting not only to be able to read the minds of more and more *targets*, but in a wider *radius* as well. I could tell his area of effect was expanding, because about three days (and about three *courses* of each wall) into my keep construction, I remember looking up at the high sun and thinking how great a nice drink of ice water would have been, but decided against aquamancing myself one out of thin air, as I didn't want to slow the progression of the work by splitting my focus. Not *two minutes* later, Kyle was riding his horse into sight with a tall, wooden mug of ice water from my cabin's refrigerator. "Awesome!" I rejoiced as I reached for the water. "Your magic reaches all the way up *here*, now?" "You bet, big brother!" he replied, slightly out of breath. "I was just about to quit training for lunch, too, so you're lucky you thought what you did *when* you did!" "I guess so!" I laughed, after finishing a refreshing gulp. "Man, this is coming along *well*!" he admired the work I'd done on the keep. "Oh yeah, little brother - it won't be too long before we'll be moving in up *here*!" "Long live Xeresgate!" he cheered, rearing his horse back toward camp. "Long live the Truth!" I answered.

Running Bear had taken to exercising himself daily with runs to the top of the northern cliff, under which I was working. Once there, he would spend mere minutes loosing what looked like a barrel-sized sheaf of arrows from the English styled yew longbow that I had crafted for him (as a better option than his hunting short-bow). He practiced tirelessly - always running back down the cliff to gather every last arrow - until he could notch, draw, and loose an arrow in under a second. Then, he worked on long-range shots, with the goal of hair-splitting accuracy. I came out from my cabin one morning to see that he had been firing at a target in front of the fire pit. *Ten whole arrows* were in the black bull's-eye, so when he ran into camp to collect the arrows and let out a sigh of disgust, I asked, "What's the matter? You got ten bull's-eyes!" "I got *none*," he said, pointing to a white dot in the absolute center about the size of a freckle.

62

These were the dedicated citizens of Xeresgate... the very first Xeresgatians. I was proud to serve the new nation right alongside them. Though I was their King, it was the one of the few distinctions that separated us. Regardless of culture, age, or wealth, we all worked toward the common goal of a society built on *Absolute Truth*: those things which are readily, naturally apparent (that society generally chucks by the wayside whilst pursuing avaricious, barbaric, or biologically antithetical ends).

It took me a little less than a month to finish the keep to my satisfaction - even the inside (less any overt decoration). There was a wide interior hall with 8-foot-tall windows made of solid pyro- and erde-manced glass a foot thick (forged around metamanced iron bars for support) with three windows on the eastern and western walls, and two on either side of the main door. There were eight stone braziers for light at night as well: two between the windows on each side of the hall, with an additional two near the entrance, and two more near the throne platform's base on either side of its stairs. The throne itself was wodemanced out of fir and then gilded, using ancient gold plating techniques. Two cushions were set in the throne, made of dyed-red deerskin and filled with the softest cotton that I had bought from Frank and his new flock.

The door at the head of the throne hall was a double door (ten feet tall!) made of the strongest fir beams on my land, each manipulated by wodemancy to be a dark, imposing brown. The beams were then bound together by wrought-iron crossbars, riveted all the way through the wood (with heavy iron rings for handles on both sides). The crossbars attached to iron hinges metamanced into the solid stone behind them, and made to only open outwards. Once closed, the mammoth doors had two wide, iron cradles that held the massive, iron-reinforced fir beam that could *keep* them securely shut. The hall itself had solid stone pillars (4 on either side of the path to the throne) that I had erdemanced at the top and bottom in designs fancy enough to have made Corinthian marble sculptors jealous.

The entire roof was made of a singular slab of stone, through which I had also erdemanced holes large enough for the four staircases at each corner of the throne hall. The top had an entirely crenellated battlement (surrounding all three sides *not* attached to the cliff behind) complete with machicolations all around and an extended brattice over the entrance. The main living quarters were housed in an additional level built in from the battlements by a 6-and-½-foot wide walkway all around. This left an 83x83' area to quarter, that (after building out from the cliff with more foot-wide stone blocks), left us each with rooms having about 1620 square feet apiece... *quite a step up* from our cramped cabins! Kyle and I took the northwest and northeast rooms, respectively (as I figured that the King and his Advisor should have the closest accesses to the throne platform). Running Bear and Flowering Bear Grass took the southeast and southwest rooms so that they'd have the closest access to the front battlements, as R.B. had become quite the skilled archer, and B.G. would need to see the future intents of any visitors as soon as they made themselves known.

As I had used the top bedrock stone from the cliff behind the castle in its construction, it had lowered the top of the cliff to be even with the level of the Court quarters' roof. If it weren't for the additional battlements placed atop *that* roof, animals or invaders could just walk right onto the very top of the castle (After the battlements went up, potential assailants would have to vault four feet into a crenel between two merlons before they could breach the northern defense.). When Running Bear saw this seeming design flaw, he asked: "So why have it like that? Why not make the wall higher, or lower the cliff with your magic?" "I think it's better this way," I replied. "When it's cold (for most of the year), the flat stone will be an icy, treacherous surface. And if they *do* manage to get far enough, I can always turn the stone beneath their feet into molten rock, which would melt any foolish foot soldiers before they're even close enough to engage!" "Hmmm!" he grunted his support of my tactics. "So that's why the only stairs leading to this upper level end right by your bedroom door?" "You got it," I winked.

"Just out of curiosity..." Kyle had quietly approached from behind us. "What if *tanks* roll up that hill *instead* of foot soldiers?"

"Well, Kyle, that would be rather difficult, considering the only American military base close enough that *supports* tanks is far further away than even the closest *air* bases... and even **they** are hundreds of miles away." B.G., who was in turn following Kyle up the top battlement stairs sounded off as well: "Sure, but jets or even drones could be flown in here across that distance in a matter of seconds. What's to stop them?"

"I'm glad you asked that, B.G.," I grinned, ready to show off my latest magical advancement. "Do any of you have a digital watch on you?" Kyle and R.B. shrugged while B.G. produced one from her back pocket. "I used to look at it around people in town when they weren't watching me, and then when they'd turn back around, I'd look up at the sky like, 'Hmmm! Big sun disk say it 12:25!' They were pretty stupid; no one ever *didn't* fall for that," she shone a toothy smile at us. R.B. grimaced in disapproval, but I couldn't help but chuckle. "Well, does it still work?" I asked. "Oh, yes sir! I put a new battery in it just last month." "Do you mind if I make it **never work again**?" "Only if you don't let me watch!" she was already excited to see. "Awesome; now you guys stay back here." I crossed to the southern end of the upper battlement and placed the watch on the center merlon before returning to the group. "Now keep behind me - I've managed to focus this burst of Electromancy to where there's a shielding about the size of a TV station radar dish behind which you won't be affected. Every other part of this is like a focused EMP."

I turned back toward the watch, preparing to fire. "What would happen if we were in *front* of this EMP?" Kyle managed to be curious enough to stop my concentration. "Most likely some involuntary muscle spasms, or (if I upped the intensity) electrical burns." He scooted a bit further back. I focused again and then fired a short burst of Electromancy as an instantaneous, barely-visible blue orb that expanded outward from my hands, shielded only from expanding backward toward *us* by my concentrated focus. The watch didn't move. "Well... *that* was kinda cool," B.G. remarked. "How's the watch?" I walked over to the merlon to check the face of the watch. "Powerless."

63

Flowering Bear Grass asked how I'd be able to save us from a supersonic jet or drone attack with an EMP. Kyle added that any EMP effective enough to shield us from any such attacks would likely scorch us, Frank, Mimi, all the ranch hands, scores of innocents in the town below, and likely every other living animal (including *all our livestock*) on or around the mountains. "How exactly can that be a *practical* means of defense: using your electrical magic?"

"Electromancy," I corrected him. "Yeah; that. How?" he quipped. "Well, considering I need it on a several miles wider scale than I'm currently capable of, it wouldn't even be effective at *this* stage. *But*... every time I increase the power output, I'm working on increasing my shielding capabilities at the same rate. By the time I surge one of these pulses high enough (like an HEMP), I'll have enough shielding capabilities to protect our entire *mountain range* from its effects. "What about the planes?" Running Bear spoke up. "Wouldn't they crash to the earth (possibly killing people) after they lost power?" "Possibly, brother... but I'm working on my Metamancy as well, hoping I can use it to levitate any falling, disabled vehicles. That way, even if it's a *manned* strike, I might still be able to save the pilots."

I waved my hands in front of me, dismissing the hypothetical. "But that's all irrelevant anyway, right? When's the last time the U.S. carried out a strike *inside* its own borders? And we haven't even done anything to *incur* the wrath of the current presidency, so it's kind of a moot point. The only reason I bring up the new magic *at all* is that I want you all to feel safely inside the first Xeresgtian edifice... from all threats foreign and domestic." "Oh, *we do*!" Running Bear soundly slapped the merlon he was leaning against. "This keep is an imposing fortress all by *itself*!" We adjourned the rooftop meeting to gather some more wood up from the cabins to the keep before nightfall, as I wanted to see whether or not the braziers in the throne hall would produce sufficient enough light at night for nighttime sessions of Court - or for feasting, should we feel the need to convert it to a feasting hall for a special occasion. Once we'd all made nice, solid log pyramids in each brazier, I stood in the center of the hall and told everyone to duck.

I shot eight individual fireballs in rapid succession: one at each brazier. *FOOM!* *FOOM!* *FOOM!* *FOOM!* *FOOM!* *FOOM!* *FOOM!* *FOOM!* I hit them all perfectly, and the room lit up brightly with the dancing flames of eight glorious fires. Everyone cheered, as it was the closest thing we'd seen to fireworks in quite some time. I happily strode up the three steps to my throne to sit on it and imagine a Court full of loyal citizens. Kyle sat with his back against one of the throne legs, staring into one of the blazing braziers. Running Bear sat with his arm around Flowering Bear Grass on the steps, looking fondly about the hall. "You know what this place needs?" "What?" I asked him. "More chairs." We all laughed.

"You know what *I'd* do?" B.G. chimed in. "What, B.G.?" "*Decorations!* This place would look super in some nice colorful banners, and flags, and..." she stopped shortly. "***Wait a minute!*** King Kai, what *is* the flag of the kingdom of Xeresgate? Do you know yet?"

It was something I had actually thought about for quite some time. Ever since the word "Xeresgate" first escaped my lips, I had been mulling over the design of its flag (mostly during lunch breaks from constructing its Royal keep). I decided to keep to my first known national roots and honor the discipline of Wu Xing, while centering on the history of my family and introducing the idea of new Royalty. I explained to them how the silver and gold Taijitic Seal would be represented in the flag's center, and stretching forth from that circle seal would be four widths of Royal purple, extending into its corners. Then, atop the flag would be a quadrant of red for southern full yang, to its right would be a quadrant of green for eastern new yang, on its bottom would be a quadrant of black for northern full yin, and on its left would be a quadrant of white for western new yin. "All that, and each color would be outlined in a majestic blue... just because it's beautiful," I finished. They all looked at me, mouths agape, as if I'd said that I met the Devil. "Good *god*, Kai! You've really, ***really*** thought about *this* one!" Kyle spoke first.

"Yes, little brother, I have," I told him. "A flag is a unifying emblem - a standard to be raised high in battle, saluted proudly by its kingdom's warriors, and an ensign to be looked to when you're lost and struggling to find home. It is how we know that we are *one people*, and our hearts strive *together* for peace and the pursuit of Absolute Truth." "That was so poetic!" B.G. wiped a tear from her eye. "Hear, hear!" cheered R.B. Kyle began our battle cry: "Long live Xeresgate!" We all replied, "Long live the Tru..."

A thunderous knock resounded through the mostly empty hall. Someone was at the front entrance, and proving that the wrought iron door handle rings could *also* be used as incredibly practical door knockers. I sprung into action: "R.B. - take your bow; climb the battlements; see who it is." "*Right!*" "B.G. - read us all again and see if anything's changed from this morning. Make sure we're in no danger." "*Yes, sir!*" "Kyle - come with me to the door so you can read the person's intent on the other side." "Right away, big brother!" I drew my Ulfberht sword out from behind my throne. "Let's go greet our guest." By the time Kyle and I started toward the door, Running Bear was halfway up the staircase toward the battlements. Once we'd make it to the door, I heard B.G. yelling from the foot of the throne: "We're still fine, but that woman wasn't there this morning when I read!" "*Thank you!*" I shouted back. "Wait, what?" Kyle grabbed my arm. "It's a *woman* out there?" I heard the creak of R.B.'s bow as he aimed through the machicolation at the edge of the entry brattice. "***Who goes there?!?*** Declare yourself or limp home with an arrow in you!" he roared. I heard the short, muffled shriek of a woman taken off-guard by a master archer. "***Stay your bow, R.B.!***" I commanded. "It's just a *woman*."

"She's just here to deliver something... and she's very frightened right now," Kyle read. "She's thinking of running without giving you what she was sent with." "Ma'am?" I called through the door. "It's all right. I'm going to open the door now, so just back up a bit so it doesn't hurt you when it opens." Kyle nodded that she had done so. I metamanced the reinforced fir beam out of its cradle and propped it up long-ways against the wall. I cracked the heavy door outwards, and it creaked under its weight (and for lack of the oil that I'd neglected to put on the hinges). Outside was a fetching, busty redhead quivering in the night air. "*Vera??*"

64

"Yeah, it's me," she laughed weakly, nervously. I opened the door further. "Well, *come in!*" I invited her. "Warm yourself over a brazier here." She rubbed her arms as she entered. "Thanks." Kyle pulled the door closed behind her. I decided to leave it unbarred.

"We could really use some outside braziers for things like this!" Running Bear reported, as he descended from the battlements. "Or some torches... something. There's not enough light coming through those windows to identify people." "Duly noted, R.B.," I replied. "Now could you please come introduce yourself to the woman from town that you scared half to death?" He quickly crossed to us as B.G. came to inspect the newcomer as well. "Sorry about that," he apologized. "Can't be too careful when someone's brazen enough to knock at the door of a keep, after all!" She bore up bravely, considering the muscular, imposing Native towering over her. "I forgive you. I guess I didn't really *know* how loudly those big rings would actually *knock* until it was too late and already done!" "Quite all right," I reassured her. "And R.B. - though I *will* make it my next construction priority to get some torches out there, *please* don't draw on anyone else before you've at *least* discovered that they're a threat."

He clasped his bow to his chest. "Yes, my king." "Ooooo," Vera cooed in sing-song. "So you're a *King* now, eh?" R.B. growled, sensing someone making light of his King. Kyle saw his grimace and put his arm around him, tactfully attempting to lead him away from the woman. "*Hey* R.B. - why don't you come show me how to do a shot or two over here on that target of yours we brought in earlier? You know *I* need the practice!" "*Hmmph!*" he grumbled. "If anyone *does*, it's definitely *you*." They pulled apart from us and headed over to the side of the hall where he'd set up a small target earlier in the day. Just as they left, B.G. made it to our sides.

"So *this* was the woman outside?" she eyed her up and down. "Yes; I'm Vera," she extended her hand. "Nice to meet you." "Kinda *chesty*, huh?" B.G. continued sizing her up without shaking her offered hand. "I *guess* that's okay if you *like* that kind of thing." "***B.G.!!***" I reprimanded her. "*Behave* yourself in the throne hall!" "I apologize," she pouted, finally grasping Vera's hand and shaking it properly. "Vera, I'm Flowering Bear Grass... his Majesty's Royal Strategist." "Wow," she reacted. "Kind of *young* for a strategist, aren't you?" "I turned 18 this month, you... you..." B.G. was getting agitated, so I stepped between them. "*Women!*" They looked up at me. "Not *here*. Okay? Not here." "Sorry," they begrudgingly uttered in unison. "B.G., why don't you go and wait by the throne?" "Yes, King Kai."

"Holy *shit*!" Vera looked over my shoulder at the gilded throne. "You have a **golden throne??**" I could tell, with her focus off of me, that she was taking in the medieval spectacle of the hall for the first time... the ornate stone pillars, the two men practicing archery, the sheer length of it, and the many blazing braziers. "I'm sorry, Vera... did you come here for something in particular?" I tried to remind her. "*Oh! Yes!*" she shook herself away from admiring the hall. "I was told to give you this."

She pulled a tape-sealed envelope from her back pocket and handed it to me. "You know, this is **really** nice - especially for *these* mountain parts. I'd bet you could charge every person in town ten bucks just to come and look in the window!" I had already opened the letter and had begun reading. "I kind of doubt that, considering this." "Huh?" she asked, clueless. "Do you know what's in this envelope?" "Sorry; couldn't tell ya. I was just picking my Dad up from one of those boring town hall meetings and came in at the end. I don't know *what* they were talking about *before* I got there, but when *I* walked in, they were all like, 'Hey, Vera... why don't you take this envelope up the mountain to Malachi Hunter?' and stuff." "So they sent you all the way up here *alone*? At **night**?" "Well, my Dad got kind of a late start driving the pickup up the mountain, but then right before sundown we came across this wall of firs that looked like someone had just braided a bunch of trees together and he just told me, 'I'll wait for you here, darlin'. I don't think Mr. Hunter takes too kindly to men on his mountain. You hurry back now, ya hear?' I had made it up to your cabins down the hill a bit when my flashlight here quit on me, but fortunately, I saw the lights flickering in your castle and came on up."

"It's just a keep," I explained. "Well *whatever* it is, it's impressive!" "Well, let me tell you what they gave you to deliver to me. It's a **summons** to appear before a town judge for the violation of *all* the trumped-up charges that you all's crooked Mayor Ed had put on me *before*, with the addition of several federal *felonies*. He's also included a personal note along with it," I pulled it out to read aloud. "Mr. M. Hunter: You are hereby ordered by the town proper to leave your land immediately and stand trial by a jury of your peers for the many charges laid against you. Should you ignore this order, or take any force or untoward action against the town or any of its residents, you will be subject to be remitted to the custody of federal authorities - or forcibly eliminated to keep the general peace. Signed, The Right Honorable Mayor Edward Ahgoh." She was visibly aghast, having had no idea the insulting nature of the contents of the envelope she had brought. I held up the papers. "This is a declaration of *war*; make no mistake, Vera!"

Running Bear heard from across the hall. "Whoa, what? *War??*" He plucked his bow from Kyle's hands and sprinted to my side. Kyle and B.G. began to follow suit. I spoke loudly enough for the whole hall to hear me. "The asshole Mayor of the town in the valley has decided that he has the authority to call me out from my own land and my own home! He would take your King and try him in some backwater court..." I turned to Vera, "No offense." She shrugged. I continued, "...by a rigged jury on falsified charges that would surely strip me of my land, fortune, and people. *Will we allow this??*" I rallied them. "*NO!!!*" they cried in unison. "*Will we let some fascist small town dictator ruin the kingdom of Xeresgate??*" "*NO!!!*" they yelled again, closing in like a huddle. "*Will you fight with me to protect our kingdom at all costs??*" Kyle shouted, "*LONG LIVE XERESGATE!!*" R.B. and B.G. answered, "*LONG LIVE THE TRUTH!!*" The war cries had made Vera take an uneasy step or two backward. I motioned for Kyle to fetch me a torch, which he did. I burned the letter and summons over it, and then handed the torch to Vera. "If your flashlight's not working, you'll need this. You should go."

65

For the next week or so, there was no word or action from town. I had B.G. read all our futures a week in advance at every hour of the waking day, because (as we'd learned from Vera's approach) if we were to be read *early* in the day and a decision was made in town *later* in the day, there was no way to see how it would affect us (as those events had not yet been set in motion and, as such, *were not yet the future*). Given that fact, I'd say that we were ***extremely*** fortunate that the evil Mayor's *first* hunting party didn't decide on a *different* lethal plan of attack during their hour-long approach, or I'd be a much graver man today.

Still, we had to begin keeping a night watch as well - for I couldn't ask the poor young B.G. (***already*** stretched to her magical limits) to have to read us during the time she'd have otherwise been *sleeping*. With each of us men standing a four-hour watch on the upper battlements, we all still got a good eight hours of sleep apiece. All the same, it was a tense time. We felled every tree within a 100 yard radius of the keep and (after Kyle suggested an improvement on Running Bear's idea) I erdemanced stone braziers for *outside* of the keep as well - so many that it seemed to light up the mountain at night. "I'm glad you're here to grow and split the wood with your magic, brother; because with this many fires at night, we'd *all* have to be chopping *all day* just to have enough fuel!" Running Bear noted. I had become what I would call "moderately-skilled" in Wodemancy, Pyromancy, and Erdemancy, and quite advanced in Electromancy and Metamancy during this time. And even though the preparations for war had not given me much of an impetus to practice my Aeromancy and Aquamancy skills, I felt them growing inside of me at a much slower rate. I can only relate it to how much easier other languages become once a person has gained a working knowledge of 3 to 4 of them. That's how my magics were beginning to feel to me - like a natural, innate extension of who I was.

I rode out to the cattle hands to have them gather up my herd into a corral I'd built within sight (but downwind) of the keep so that I wouldn't have to keep them employed where they weren't needed. I paid them each 2 gold (*Yes*; I'd set up a nearby smelter/mint already.) for their last month of service as a thanks for their good work. I managed to keep Old Bob on at the new corral (for 1 gold a month) to keep a watch over the herd's health and what-not, and would sneak in around nightfall to wodemance some new, fresh grasses for them (so that they wouldn't need to be *herded* to always have good grass).

B.G. had taken the time during the interim to go back home and get a few things from there that didn't require electricity (as the keep was purposefully **not** outfitted with it, so as to not get used to a lifestyle that could be *crippled* in the event that we'd have to defend ourselves via EMP). She'd even managed to scare up a few lengths of cloth in the proper colors for mock-ups of a Xeresgate flag and some seasonal banners (We'd agreed to hang long, blank banners in the throne hall in the corresponding color to the Wu Xing season in which we found ourselves.). When she returned from home, I could tell something was on her mind. "What's wrong, B.G.?" I inquired.

"I feel like the worst kid in the world right now." "Why? What happened?" "Well, Dad and I have been here with you so long - I mean, don't get me wrongly, it's been like some kind of super-fun *summer camp* - but **both** of us had totally forgotten about Mom!" When I thought back on it, I *did* seem to remember Running Bear mentioning that he had a wife, but I couldn't remember a single time *thereafter* that he'd brought it up again. And it had been a **while**.

"So... is she ill again, or is she short of supplies or something?" "Well, it's not that. She's fine for supplies and has access to all of Dad's money that he's made as your cattle hand all this time." I gave her a confused look that she answered simply with: "Joint accounts." "*Ahhh*." It's just that... well, she's my *Mom*, and no matter how much grief she generally gives Daddy..." (I was beginning to see that this was a "summer camp" for *Running Bear*, too!) "...I still love her and I don't know what's gonna happen between us all now that we're with you here in Xeresgate. I mean, should we be separated *forever*, or does she need to come and stay *here*, or what?"

"Well, we're not an *island* kingdom way out in some foreign waters or something. So I'd never *forbid* you from going to see your

Mom whenever you want. But this is a *special place*, and we can't just grant access to people who don't share our quest for Truth, or people who've not proven themselves (or their usefulness) to us," I tried to explain the situation as tactfully as I could. "Yeah... I guess that makes sense," she pouted, unhappy with my answer. "I'll tell you *what*, though, B.G. Just as soon as we're done with this awful business with the town Mayor (or *whatever* goons he sends our way next), I *promise* you that I will make a way for there to be an upper town and a lower town in Xeresgate. The upper town will house the Court - people who've proven their loyalty and special usefulness to us, and the lower town will house people still trying to prove those things, who *also* believe in and strive for the Truth as we do. That way, if your Mom agrees with our laws and ideals, she will be welcome to stay there. And even if she *doesn't* (like I said), I would **never** forbid you from going outside the town to visit her. Okay?" "Yes, my King," she answered, making certain that she was duly respectful.

I decided not to bring up the question of Running Bear's wife with him, feeling that if it was truly important to him (or that if he desired my counsel in the matter), then he would come to me with it. He never did - for the entire time that we prepared, fortifying against the town - so I let it go for the time being. As we prepared, it seemed like he got ever more accurate with his bow, until it got to the point that he was not only *hitting* the small white dot he'd painted on his target's bull's-eye, but was *splitting arrow shafts* from hitting the same mark repeatedly! I asked him if he thought he'd mastered that English-style, heavy-draw, yew longbow yet on the day in which I noticed his extreme marksmanship, and he simply replied: "As long as I own *two* un-split arrow shafts, I have yet to truly master this weapon." "Well, don't forget to keep making new arrows, or else you'll run out of ammo for the weapon you've mastered!" I laughed, half joking. He eased the draw on the arrow he was aiming with a look on his face that revealed that he *clearly* hadn't thought of that. "I think I need to go make some more arrows," he said stoically, then immediately marched down the cliff to the forest.

66

The next day, after some long overdue coffee and conversation at Frank's place (with the only other two friends I was beginning to feel like I had for *miles* around), Mimi graciously offered me some seeds for planting - of the *best* of her vegetable and herb gardens. I humbly accepted, and invited them to dine with us soon at Xeresgate. "So your kingdom's already *built*, huh?" Frank asked, a bit surprised. "Oh, not even *close*!" I admitted. "But for now, the keep is up, and..." "What do you mean 'for now'?" he interrupted. "What'd you build it out of... straw?" Mimi giggled. "No, but now that you mention it, we *are* having more trouble with Ed Ahgoh."

· "I prob'ly shoulda told ya that that back-stabbin' jackass woulda had more tricks up his sleeve! I swear, if there was some way to get that sidewinder outta this town for *good*, I'd..." his thought was broken up by the ringing of their home phone. Frank reached out and slapped the switchhook of the mock old-timey phone (almost exactly like the one at Jim Bob's work) nearby. Annoyed to be interrupted, he nevertheless picked up the handset. "*Hello?*" As he spoke to the person on the other end, his near-furtive glances over at me told me that the call had to do with *me* before he even hung up.

"That was my son," he said, gravely. "The Deputy?" "Yep... turns out there was some kinda disturbance up at your castle..." "Keep." "Yeah, that. Anyway, the town is mostly too scared to move against you, and because you decided to go against the Mayor (Which, trust me, *I woulda done, too.*), he's been able to whip the town into a paranoid frenzy against you. They sent out a hundred-person petition to the *Governor* just to have him involve the Feds. Now, I've never met the Governor, but I've also never heard of a bad law he's approved of. Even so, he very likely doesn't know what's goin' on up here. I doubt he'll flat-out ignore a plea from a town under his governorship, but he might just recommend a Federal inquiry team. It might be a small measure, but I've had my own problems with the gub'ment, as I think you know." I nodded in recognition. "I love you like a son, Malachi, but I can't afford to jump into this by your side. I hope whatever God you pray to is behind you, and you know our thoughts and prayers are with you as well." I chuckled, "Well, though I'd prefer your *guns* were with me, I'll settle for that." He extended his hand for me, and I shook it strongly. Then, grasping it with *both* of mine, I said resolutely: "You *know* that should you ever decide to come under my auspices, that I would defer to you as a *Father* and defend you with my own life." "Yes I do, Malachi. And while that day isn't *today*, I really *do* hope it'll be soon."

I was almost out the door when I remembered that I had a gold coin of Xeresgate in my pocket. "*Oh hey!* Check this out," I flipped the coin at him. He caught it with both hands, and then showed it to Mimi over his shoulder, "Mmmm... shiny!" She almost perched on his shoulder and cooed, "*Ooooo!* Is that real gold?" "You bet, Mimi!" I told her. "Should Xeresgate fall in the near future - for *whatever* reason - I hope you'll keep that in memory of what we've tried to do here in these remote mountains." "It would be my very great honor," said Frank, who then smirked. "It'll be the last thing I ever pawn." "*Thanks!*" I laughed.

I left Frank's with the warm feeling you have after you've had a good time of fellowship with close friends. Freedom's saddlebag was filled with a combination of both the fresh-baked breads and the bags of seeds that Mimi had generously given to me. My intent was to grow a delicious garden of herbs and vegetables just like hers, perhaps ushering in a future in which I would be able to use my Wodemancy to help with problems of world hunger. As I was lost in thoughts of my hypothetical charity work, B.G. was frantically riding her Father's horse toward me. "King Kai! *King Kai!*" she shouted as she rode, rousing me from my daydream. "What is it?" I asked as she arrived, breathless. "The future... read it... those men..."

"Calm down, B.G.," I settled her. "What has you so upset?" She swallowed, took a deep breath, and then exhaled with the kind of stutter that your breath has after crying or when you're terrified. It seemed she was on the verge of *both*. "I just read... just read tomorrow. It's *changed*. Two men in black suits and ties show up to the keep. I couldn't hear what you said from the battlement, but you raised a fist at one of them, and the one you *weren't* watching drew a gun from a chest holster and fired a shot through your forehead before my Dad could even notch an arrow!" Her eyes began to well up with tears. "I could tell... you were dead before you hit the ground." I guided Freedom close to her and reached over to hug her. "It's gonna be okay. We know the future isn't set in stone; now that we know, we can prepare," I comforted her. "I know... I just... I guess I was starting to think we were *safe*. And I don't want to lose you. You've been so good to us." "It's okay, B.G.," I lifted her chin to meet my gaze. "...Chief Strategist. Let's go and *change the future*, all right?" She sniffled, and then vigorously nodded her assent. We rode back to Xeresgate and left our horses in the new corral with Old Bob, who sat on his own horse, looking out at the beauty of the surrounding mountains. "You know, castle or not, this is some mighty fine country 'round here. I'm sure glad you got it, Mr. Hunter, instead o' some smoke-spewin' corporation or somethin'." "Well thanks, Bob. I always hope to do the land justice. And I *hope* you don't mind all the fires we set in our braziers at night." He waved off the implication like it was nothing, "Shoot - I always *did* like the smell of fresh wood smoke! I just hope it ain't doin' any damage like my granddaughter tells me about these greenhouse floro-carbons or whatever. Says we'll all be bakin' under a hotter sun someday or *somethin'* like that." "I'm pretty sure she has a point. I'll have to look into that once a proper peace has settled in." I gave him a casual two finger salute and he tipped his cowboy hat to me as B.G. and I made our way back to the keep.

I began practicing with Running Bear until I had prepared an electromantic deflection shield with a magnetic force so strong that it bounced off a heavy-iron arrow that he'd loosed at me (*full draw*) from ten paces as if it were a *toothpick*. With my permission (and my shared curiosity), he asked to fire a similar arrow from **behind** the shield, and - surpassing even **our** expectations - the force propelled the arrow forward at such a high speed that the arrowhead pierced into one of the throne hall's solid stone pillars a good *half a foot*, which shattered the arrow shaft against the outside of the pillar like a cartoon, splatted against a brick wall. We looked confidently at one another and I declared, "We're ready."

67

The next day came, and B.G. read our futures early and half-hourly, all the time insisting that we now made it through and that I was to do: "something *impressive*... I don't want to spoil it for you, your Majesty." I decided to let her enjoy her secret and be content with the fact that I was to *live through the encounter* in this future. I positioned myself over the barred keep entrance on the lower battlement, as I'd never intended to grant the government lackeys admittance to my place. It was courtesy *enough* that I was allowing them to trespass on my land in order to speak to me. Kyle took a hidden position behind the door, from where he said he could now read minds all the way down to the widow Athelas' place on the edge of town. Flowering Bear Grass stayed behind us on the battlement, seated against the Court quarters' wall on the outside of her Dad's room in such a way that she could neither be seen over the crenellations nor through any of the lower machicolations. Running Bear stood sharply behind me (with an arrow already notched, and his hand ready to full draw in an instant) at an angle from which he could see any car pull up and have a full aiming view of any potential threats.

It wasn't far into the morning hours when I saw a black sedan pull up alongside the lower hills' cabins. I could see the men knock at my cabin's door before positioning themselves to the sides of it and drawing their firearms. Not wanting to have my old door kicked in (*or* have them going through my old computer - which I suddenly remembered), I aeromanced a path (through the long distance of air between us) as free from refractory or inhibitive particles as possible so that my voice would carry over the hundreds of yards as clearly as a signal over a fiberoptic cable. "*HEY*... you two! I'm up the mountain here at the keep." As soon as I saw them turn to look, I waved a banner of red (one of the ones B.G. had been working on for the summer decoration of the throne hall) over my head to prove that I had been the one that had said it. After a few seconds of disbelief, I saw them get back in their sedan and drive up to us at the keep. I had practiced the night before, holding a strong electromantic shield for up to an *hour* before tiring myself out, so I was *hoping* for a short conversation.

They parked so that they could see me above the crenellations through their windshield. They got out of their car in unison: two large white men with matching short, brown haircuts and black suits, who were so ridiculously muscular that they looked like they *lived* at a gym. "What are you guys, *Men in Black* on steroids?" I joked. Their unflinching expressions revealed that they were clearly in no mood to joke around. The man from the passenger side removed his ID from his inside suit pocket and spoke, "Malachi Hunter? FBI. We need you to come with us and answer some questions." "***NOT TRUE!!***" I heard Kyle shout from below us. "*They're going to capture you without trial and throw you in Guantanamo Bay under a random alias!!*" They looked down at the entrance door, behind which was someone obviously giving away their mental secrets, and then back up toward me. The man spoke again more candidly, "We do not want to use force, Mr. Hunter, but if we must, we will." "I don't wish to use force, either, so if you still desire to leave here as *whole* men, I suggest you turn around and *do so* at this time."

He was done splitting hairs. "*You are **commanded** by the United States government to surrender yourself at this time, Malachi Hunter! If you do not, **all** of your lands will be forfeit, and any of those who have assisted you in resisting us will be regarded as **enemies of the State**!*" I wanted it to be over quickly, so I taunted them: "Your State has **no** *authority here*, and if they wish to further trespass on or invade the sovereign kingdom of Xeresgate, then they will answer to *ME*!!" I heard B.G. and Kyle both warn: "***GUN!!***" mere fractions of a second before they both drew on me. I instinctively amplified the electromantic shield in front of R.B. and myself as I saw several shots ricochet off of it mere inches in front of my face. Running Bear had full drawn his longbow in an instant after hearing the gun-warning, loosing an iron "full-pounder" arrow through the shield with such accuracy that it had *severed* the firing arm (of the man who spoke) right at the shoulder. Before the man could even yell out in pain, R.B. had notched a *second* full-pounder arrow at full draw and fired through my shield, cutting the *second* man's humerus from his shoulder socket. They both were yelling, grabbing at their wounds, their arms hanging limply in their torn sleeves by fragments of flesh and a few partially-severed ligaments.

I lowered the invisible shield (*finally*) to address them, as they did their best to stifle their moans of pain. "The government exists to **serve** its people, not to humiliate and intimidate them! I will leave you alive so that you may tell the corrupt government that sent you - *Xeresgate proclaims its independence!* We govern **ourselves** now. We wish nothing but *peace*, but do **not** think that you can attack us with impunity. The consequences..." I motioned at their arms, "...will be **severe**." They began to move back toward their car. "Let me help you with that," I said, metamancing the doors and roof off of the car. I levitated them above the car and then crushed them into a single, crumpled ball of metal, which I then rolled down the hill into the western forest. "You both know that it's a 15 minute drive back to town, and let me tell you - I'm not sure the clinic doctor there is entirely competent. Even if you sped, you could easily die from blood loss before you could be properly tended to." They looked at each other horrified, knowing it was true. "Well, *help* us! *Please!!* We were just doing our jobs! Please have mercy!" the man (who had not yet spoken) begged.

"Please help them, my King. Show the world that we are just," B.G., who had risen to stand by my side, pleaded with me. I turned to R.B., who nodded his agreement. "There's only one thing that I can do," I said sorrowfully. "I can flash-cauterize your wounds. It will hurt a great deal (and for days afterward), and it *may* damage the flesh beyond where you may have those arms surgically reattached... but you *will* live long enough to have your government try." "Yes, Mr. Hunter - do that please," the second one replied. "*Do it!*" the first man steeled himself, opening the space between his arm and shoulder for maximum exposure. I mentally prepared a pyromantic flame of white-hot heat to target each of their wounds as directly as possible, and then released it for one second. Their screams were instantaneous, and the acrid smell of seared human flesh filled the air, but they were *alive* and would remain so. "Now *hurry back to town*!" I urged them. "If you want to *save* those arms, *put them on ice*... and I'm pretty sure the clinic has *Morphine*!" Amid their own stifled cries, they got in their car and sped off toward town.

68

Kyle joined us on the lower battlement as we watched the FBI men speed away from Xeresgate. "I'm pretty sure I know enough about how our government operates to predict that they're not just going to let this go," he observed. "Yeah - it's going to take more than two badly injured men before the U.S. *government* gives up on anything," I agreed. "B.G.?" She was already ahead of me, reading us all quickly... as far as she could. When her eyes opened, they were as wide as saucers.

"We all stay here for the next two days, but then the morning after that, it just goes *black*. Either there's *no future* three days from now, or we're all *dead*," she relayed.

"I know!" Kyle spoke up. "I officially plan to go down the mountain on the third morning (as far as I can go and still see the keep and campsite areas) and then watch to see what happens! Now read *me*, B.G.!"

Flowering Bear Grass did as she was instructed, and then opened her eyes with a gasp. "Three drones that I could barely make out against the daytime sky flew over the keep and campsite areas, and fired *three missiles* simultaneously. Those things were so powerful that they wiped out *your entire mountainside*! As far away as Kyle was, his clothes *still* caught fire from the intensity of their heat!"

"Were they nukes?" I asked, *still* a little shocked that our government would attack an expatriate on U.S. soil so close to other civilians. "No, sir. No mushroom clouds or anything; they were just *really* intense weapons!"

"All right guys, just to be safe, I want you *all* to go to Frank's place and hang out that day. I'm going to attempt to electromance an HEMP strong enough to disable those drones, and I don't want you all to be here in case I can't - or something goes wrongly," I said solemnly, as if I were saying goodbye.

"Pardon my insurrection, your Majesty, but *no frikkin' way!*" B.G. snapped. "I *need* to be here in case they change their plans at the last minute, remember?" "*B.G.*, you have to..."

"Not happening, brother," R.B. interjected. "I'm her Father, and I'm telling her *not* to go, because *I'm staying with you, too.*" "But..."

"We're *all* staying with you, big brother!" Kyle added. "If your dream of Xeresgate dies, I don't *want* to live in the world that remains!" "*YEAH!!*" R.B. and B.G. agreed. Kyle motioned for the others to cheer: "*LONG LIVE XERESGATE!!*" The thought of letting them down and possibly costing them their lives weighed heavily on my heart, so I didn't answer the cry immediately. Kyle poked me, "Come *on*, big brother... don't leave us hangin'." I took a deep breath and thrust my fist defiantly into the sky: "*LONG LIVE THE TRUTH!!*" They exulted happily, and then we began our preparations.

Knowing that it could easily be the last days any of us had on Earth, I had my fattest cow culled for us to enjoy all the Kobe beef we could eat, and the wodemancing of the seeds that Mimi had given me made for some of the best tomatoes, green peppers, potatoes, and other delicious treats of the earth that we'd ever had in our lives. Our fires seemed brighter, the air seemed sweeter, and we knew that - live or die - we would all be joined in spirit for an eternity.

The day came, and I had prepared as fully as I possibly could. I had prepared my focus to spare the electronics below the height of the keep, and had enough energy to shield the entire keep from electric burns. B.G. read me near-*constantly*, and had adjusted her plans by the second to be able to see when was the perfect moment to have me release my HEMP.

I remember the seconds leading up to the final strike seeming like *eons*, but at last B.G. screamed, "*NOW!!!*" I channeled every ounce of psychic power necessary high into the sky where the epicenter of the HEMP was a mile directly over our heads. An orb of light blue electric energy expanded instantly outward across the sky and down toward us, the keep being shielded from it by my simultaneous Electromancy.

Instead of merely flying over and dropping their payload, the now-fried circuits of the drones left trails of smoke as they fell from the sky. Some quick Metamancy later, they were harmlessly landed in a nearby field. The men rode our horses down to the site, where I aquamanced blocks of ice around each one, *just in case*. After removing and ensuring each warhead was permanently disabled, I melted them all down, releasing a video of the whole thing to the internet group "Anonymous", as I was relatively sure that they could "get the word out" about this atrocity *far* sooner and faster than I could.

Once we were back at the keep, B.G. read that the week ahead was free of troubles, and we all breathed a deep sigh of relief.

69

Unbeknownst to us at the time, the United States President had already been informed of this situation that was seemingly unconquerable, even at a large-scale level, in this mountainous state of the union. As his light-skinned advisor bent over his shoulder, pointing out the best possible plans of action on a memo already lying on the President's desk, Nathan Fillion appeared before them. They shot each other a look of disbelief, and the President went to reach for an alarm button under the desk.

Nathan's standing position changed in a *blink* before he advised: "I wouldn't do that yet, Mr. President. You have a problem that only *I* can solve, and I think it's *time* we discuss my services."

TO BE CONTINUED...

About the Author

Guys, do I *have* to write this section? Shouldn't my writing just speak for itself? Wait, *what*?? You're ***recording*** this?? All right, well skip that part and just start from here...

Michael R. Holt - the man, the mystery, the legend, the genius...

Nah, that's too much. Start over; start over!

Michael R. Holt is many things to many people; mostly to himself...

Nope! Too real... Okay, okay - I got it...

Michael R. Holt is just a simple writer, who believes in the magic of written and spoken words. He's been a fan of medieval times and everything associated with them (before all that gunpowder business) for as long as he's known of them. He used to think that he was a descendant of perhaps Lü Bu and/or Genghis Khan, but then he heard that those guys may have murdered and raped people, and then he changed his mind about the whole thing.

No, no, no... you can't say "rape" in an "About the Author"... they'll think I'm joking about it and try to crucify me like they did Tosh. Hell, I might as well tell the NSA that I'm a turr-rist or something.

Look, just throw something in there that says I love to write, I hope to suspend disbelief enough for my readers to get lost in the narrative, and that I hope they end up loving my characters as much as I now do. That, and I hope I don't get sued by Nathan Fillion.

Seriously, you guys... how cool would it be if he and I starred in a movie based on this book together? ***Badass***, right?

Yeah, well *you're* ugly, too! I'm done here; just make it look professional.

*Afterward: Oh, that dictation team is **so** fired.*

www.ingramcontent.com/pod-product-compliance
Lightning Source LLC
Chambersburg PA
CBHW031331170626
46807CB00002B/649